P9-BZW-012

When Caleb smiled, all those years that had passed felt like nothing.

The crush she'd had on him at twelve reared into the present. She tried to be calm, to keep it all business. But he'd asked a question, one she'd rehearsed answering on her flight to Cody. Now her mouth felt dry.

He smiled at her, slightly crooked. "Is this job condition of yours top secret?"

"No, of course not," she said. "But it's something we need to agree on before I can go further."

"Is this condition a huge problem?" Caleb asked, the smile gone.

"Maybe for one of us, or possibly both," she said, surprised that her voice sounded pretty normal.

"Okay, let's get to the bottom line," he said, his dark eyes narrowing on her and not touched with any humor now.

Harmony braced herself then laid it out. "I have a daughter, Joy, and I can't be away from her for Christmas."

Dear Reader,

For the generations of Donovans born and raised on the Flaming Sky Ranch in northern Wyoming, family has always been and will always be everything.

For Caleb Donovan, one of the three Donovan sons whose lives revolve around the rodeo, family helped him through healing when he was injured bull riding—and when he had to face walking away from the rodeo and building a different life. Harmony Gabriel has been running from her past most of her life. Just when she thinks she's outrun it and is trying to build a family with a little girl she's adopted, she comes face-to-face with Caleb Donovan, a man she knew in her past. A man she never wants to find out who she used to be.

Two people who are building their lives but going in different directions. Caleb's expanding his business and concentrating on being a success on his own. Harmony's choosing her daughter and her business over everything else, including love. Gradually, they find what seems impossible, what should drive them apart, and it's actually the very things both of them have been looking for: love and family.

I hope you enjoy the journey of Caleb and Harmony as they come together to start a new life at Flaming Sky Ranch.

Mary Anne Wilson

HEARTWARMING

A Cowboy's Christmas Joy

—

Mary Anne Wilson

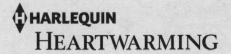

HARLEQUIN
HEARTWARMING

If you purchased this book without a cover you should be aware that this book is stolen property. It was reported as "unsold and destroyed" to the publisher, and neither the author nor the publisher has received any payment for this "stripped book."

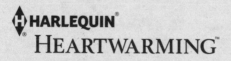

ISBN-13: 978-1-335-58477-9

A Cowboy's Christmas Joy

Copyright © 2022 by Mary Anne Wilson

Recycling programs for this product may not exist in your area.

All rights reserved. No part of this book may be used or reproduced in any manner whatsoever without written permission except in the case of brief quotations embodied in critical articles and reviews.

This is a work of fiction. Names, characters, places and incidents are either the product of the author's imagination or are used fictitiously. Any resemblance to actual persons, living or dead, businesses, companies, events or locales is entirely coincidental.

For questions and comments about the quality of this book, please contact us at CustomerService@Harlequin.com.

Harlequin Enterprises ULC
22 Adelaide St. West, 41st Floor
Toronto, Ontario M5H 4E3, Canada
www.Harlequin.com

Printed in U.S.A.

Mary Anne Wilson is a Canadian transplanted to California, where her life changed dramatically. She found her happily-ever-after with her husband, Tom, and their three children. She always loved writing and reading and has a passion for anything Jane Austen. She's had around fifty novels published, been nominated for a RITA® Award, won Reviewers' Choice Awards and received RWA's Career Achievement Award in Romantic Suspense.

Books by Mary Anne Wilson

Harlequin Heartwarming

Eclipse Ridge Ranch

Under a Christmas Moon
Her Wyoming Hero
A Cowboy's Hope

The Carsons of Wolf Lake

A Question of Honor
Flying Home
A Father's Stake

Visit the Author Profile page
at Harlequin.com for more titles.

~Tom~

Dreams Found

Dreams Lost

Love Is Forever

CHAPTER ONE

A PERSON CAN'T outride their past. Harmony Gabriel had heard that for the first time when she'd been twelve years old, and her name had been Harriet Randall. Early one April morning over seventeen years ago, a caseworker from Wyoming's Family Services had taken her out of protective care to a small white bungalow just outside Cheyenne. That's when she'd first met Letty Gabriel, the grandmother that she'd never known existed. She'd always thought that she and her father, Lester Randall, had no family. He told her that over and over again.

Grandma Letty had taken her in with open arms, shown her unconditional love, and her dad, whom she'd always called Les, had never shown up again. For a long time, she'd been afraid he would come back and take her away with him. That's when adoption proceedings had begun on grounds that

Les had abandoned his child. A year later, Harriet Randall became Harmony Leticia Gabriel, a name she'd chosen for herself at the adoption hearing. Her life as Harriet was left behind, but there were times when old memories intruded and brought back the twelve-year-old who'd been so ashamed of her father.

A person can't outride their past. She wasn't exactly running from her past, but she wasn't going to let it find her, either. Especially not in her office of the company she'd owned for five years, Perfect Harmony Events Planning in Cheyenne. On a December day, she was staring at the flashing red light on the phone console, and it seemed a perfect warning not to take the call.

Mandy Thompson, her friend and associate in the business, had put the call on hold for her. She looked across her elegant glass-topped desk at Mandy now. She could almost hear the footsteps of her past getting closer. "Are you sure he gave his name as Caleb Donovan?"

"Yes. That's why I needed to talk to you. It's not an unusual name, but it's unlikely there are two Caleb Donovans calling from

Cody, where he has a business. He needs help with an event and made it *very* clear money was not a problem. The venue— he called it Pure Rodeo—is located just south of the Flaming Sky Ranch, midway between Cody and Eclipse. It's new construction and he owns it. I thought he'd hang up when I told him we couldn't do it, but he insisted on speaking to my superior." Mandy added, "All things considered, it sure sounds like he's your Caleb Donovan."

Mandy was right about everything except her last opinion. "He was never *my* Caleb Donovan." She'd had a crush on him—that was true—but he'd never even spoken to her back then when her father had worked on the Flaming Sky Ranch. She remembered Caleb staring at her after the sheriff had put her in the front seat of his cruiser, and then pushed Les—who was falling-down drunk—into the back seat behind a metal mesh safety screen.

"I guess I can accept the fact that he's calling by some weird twist of fate," she said. "But honestly, I don't want to talk to him, even if he insisted on speaking to the owner. I can't change the fact that we're fully booked and can't take on a new client."

"He was determined, and I sure didn't want to hang up on him, especially if he's one of *those* Donovans. If he was mad about being cut off, he could give us bad press, which we do not want. They've been on the Flaming Sky Ranch forever and just about everyone in the state knows them. We don't want to offend them."

"I agree," Harmony conceded. Grandma Letty, who had passed two years ago, would have told her, *Put on your big-girl pants and take care of it instead of letting it eat at you.* That had gotten the older woman through a life of ups and downs, and she always did what she had to do. The man on the other end of the line would never know who he'd talked to.

"I'll take the call and tell him the truth, and that should be that." The light was still flashing red. He hadn't hung up. She looked at the large computer monitor on the desk to her right, and she saw her reflection in the blank screen. The woman looking back at her was wearing her big-girl pants, even though they looked like a slender black skirt she'd matched with a simple white blouse.

She fingered her lucky locket, a small oval that held a picture of Grandma Letty on one side and a picture of her daughter, Joy, on the other. The two most important people in her life, past and present, were always close to her.

She ran her fingers carelessly through her short blond hair that only emphasized the flyaway style of her pixie cut. The freckles across the bridge of her nose had faded enough over the years to be indiscernible unless you knew they were there.

"Do you want me to sit in on it with you?" Mandy asked.

She smiled as she turned to face the desk again. "No, it's okay. But do me a favor and go and check on a certain little person to see if she's still asleep."

"Last I looked, Joy was asleep hugging Mr. Winky."

The thought of her small daughter holding her rainbow unicorn reminded her that now was what counted, not something that had happened years ago. The past was nothing, and the present was good, better than she could ever have wished for. Joy was healthy and happy and beautiful, and the center of Harmony's world—a world she loved more than anything. "Let me know when she wakes up."

"I will, and good luck," Mandy said before she left the office.

You can't outride your past. Harmony obviously couldn't, but she could outride the fear of it, which still reared its ugly head at the most unexpected times. *Think on the good things.* That was something else Gramma Letty had told her more than once. She'd do that now and let Caleb Donovan down gently.

She finally tapped her earpiece and adjusted the microphone closer to her mouth. "Mr. Donovan?" Thankfully, her voice sounded pretty normal and businesslike.

"Yes, Caleb Donovan."

Nothing about the deep voice sounded even vaguely familiar. But then again, the caller wasn't a lanky teenaged boy anymore. Now he was a grown man, maybe thirty-three or thirty-four years old. "I'm Harmony Gabriel, the owner of Perfect Harmony Events Planning." It felt good to say that to a Donovan. "My associate said you called about an event you wanted us to cover this month and requested to speak with me."

"Yes, I do want you to cover a party for me."

"Since it's in December, we can't help you. We're fully booked until the middle of January." The past few years had been hard ones for the business, but it was finally coming close to what it had been before. She was thankful that the revenue from the holiday events would keep Perfect Harmony from posting a loss in the fourth quarter.

She heard Caleb exhale before he spoke. "Ms. Gabriel, I only need your help for one evening for an anniversary celebration for my parents. I own the venue, so that's all set, but I need professional help for the rest. I want the party on Christmas Eve. That's when they were married."

It was for Dash and Ruby, but their son was on a fool's errand if he expected anyone in the business to have openings for Christmas Eve. It was a few weeks away.

"I'm sorry. We can't." There was silence

on the line for a long moment, and she wondered if he'd hung up. But the red light was glowing steadily. The line was still open. "Mr. Donovan? Are you still there?"

"Yes. Is there any chance you know of another company I could contact, even if it's out of state?"

"Sorry, I don't—"

Mandy unexpectedly hurried back into the room with a sheet of paper in her hand that she handed over to Harmony. She scanned it: "Something you need to know NOW! Tell him you might be able to help him."

Harmony had no idea what Mandy was talking about, but she didn't hesitate saying, "Mr. Donovan, I need to check on something that might be of some help to you. It's a slim chance but let me find out."

"What is it?" he said quickly.

"I don't want to say until I know for sure, one way or another. Will you hold while I can verify it?"

"Yes," he responded quickly.

She hoped Mandy was right about maybe helping him. Putting her mic on mute, she said, "What's going on?"

Mandy pressed her hands flat on the desktop and leaned in closer to Harmony. "I just took a call from Marla Brewster, the bride in the Brewster-Wayne wedding. They're canceling everything. She made it clear that there would be no reconciliation. They won't fight forfeiting their deposits, and she apologized profusely for the cancellation. So, no rehearsal dinner, no wedding and no reception at the Carstairs Compound."

Harmony was stunned. She hadn't heard from the planner assigned to it, Louise Fletcher, about any second thoughts by the couple or their families. "Why didn't Louise let me know right away if they were having trouble?"

"Because she didn't know anything until I called and told her about it. She was totally taken by surprise. She's going to close down at Carstairs and hire a team to get the rentals returned and clean up everything."

The Brewsters were one of the wealthiest families in the Jackson Hole valley and being hired to do everything for their daughter's wedding had been a huge coup for the company. That had just gone up in smoke, but Harmony realized that maybe it wouldn't be totally devastating for the company. Mandy verbalized what she was thinking.

"This might not be too bad," Mandy said. "Not as much money, but not bad money, either. We might be able to pull victory out of the jaws of defeat if Caleb Donovan signs up with us."

"Exactly," Harmony said.

"The Donovan party won't be as elaborate as the wedding, but it could be a pretty good way for us to minimize our losses and get some very favorable notice in the area. With the big rodeo in July, the parties pile up, and we could get a few of the bigger ones if we play this right." Mandy had been a business major in college, and she understood numbers.

"Okay. We have to move quickly. More good news is Louise is available to take it on, and it's way up north, so I don't see me dealing with the Donovans except to back Louise up, and she hardly ever needs that. Call Louise back and let her know what's going on, and I'll get the basics of the request for you from Caleb."

Mandy nodded. "I'm on it."

"Oh, tell Louise to call me when she gets back today. We don't have a lot of time to get anything done by Christmas Eve. Twelve days, that's all. I'll set up the call with Caleb for Louise to lay everything out for him. Tomorrow morning would be a good time to get on this."

"Okay, I'll get her briefed. She probably won't be back in Cheyenne until late tonight."

"Ask her to give you a time she can do a video call with Caleb tomorrow morning."

"Aren't you kind of curious about the Donovans now?"

"No, I'm not. They're obviously still rich, have the ranch and they have good deal of fame."

"Wouldn't you like to see how Caleb turned out?"

That stopped her. She imagined Caleb would be tall and strong with dark eyes, dark hair and a year-round tan. She stopped right there. "No, I don't want to. I just want Caleb to get what he wants if we do his event. That way, we'll get what we need out of it. I've had him on hold long enough."

Mandy was on the move and out the door before Harmony could blink.

Harmony took Caleb off mute. "Mr. Donovan?"

"I'm still here."

"I think we might have good news for you after all. We just had a cancelation that clears up our calendar from tomorrow until the day after Christmas. Since your party is in that time frame, I don't see why we couldn't fulfill your request."

He didn't hide his relief when he sighed and said, "That's great to hear."

"I think we could start as soon as tomorrow."

"Tomorrow," he said. "Perfect."

"Good, then tomorrow it is."

"Now, what do you need from me besides money?"

She grinned at that. "First, before the money comes into the picture, you'll need to either meet with your planner down here in our office or have a video call so she can find out just what you expect and what we can do for you. I know that's quite a trip for you coming down here, but the faster we get in motion, the better things will be."

"I can be there in two hours," he said, taking her off guard.

"Excuse me?" Didn't he still live at the ranch or maybe Cody?

"I can be at your office in Cheyenne in two hours. I'll fly myself down and get this going faster."

She hadn't expected that and tried to think. "That would be fine, except your planner, Louise Fletcher, won't be available until tomorrow morning. There isn't any need for you to fly down. Louise can do a video call as soon as she's free to do it. Tomorrow morning would be the earliest she could take care you."

"What time will she be there tomorrow?"

"At the office?"

"Yes."

"Any time after ten o'clock. If you decide to go with us, as soon as the agreement is signed, she's on the job."

"When will she be here to start on-site?"

He really was anxious. "Monday morning."

"No, no, no," he murmured. "That's the whole weekend lost."

"I'm sorry, but—"

He cut in. "I'm flying down tomorrow so she can fly back up here with me after the meeting."

"That would be a good idea, except Ms. Fletcher is terrified of flying. She'll drive up to your place and go from there with the planning."

He was silent for a long moment before he responded. "That's unbelievable," he said.

"Tomorrow's Friday, and what if she drives up and gets there first thing Saturday morning? I think that could work."

"I guess it has to," he said, obviously not happy, but not about to cancel everything because of bad timing.

"All I need from you is general information to pass on to Louise."

"Okay."

She turned on her monitor by the phone and opened a new account template to fill in his personal information. The address he gave her for the venue turned out to also be his personal address. So, he lived at Pure Rodeo. That was interesting.

"How long will this meeting take?" Caleb asked.

"Oh, around an hour. If you both agree quickly, it can be shorter. Louise explains everything involved—pricing for the theme, food, drink and entertainment, anything special you request. So don't hesitate to ask for what you want. There's limits to what we will or can do, but believe me, she'll try."

"Understood."

A man of few words, the way she remembered his dad being. "She can do everything needed and take your good-faith deposit right then."

Her door opened and she paused. "I'm sorry, can you hold for just a minute while I make sure ten o'clock is good for Louise?"

"Sure, why not," he said easily.

She almost smiled when she put him back on mute. As Mandy came into the room, Harmony heard Caleb humming in her ear. She couldn't name the song, but she'd heard it before. "Mandy, find out if ten tomorrow morning is okay with Louise for the meeting with Caleb here."

"Louise is going to be here at eight tomorrow, sharp."

"Great. Let her know about the meeting

time and the possibility that, if he signs on, he needs her up at the venue at least by Saturday morning."

With that taken care of, Mandy left, then Harmony took Caleb off mute. The humming stopped as soon as she said, "Mr. Donovan?"

"Yes, I didn't hang up."

"Thank you for that," she said.

"What else do you need from me right now?"

"Will you be bringing anyone with you for the meeting?"

"No, I don't think so. Why?"

"We want everything to be easy and comfortable for the client, and if you're bringing your spouse or children or both, we want to be set up for that. We can offer childcare, if needed."

"No, that is definitely not needed. I'm not married, no kids. I'll be on my own for the meeting."

"Okay, not married," she found herself repeating, a bit surprised Caleb was single.

Then she got back to business. "Just two general questions. How many guests will you invite, and what theme do you want for the party?"

"Around seventy guests, give or take a couple."

"How did you find us?"

"From a friend, Chip Ewing. He's from near Jackson Hole. His ranch is on the Snake River. It was a party to announce he was going to run for political office."

She recognized the name immediately. Mr. Ewing had been elected to the state senate seven months ago. His event had run for two days at his ranch and had been very profitable at a time when money had been scarce for the business. "Yes, I remember Mr. Ewing. He and his family were really good clients, and I'm happy to hear he was so satisfied with our work."

"He thought if anyone could help me, you could. I'm glad to see he was right. Now, the deposit—card, cash, check?"

"A credit card or a check would be fine."

"Okay."

She really wanted to ask him something that she'd been wondering about before she let him go. "How many years have your parents been married?"

"Forty years on Christmas Eve."

"That's incredible." She had seldom seen Dash and Ruby on the ranch when they hadn't been together, working or riding or sitting in the media box when Dash had been the announcer for the rodeo events. They obviously knew how to make a marriage work. "I can understand why you'd celebrate that."

"Do you know what the gift is supposed to be on a fortieth anniversary?" he asked.

She had a feeling he already knew but wanted to see if she did. "Rubies."

There was a low chuckle that she liked. "Well, what a coincidence. My mother's name is Ruby."

"A very nice coincidence," she said.

The door opened, and Mandy came across to the desk. When she laid another piece of paper on the glass top, Harmony glanced down at five vendor names they had thought they'd use for the wedding. Now the list was headed with "They all want in!"

Harmony smiled and nodded. Having those vendors willing to possibly follow them to the Donovan party was a gift for

Louise. A lot of time in planning was spent on finding the right vendors. Harmony gave her a thumbs-up sign, then Mandy waved goodbye and left again.

"Do you need to know anything else, ma'am?"

Ma'am? She wondered how old he thought she was. She needed more information. "Oh, yes, I forgot, the theme you want. Is it just family or couples? Adults? Children?"

"Yes on family, along with a lot of local friends and some coming in from out of town for the party. Absolutely no children."

She was surprised by that. She would have thought kids would be part of it all. Even as a child, she'd seen how important their sons were to Ruby and Dash. Back then, everything they did was centered on supporting their sons' love of rodeo and building a strong family. She entered the information and underlined "No children attending." Whomever he invited or didn't invite was nothing to her, as long as he agreed to hire them for his event. Then she'd get back to life without a Donovan in it, but his money would do a lot of good. That made her happy.

"Mood or theme, Mr. Donovan? Do you have a preference?" Harmony asked Caleb.

"Traditional Christmas meets the rodeo." He chuckled to himself, and she liked the sound of it. "Now, that sounds weird, doesn't it?"

"No, not at all." She'd had much weirder requests before. "Louise will get it sorted out to make it what you want. I imagine you want the mood to be geared for adults."

"Yes and no. My parents are fun and a bit crazy, very much in love after all these years, and their friends are a cross section of what their life has been. My whole family's involved in the rodeo. But the party is about their life together, and that means great music for dancing, maybe a remake of their first meal after they were married, but mostly just being with people who were and are important to them in their life together."

Harmony closed her eyes as he spoke. She'd always envied the Donovan boys living on a beautiful ranch and having real parents in their lives. All she had was a father who was one of the best horse trainers in the state and one of the worst drunks. She'd never known her mother, who had died when she was just a bit older than Joy was now. Les wouldn't even talk about Adelle. It seemed too painful for Grandma Letty to talk about her daughter, her only child, who'd run off with Les and disappeared from her life.

As Caleb had been talking more about his parents, she'd felt a pain deep inside her. A sense of loss that she tried to push away, but when she started to say something, anything, she found the words almost choking her. She coughed, and then managed to say, "One more thing, if you'll hold again?"

"I'm a pro at holding," Caleb said with that touch of humor in his voice that only made her feel worse. "Thank you," she said quickly and muted the call. "Breathe," she told herself and tried to inhale and exhale as she sank back in her desk chair. "Just breathe." That feeling had come out of nowhere and threatened to overwhelm her. It had never happened before, but it almost shut her down. She steadied herself, took another breath and told herself she was okay. This would all work out and life would go on, with the business in the black at the end of the quarter.

CHAPTER TWO

CALEB SAT BACK in his computer chair behind the desk. He'd made the call to Perfect Harmony Events Planning from his office at C.D.'s Place in Cody, and he was working on trying to be patient. He'd been foolish to think he could pull off a great party that wasn't a repeat of the ones he gave at C.D.'s Place. Beer, barbeque and some great bands were all he needed to make any party a success there. But he wanted a whole lot more than that for his parents. Harmony Gabriel had been his last chance to pull that off, and he was close to sealing the deal...if she ever came back on the line again.

He was startled by a sudden blast of country and western music coming from the dining room as his brother opened the office door and leaned against the jamb. "Well, get in here, and shut that door behind you,"

Caleb said. "I didn't pay all that money for soundproofing for nothing."

A thud sounded and the music was gone as Max closed the door behind him. "I'm early, I know, but the meeting I had with the mayor was cut short." As the sheriff in these parts, Max occasionally met with the mayor. "So, what's going on with you?"

"I'm on hold for the umpteenth time on the same call."

"Hang up. Let them call you back."

"Easy for you to say. I can't afford to cut them off. I've got too much time invested in this call, and I'm pretty sure I finally found a company to take care of the party for me. Go on down and get started eating your dinner. I'll catch up."

"I'll do that," Max said. "Hope the party's a done deal for you soon."

"Me, too." He didn't know what he was thinking at first, trying to do it himself. "I just don't know how to throw a party that isn't centered on C.D.'s Place. I want it classier, and a lot better than free beer and barbeque. Right now I'm in the middle of discussing a few things with the owner. Their offices are in Cheyenne and

I'm meeting with the planner down there at ten tomorrow morning."

"Well, good luck. Mom and Dad deserve the best, that's for sure."

"Agreed. Say, Max, I need you to take your badge off if you're sitting at the bar again. You know how it makes some guys uneasy to see the county sheriff sitting next to them."

"It's not the same reaction Coop gets when he drops by here."

Caleb chuckled. "True. A big rodeo star trumps a sheriff any old day."

His twin brother was a five-time world champion in bareback bronc riding with a ton of other wins he took along the way. Most people thought he'd get number six soon.

"Are you taking Heather to the party?" Max asked.

His enthusiasm dampened a bit at hearing the name. "I don't know. Maybe. She's been out of town, but I think she'll be back for Christmas." He liked Heather well enough but wasn't looking for anything serious, and he got the feeling she was. "Mom and Dad aren't crazy about her, and it's their party. I might just go stag and forget about a date. Who are you taking?"

"Miss Wyoming." They both cracked up at that. Max would be going stag, too. "What's this company you found for the party?"

"Perfect Harmony Events Planning. The owner's the one I'm dealing with. She seems pretty good at what she does, but she must have a love for putting people on hold."

"Well, when she's back, turn on the Donovan charm and make sure you don't give her a clue how desperate you are. One important piece of advice is do not beg. Cowboys never beg."

"Get out of here, Max."

"Yeah, I'm hungry. See ya."

The music blared again only to be shut out by the thudding of the office door closing. The truth was, Caleb was a bit desperate, and he didn't know if he was above begging. He needed this party to go off without a hitch.

"Mr. Donovan. I'm back." The voice on the other end was smooth and low. "Sorry to keep you waiting."

Instead of saying what he wanted to say, *It's about time*, he made himself say, "Not a problem."

"I need some more information, but it's not a lengthy list."

He didn't mind just listening to her talk as long as she stopped putting him on hold. Her voice had intrigued him from her first words over the line, and the more she spoke, the more intrigued he was. "Fire away," he murmured.

He'd enjoy listening to her while they spoke, but his goal was to give his parents the best celebration ever. It was business pure and simple, but he did wonder what the woman behind the voice looked like. Maybe he'd see her sometime if the party became a reality.

"You mentioned you live at the venue site?"

"Yes, I also have quarters in Cody at my business there. It makes life easier for me."

"I can see that could make things easier."

Her tone was soft with a slight huskiness, and very easy on the ear, but also businesslike and direct. This *is* business, he reminded himself. "Next question."

"At what times do you want the event to start and end?"

"Since I own the venue, we can have any timetable that works the best. I was thinking of starting later in the afternoon and going until the last guests leave."

"Hmm, so tell me about this venue."

She must have a cheat sheet of questions to ask a prospective client. "Have you heard of C.D.'s Place in Cody?"

"I don't think so," she said.

That surprised him. She had to be one of the only people in the state who hadn't heard about it, especially since Coop's fans flocked there in hopes they'd catch a glimpse of him. "I opened it about ten years ago, and now I've expanded to a second location. The new place, Pure Rodeo, just completed construction on land halfway between Cody and Eclipse. The Cody location shows all the sports, but rodeo is favored. However, the new place is what the name says, pure rodeo. It's going to be open when the rodeo circuit shows are anywhere in the state. We'll do full video coverage of the rodeo, no matter where it's taking place. I'm thinking it might be smart in off times to expand to weddings and private parties. It's set up for catering and the kitchen can handle up to two hundred plates."

"That sounds impressive for a bar."

Saying it was a bar was like saying the *Mona Lisa* was just a painting. "I like to think of it as a destination place for everyone who loves the rodeo and that life. It is definitely not just a bar."

He looked down at the red T-shirt he was wearing with jeans as faded as the shirt was. But the logo for C.D.'s Place still showed up well on the cotton: a midnight-black horse with mane and tail flowing, racing across the front with flames coming out of its back hooves. He was tempted to send one of the T-shirts to Ms. Gabriel to give her an idea about what Pure Rodeo was all about.

"Of course it isn't," she said with just a touch of dismissiveness in her voice.

Because she sounded good saying that, he let it go, but he'd forget gifting her a shirt. The woman lived in a city that hosted the largest rodeo in the world every July during their Frontier Days celebration. But she seemed to have little to no knowledge about the rodeo. "So, is there anything else?"

"The food. You mentioned the dinner?"

"Prime rib with roasted potatoes. That was my parents' first meal after they were married. They splurged for the occasion. Every Christmas Eve since then, they have it for dinner."

"That's nice," she said. "Flowers. Do they have a favorite flower?"

"When they had that dinner the first time, there was a poinsettia on the table, a small one. My mom always gets them for Christmas—they always have one at the table for their anniversary dinner."

"Oh, that's really…sweet," she murmured. "I'll be sure to pass that on to Louise along with your desire to have a traditional Christmas-slash-rodeo theme, and she can go from there."

Harmony Gabriel was very calm and efficient, laser focused on her work. "Does your planner know anything about the rodeo?"

"Absolutely. She's a real fan."

That was a relief. "You believe your company can support the theme I want?"

"Certainly. We bring wishes to life. We don't have to slay a dragon to put on a great World of the Dragon party and win an industry excellence award for that event. You can check our references if you want me to send them to you or look us up in the Better Business Bureau."

He wasn't going to do that. But he was nervous about the whole thing. He figured honesty was the best policy at the moment. "I owe my parents so much that I'm getting nervous about being able to give them everything they want." He hadn't admitted that to anyone, not even to himself until a few days ago when he'd started his hunt for a party-planning service. "That's why I decided to find a professional to do it for me. I don't want to blow it."

There was silence, then Harmony said, "Oh, Mr. Donovan, you have no idea how nervous some of our clients get. When it's all for family, for the people they love, they feel just the way you do. They want it to be perfect in every way. Now, we both know perfection really can't be had, but you'd be surprised how perfect your parents will feel their event is. It's emotions and caring and the love involved in it. That's what counts. We'll give you our very best. I promise you that."

He sat in his office alone, stunned. He'd never dealt with anyone who sounded so genuine when he was bargaining for business services. She'd said nothing was perfect, but what she'd told him was perfect for what he'd needed at the moment. "Thank you," he said. "I needed that."

There was a soft laugh in his ear before she said, "Well, I'm glad I could help, sir."

He smiled at her smooth response. "I am, too."

"Good, then I've done my job."

She sure had. He closed his eyes tightly as he thought, a voice was a voice, and when it came from a good businessperson, it was just that, the voice of a good businessperson. She knew what to say, how to say it and when to say it, and she had the voice to say it. Then she spoke again, and she burst his bubble. "Basically, you want a traditional Christmas, with Western influences."

Obviously, Harmony Gabriel could say the right things until she didn't say the right things. Caleb sat back in his chair, put his feet up on the only cleared spot on his desk. He was making an effort to ease the stiffness in his right leg, which he still dealt with years after an injury when he'd been bull riding. It was starting to throb. He needed her to understand what he wanted, and he made sure he kept any annoyance out of his voice.

"Western is great, obviously, but I want it rodeo *specific*." He emphasized the last word intentionally. "Traditional Christmas is pretty self-explanatory." He tried to lighten his mood with an addition meant to be funny. "But nothing cheesy, ma'am."

Regrettably, she didn't laugh at all, but spoke in a clipped tone she hadn't used before. "It will be both classical and classy, sir."

He'd blown that. "Yes, but not stuffy." He wasn't joking now. "No one there will be stuffy, not my parents or their guests."

She was quiet for an awkward moment, then said evenly, "Of course not. It's a celebration. That's a fun, happy time." He heard her exhale before saying, "I have no more questions. You can go over everything with Louise tomorrow at the meeting."

She hadn't hung up on him or told him to go away, but the call was ending, and he was relieved he hadn't annoyed her enough to have her cancel everything. "I'll do that and talk to her about coming up at least by Saturday. That leaves ten days until Christmas Eve. I'm hoping to not waste time."

"Of course. I understand." There was a touch of discernible patronization in that voice now, but it was gone when she kept talking. "Maybe she'll be able to drive up tomorrow afternoon and be ready to start everything early Saturday morning."

There was no way he'd push too hard, so he let that go and changed subjects before she ended the call. "You said it's an hour for the meeting?"

"Give or take, depending on how much you all agree on, or don't agree on. Louise agreed to ten o'clock for the meeting."

Her voice was never raised, staying low and composed. She must be able to do this business in her sleep. "I'm sure things will go smoothly."

"We always hope so," she said. "Oh, I remembered something else I need to ask you about. Louise will be staying up there until everything's finished and you sign off on it. What would you recommend for her lodgings?"

Something came to him that made perfect sense. "I have an offer but don't know if Ms. Fletcher would be okay with it. Cody has some good places, but they usually get full around Christmas. The B and Bs sure do. A lodge south of here closed down a few months ago, and the dude ranches are booked way in advance.

"My offer is, I have a second floor where my office and living quarters are. Construction's just finished, and I haven't moved in there. It's furnished, ready for occupancy, and Ms. Fletcher is welcome to use it for the duration of her stay. She'll be right on-site without having to commute at all."

"That sounds good, if it won't put you out too much."

"No, not at all. But maybe she won't want to be there 24/7."

"I can tell you right now, Louise would like being on-site without a commute. She could get feedback from your parents, and the more she knows them and you, the more she can read the vibe. She's very good at reading people."

Caleb shifted to take his feet down and rub the knee that was throbbing. Glancing at the bank of security system monitors on the rough plaster wall directly across from his desk, he spotted Max. Scanning the other screens, he could see a lot of after-work customers filing in, and the live band was warming up near the dance floor. "My parents are pretty easy to read. They love each other, their family, our ranch and the rodeo. It's that simple," he said as he watched Max at a table near the bar. His badge was out of sight. Some customers preferred not to eat and drink near the sheriff of Clayton County while he was on duty. Max had forgotten to hide his badge a few times. Reminding him never hurt.

He heard a low sigh over the line, and something about it caught at him the same way her voice had at the first. "That's special," she said in a half whisper.

"Yes, it is." He eased himself to his feet and turned to the windows that ran along the outside wall of the office. The view beyond the city of Cody was beautiful with rolling foothills and mountains far off in the distance. The day was clear and cold, and he could make out the cars going in the direction of Yellowstone Park.

Then he refocused on his image overlapping the view. His longer dark hair was mussed from running his fingers through it, and the red T-shirt and jeans didn't exactly scream *owner*. He looked like a laborer or ranch hand who'd stopped in for a drink on the way home from building something or working cattle. Maybe he should dress up a bit to go down for the meeting tomorrow. Or maybe he'd just be comfortable.

"Do you have any questions you need answered before the meeting?" Harmony asked.

He stared off in the distance again. "No, just tell me where to go when I drive away from the airport tomorrow morning."

"I'll text you directions as soon as we hang up. I'm really pleased that it looks as if we can help you with your gift for your parents."

She'd never know how pleased he was that

the deal was almost sealed. "I appreciate you finding a spot for me." Who knew, maybe he'd get to meet Harmony Gabriel in person tomorrow and see the woman behind the voice?

"Can I give you some advice, Mr. Donovan?" she asked.

Advice? That sounded interesting. "I'm open to anything," he said, and then realized that sounded a bit off. "I mean, you know your business so any advice to make this all work is welcome." He was amazed at how quickly he could walk that back.

"Remember that Louise is there to make the holidays easier for you and to make your parents happy. Don't hesitate to ask her for what you need. She takes criticism well, although she usually doesn't get it, but let her take on the highs and lows, and you just go along for the ride."

He liked that idea of having the load off his shoulders and hoped that was the way it played out. "So, all I have to do is show up tomorrow, take the meeting, sign off on everything and give you my good-faith deposit."

"That's it. Now, I'll let you go. Thanks for

choosing Perfect Harmony Events Planning, and happy holidays."

"To you, too," he said as the line went dead.

He sat there for a moment. No matter what, he was going to sign those papers tomorrow. No haggling, no fight to lower expenses. That was all on the shelf as long as what he saw and heard tomorrow sounded good. He leaned forward to put his cell down on his cluttered desk right when it vibrated, announcing a new text had come in. He checked and it was from Perfect Harmony Events Planning with the promised information. Ms. Gabriel was very efficient, and if he did get a chance to meet her, he'd tell her that. What mattered was he finally had hope that this would be a very merry Christmas Eve.

HARMONY WAS IN her corner office on the fourth floor of the Walker-Daggot Building at six o'clock going through the notes on the Donovan assignment to pass on to Louise. Joy was sitting off to her right on the thick gray carpet in front of the floor-to-ceiling windows that overlooked Cheyenne. The toddler was totally transfixed by a huge Christmas tree on the roof of the medical center directly behind them. When the tree had been lit up for the first time, Joy had been thrilled watching the twinkling red and green lights dancing through its branches. A huge silver star on top glowed in the dusk of the growing night.

"We need to go home, sweetie," Harmony said with a sigh as she swiveled her computer chair around to look at her daughter. Today had been crazy, going from bad to great without missing a beat. It was over. She hadn't had a Donovan walk into the office, but she'd spoken to Caleb, and it had gone well. The company would be okay, and so would she.

"Baby? Joy?" she said, but the child wasn't paying her any attention. In her pink overalls and a fluffy white sweater, the toddler looked almost angelic with her pale blond wispy curls giving the suggestion of a halo around her face. "Joy?" she said again. "We're going home."

The toddler scrambled to her feet, but she didn't come over to Harmony. Instead, she went closer to the window to press her nose against the glass. "Pwitty, pwitty, Mama."

It was the first time Joy had made a full sentence and Harmony had never been more surprised or proud in her life. True, she had to translate *pwitty* to *pretty*, but it bordered on a miracle that the child spoke at all. Their caseworker during the adoption proceedings had warned Harmony that Joy had tested low in most measures of development. But that had been blown away when Joy had stood up by herself two weeks after coming home with Harmony and walked a month later. Now she was actually really talking.

It had been love at first sight for Harmony when she'd seen Joy in the foster home. The baby's blue eyes had taken in everything, but the child had never smiled nor spoken. Lately, it seemed Joy smiled a lot over little things, like a play telephone, or something big, like a thirty-foot-tall fake Christmas tree she could see out the windows. "Pretty, pretty lights," Harmony whispered.

Joy bobbed her head enthusiastically.

"Pwitty, pwitty," she said, then turned toward her mother and rushed at her.

Harmony opened her arms and Joy ended up on her lap. Together they sat silently looking at the lights outside, as more flashed on across the city. What a day it had been, from her losing a huge job to being in a position to help the Donovan family. What had almost scared her at first had actually brought a degree of peace when it ended. Her past hadn't hurt her but had handed her a way to help her business.

She heard the door open and swiveled around as Mandy came into the office. Joy squirmed to get down, and when Harmony reluctantly let her go, the toddler went right back to the windows. Mandy dropped down in one of two chairs that faced her desk. The only furniture in the large gray-and-white space was the desk, a computer chair, a small filing cabinet and the two stylized chairs across from her.

"What a day," Mandy said with a sigh.

"Just what I was thinking." Harmony shut down her computer. "After you ran the possible numbers on the Donovan job, our fourth quarter looks good, but the best thing that happened today is Joy just said her first sentence, 'Pretty, pretty, Mama.'"

Harmony heard her daughter speak up behind her, "Pwitty."

Mandy smiled. "She's doing well, and I have more good news for you—although the news about Joy is by far the best. Wes at Inspired Bar-B-Q heard about the cancellation and wants to put his name in for it if we can use him."

"I love his food, but Caleb isn't looking for barbeque. He wants it to be classier." Harmony sat back in her chair to slowly swivel side to side. She glanced at Joy, who was lying on the carpet now with her eyes closed. The child could sleep anywhere. "They want prime rib and roasted potatoes."

"I saw that on your notes, but I thought it didn't hurt to ask for Wes." She sighed again. "Isn't it kind of satisfying that the wealthy in the world sometimes need us to make their lives feel more special?"

Relief was a more prominent feeling for Harmony right then. "Caleb wants this to happen as much as we do. I'm pretty sure he'll sign tomorrow."

"How do you know that?"

"I just know it," she said. "You know, I'm glad Caleb called, actually. The more I remember what Dash put up with from Les, the more I feel I owe the family this party. I think Santa came early for them and for us. What's great is, I have a reason to believe in Santa—at least until Joy gets too old and the Santa bubble bursts." She'd never had a chance to believe any of that when she was a kid and wanted to. Les made very sure she knew Santa wasn't real. "I want Joy to believe in the man in red for as long as she wants to, and I'll believe right along with her."

"My girls are on the cusp of realizing that a man as fat as that can't fit down our chimney." Mandy chuckled to herself. "Milly's nine now and Missy's ten, so my time's growing short for the Santa thing."

"Speaking of time, did Louise call in again?"

"Yes, she's aiming to rest up tonight, then be here by eight in the morning."

"I'll brief her then and explain how time is really important to Caleb. I'd bet the ranch that he'll get here right at ten."

CHAPTER THREE

THE NEXT MORNING, Caleb set the twin-engine plane down at Cheyenne Regional Airport an hour and ten minutes after he'd taken off from the Flaming Sky Ranch. He'd used a courtesy car that the airport had supplied for him, found the Walker-Daggot Building, a four-story faux adobe structure, and used the curbside valet parking he hadn't expected. Right at ten o'clock, he stepped off the elevator at the fourth floor to be greeted by a woman wearing a bright red sweater almost the color of her hair. A big snowflake knitted into the front had Let It Snow! stitched in green across it.

She flashed a bright smile. "Mr. Donovan?"

"Yes, ma'am," he said and took off his hat.

"I thought so. I'd heard that Coop Donovan had a twin, and you really do look a lot like the pictures I've seen around here of

Coop." His brother was a rodeo star who often competed in Cheyenne, so he was easily recognizable. "You're very much alike."

"That's what I've been told," he said dryly.

She laughed at that. "Of course. You're identical twins."

"Yes, ma'am."

He'd chosen not to get too dressed up after all, keeping with his jeans but substituting a black Henley collarless shirt for the usual T-shirt and wearing his favorite tooled boots that he'd had for years. He'd taken time to tame his hair back from his face and chose to wear a lucky hat that Coop had gifted to him last Christmas. It was branded on the inner liner with a Flaming Coop D. label, all part of his merchandising program.

"This way," she said as she started off to their left down a corridor of bare white walls and tiling. "I heard that you flew your own plane down today."

"Yes, ma'am, I did."

She stopped near the end of the corridor at a dark wood door with a brass plaque on it. Perfect Harmony Events Planning was elegantly embossed on the burnished metal along with We Make Wishes Come True. Mandy swung the door back and led the way into a reception area with thick gray carpeting and white walls, and a Christmas tree across the room standing between two closed doors. Neither door had an identifying nameplate, and the Christmas tree added a splash of color in the bland space.

The tree was nice enough but was as fake as the garlands draped on the wall around the room. The only furnishings were a reception desk to the left of the entry door along with wooden filing cabinets and four chairs, presumably for clients to use while waiting to be seen.

As if she'd read his mind, Mandy said, "Excuse our almost empty space here. It's only because of Christmas that we have any color at all. We only moved in a few months ago, and we've been so incredibly busy that we barely had time enough to get our sign on the door and the Christmas things up."

He shrugged. "When business is that busy, taking time to decorate can't be a top priority."

The woman seemed to always have a

smile that didn't look a bit forced. He liked that. "That is exactly why everything else is boring. Well, most everything, except the conference room where Ms. Fletcher will meet with you. It was a priority, and it shows."

She motioned to the closed door to the left of the tree. "I'll show you in." He followed her and stepped into a room that was impressive. A large oval glass-topped table with eight black wooden chairs spaced around it figured prominently in the center of the room. Nothing was on the table except a small notebook sitting in front of a large computer monitor. A printer and phone console sat on a side table within reach from the chair at the end of the desk nearest the windows that looked out over Cheyenne. He could even see the airport off in the distance.

The wall to the left of the windows was covered by framed photos, and the wall across the room from it had a breakfront with a beautiful poinsettia in a brass vase in front of a round mirror. A carved wooden screen was set up to hide the corner of the room. He moved to the photo wall and started scanning the pictures.

"Those are just a fraction of our best events."

He saw framed images of aesthetically stunning gatherings. They were of everything from weddings to other kinds of formal events, indoors and out, along with more casual parties and incredible kids' parties. One showed a huge dragon coming out of what looked for all the world to be a rock cave. That was obviously the event Harmony had told him about. An award for excellence was hanging right beside it.

"They give you an idea of the variety of events we can do, although we also do small events and more private parties. Louise will be right in," Mandy said and ducked out, leaving the door open. Caleb spotted a photo of the Ewing event near the middle of the arrangement. On the white matte frame below the picture was a handwritten inscription: "Thanks to Harmony Gabriel and Perfect Harmony Events Planning for putting together the best celebration ever at the Triple Love Ranch! The Ewing family." He recognized Chip Ewing and his three boys in the photo, but not the tall woman by him with long dark hair and a deep tan, wearing jeans and a T-shirt.

He'd met Ewing's wife—Molly or Millie, maybe—an attractive brunette who had never ceased talking. For sure the dark-haired lady wasn't his wife. Then he saw the T-shirt she was wearing. It was white with a fabric-painted version of the plaque he'd just seen on the business's entry door. It was very attention-getting, and Caleb figured he was looking at the lady behind the voice, Harmony Gabriel. She wasn't what he'd imagined, but then again, he wasn't sure what he'd imagined her to look like.

He'd seen enough and turned away to look out the window with a fake Christmas garland along the top and hanging halfway down its sides. The sky was brilliant blue with not a cloud in sight. He was looking forward to getting this meeting over with after he'd made sure Ms. Fletcher knew what he wanted, then he'd sign the papers, pay the deposit and fly back to the ranch. He'd have to go up to Cody today, check out how things were going at C.D.'s, then maybe drive over to Sheridan to see if Heather was back from her trip.

He went around the table to go back to the door just as a heavyset woman stepped into the room. "Mr. Donovan," she said with a pleasant smile. She was wearing a white T-shirt with the plaque from the entry door reproduced on it, along with jeans and low-heeled boots. Her dark hair was pulled back off her tanned face into a high ponytail. "So delighted to meet you." She came closer to him and held out her hand. "I'm Louise Fletcher, and I'm here to make sure your parents have the best anniversary celebration possible."

Caleb smiled at her. "That's what I want, too."

"Then let's get down to work."

And for the next little while, they did just that. By the time Caleb was on his way back to the airport, he was feeling very relieved. Louise Fletcher understood what he wanted, and she was a huge rodeo fan, a bit in awe that he was Coop's brother. On top of that, she was coming up to Pure Rodeo today, and would be arriving around six o'clock. That gave him time to check on

C.D.'s Place. He hadn't run into Harmony Gabriel, but that idea was fading away. The party was center stage now.

WHEN HARMONY RETURNED to the office after taking Joy for a walk to stay out of the way, it was ten minutes to eleven. Apparently, the meeting between Caleb and Louise hadn't lasted a full hour. Mandy wasn't at her desk in the reception area, so Harmony crossed to go into her office. She pushed the stroller off to one side in the sparsely furnished room, then lifted Joy out of it and into her arms.

Mandy came in. "So glad you're back," she said.

Harmony set Joy on the floor and crouched to take off the child's outside clothing. Once that was done, Joy ran to the window to see the huge Christmas tree on the roof again.

Mandy motioned Harmony to the chair behind her desk, which was a Plexiglas-styled piece of furniture that she loved. "Sit—I need to tell you about the meeting."

"Did he sign?" she asked, heading to her chair.

"You bet, and he didn't argue about anything." Mandy took one of the two chairs facing her. "It's a done deal. Louise promised to drive up today and get there around six tonight."

That was a huge relief. "Wonderful."

"We're going to do quite well when the dust settles. We make a great team," Mandy said.

"Yes, we do." Harmony looked over at her daughter. The huge Christmas tree had Joy's full attention. She was ready for the lights to come on, but it was a good six hours before dusk. She had a long wait.

"Everything's working out," she said as she swiveled to look at Mandy.

"I'd say so. And Louise told me she's had great luck with the vendors. She'll have very few slots that need filling."

"Where is Louise?"

"She left. She had to go home before she drove up north. She downloaded her files on the Donovan job for you and said she'd call you once she got there to get your input."

Louise was on top of everything. Mandy asked, "Aren't you going to ask about Caleb Donovan?"

Harmony shrugged. "As long as he gets

what he wants, that's all that matters. I mean, I wish them all well." She wasn't about to admit that she'd taken Joy for a walk so she wouldn't have to see Caleb Donovan.

"All I can say is he's pretty darn nice. A great smile, really easy to work with and willing to pay for the best. He gives cowboys a good name."

She figured, with his parents being his examples growing up, it was pretty much a sure thing he'd be a lot like them. "I'm glad it went so smoothly."

Mandy looked at Joy and smiled before talking to Harmony again. "I need to contact a man named Dub, who apparently heard we had a good chance of getting the Donovan job. He wants to be considered for the music at the party. His band is called Dub's Silver Kickers. Don't ask about that name, because I don't know, but I checked on him, and he gets great reviews for the shows he's put on. I let him know that if we're going to be planning the party, we'll call when we decided what band to use."

"You do that, and I'll go over Louise's notes from the meeting."

Mandy stood but paused when her cell

phone clipped to her waistband chimed. She glanced at the screen. "Louise," she said to Harmony. "Great timing." Then she took the call. "Hi there. Harmony's back, so we can—" Mandy frowned as she listened, and then said, "I'm putting you on speaker so Harmony can hear this firsthand."

"Harmony?" she heard Louise's voice come over the phone's speaker.

"Yes, I'm here," she said. "Mandy was just telling me how great the meeting was with Mr. Donovan."

"It was amazing, but I have bad news."

Louise's voice was strained, and Harmony felt her chest tighten. "What is it?" she asked, looking at Mandy, who had dropped down in the chair she'd been sitting in before the call. She was frowning.

"I'm so sorry, but I can't do the job. I just got a call from my mother. My dad fell and broke his hip, and I can't leave town, not now. Mom's so upset, and I can't leave her alone."

Harmony felt horrible for Louise and her parents, but she also felt her heart sink that all the good that came out of the meeting was fading away and out of her reach. "Of course you can't. They need you. Don't even worry about anything, I'll take care of it." Mandy raised a brow at that.

"I'm so sorry," Louise repeated.

"No, I'm sorry your dad's hurt. Family always comes first. Give your folks my love and best wishes. Keep me up to date, okay?"

"I will, I promise," Louise said, and the line went dead.

Harmony sank back in her chair as Mandy asked the obvious question, "How can you take care of it?"

She sighed. "I'm not sure." She started to close her eyes but stopped as the blunt truth of her situation struck her. "Actually, I only have one choice, and I'm it. I can't cancel. But I can't leave Joy alone until Christmas Day. I won't leave her." That wasn't an option. "I'll take her with me and find a nanny or a caregiver for her up there. If not, I'll have to work around her some way."

"I wish I could take over for Louise, but my strength isn't in designing and planning."

Mandy was the figures and scheduling genius at the company and the planners were the creative side. "I know you would, but that wouldn't work."

"You think Caleb will be okay with Joy being there?"

"I'll do my job. I do it with her here most of the time." She knew she was talking to bolster her own courage, and she kept going. "If he doesn't like it, then I guess that's it. I'll bite the bullet and we'll stay right here and hope the loss for the quarter can be made up in the New Year."

Mandy didn't argue. "I'll start hunting for childcare for you up there, but I'm thinking that it might be better for you to leave Joy here with me until you actually get there, and Caleb finds out what's happening."

She knew that was probably the best idea for the moment. "You're right. I can't show up with her and immediately give him an ultimatum—she stays with me, or I come back and the party's off."

Mandy grinned. "The girls would love to have Joy stay overnight. They've wanted that forever and the baby loves them. So, you can go up alone and find out what the final verdict is."

Thank goodness for Mandy.

Before Joy came into her life, Harmony would have just taken over the whole job and thought nothing of it. But not now. At best, she'd be able to make it work with Joy with her; at worst, she'd lose the job. "Perfect. Now I need a flight to get me up there by five or so, a rental car and then try to arrive on time."

Mandy smiled at her. "Just call when you know what's what up there. Then we'll figure out how to get Joy to you, if he agrees to it."

"Of course. As soon as I know, you'll know."

"Hope this works," Mandy said as she left to get the flight and rental set up for Harmony.

Harmony had deliberately not allowed herself to think about the one thing she'd never thought she'd do. She'd be going back to the Flaming Sky Ranch, and the very thought of it made her feel off balance. But, she had to remember, Caleb might be the only Donovan she had to see in person. The venue was separate from the main ranch, and all of her work would be at the venue.

She'd put on her big-girl pants and face what she had to face, but Harmony Gabriel would be the one facing it, not Harriet Randall. Harmony Gabriel would do it. No one around would know anything about her other than she was good at what she did, and they'd end up with a real celebration for Dash and Ruby's forty years of marriage.

CHAPTER FOUR

UNLIKE LOUISE, Harmony liked flying and at five thirty that evening she was leaving the airport in Cody in a small SUV rental. She went through the town, barely glancing at it as she headed for the southbound entrance onto the highway. Leaving Joy at Mandy's house had been hard on her, but not on the baby. As soon as Joy saw Mandy's kids and the fort they'd made out of sheets, she'd been thrilled to dive in and roll around on the floor.

Harmony, on the other hand, had almost cried on the way to the airport. By the time she was on the highway heading south, she tried to focus on what to say when she was the one meeting Caleb at the venue instead of Louise. *I'm sorry. Louise had a family emergency, so I'm here to take over, and by the way, my daughter is coming tomorrow to stay as long as I do.* No, that seemed to be information overload. Maybe just say that Louise wasn't available, so she came up to do the job. Let that sink in, and then tell him about Joy. She was leaning toward the second option.

She was halfway to the Flaming Sky Ranch area when her cell phone chimed. She glanced at the caller ID. Mandy. She tapped her earpiece and Christmas music was the first thing she heard. "Mandy. What's going on? Is Joy okay?"

"She's very okay. Right now she's dancing with the girls to 'Rudolph, the Red-Nosed Reindeer.' She bounces and wiggles her shoulders. It's beyond cute. Don't worry, I'm taking a video of it for you."

Harmony was happy that Joy was doing well but it hurt that she wasn't there to see the baby dance for the first time. "That's... that's so great," she said, hoping her voice didn't give away her ambiguity. Mandy was a godsend to have in her life, and she was thankful for their friendship over the years. She was like family and Joy needed that. She did, too.

"I'll send the video to your phone later, okay?"

The music in the background had childish laughter laced through it. "Yes, I'd love that."

"Listen, Caleb just called the office and it routed to my cell. He wants Louise's contact number to find out how close she is."

She glanced at the dashboard clock. She had about twenty minutes to get there on time. "Give him an ETA of fifteen to twenty minutes."

"Do I tell him you're coming and not Louise?"

"No. I'd rather he found out when I got there so I can read his expression about the surprise change of plans."

"You're right," Mandy said. "Okay, I'll pass that on."

"Tell Joy I love her."

"Sure will, and you drive safely."

Harmony tapped her Bluetooth as bright headlights flashed in her rearview mirror. In the fading light of day, she could make out a huge truck of some kind gaining on her quickly. She glanced at her speedometer, and she was driving a few miles an hour under the posted seventy-mile-per-hour speed limit. She had no idea how fast the truck was going, but the gap between the vehicles was almost nonexistent now. The blare of its horn jolted her as the truck swung into the second lane, going past her so fast that her car shuddered in its back draft.

With the failing light and the truck's tinted windows, there was no way to see the driver before it pulled back in front of her and sped off until it was a mere dot of red light in the distance. "Here I thought cowboys were supposed to be laid-back and easy," she muttered to herself. Wherever that driver was headed, he didn't have any traffic besides her on the road, so why did he make such a point of passing her like that?

She forgot about the silver truck as she neared the turnoff for Flaming Sky Ranch after what seemed like miles of passing the ranch's three-rail white pasture fencing. Then she saw the wide turnoff onto a two-lane road that headed back and out of sight into the distance. She found herself slowing down instead of getting past it and putting it behind her.

At the start of the access road that led

into the shadows of the ranch beyond, a new sign spanned the twenty-foot width of driveway between two massive brick pillars on either side. *FLAMING SKY RANCH* was carved into the burnished wood and flooded with light. Below it on a secondary sign hanging from chains were the gate directions and a greeting: Come On In. Anytime Is RODEO Time!

This new entrance hadn't framed her humiliating last trip down to the highway. Her hands were gripping the steering wheel tightly and she eased them back. This wasn't the ranch she'd roamed with Duke, the horse Dash had asked her to exercise for him that summer. She wouldn't go down to the security gates again. No need to. She sped up and kept going until she knew she was close to Pure Rodeo. The white rail fencing was gone, and the area beyond it had been cleared back from the pull-off space paved with cobblestones. A huge lighted boulder, at least ten feet tall, was set on the cobbles and painted on it was a beautiful rendering of a muscular black horse rearing up. A red banner under his flailing front hooves declared, PURE RODEO! Welcome!

The glow of lights from Pure Rodeo could be seen fifty feet ahead down a wide driveway. She knew the building was on Flaming Sky Ranch property, but with its own access off the highway. The naked deciduous trees that lined the drive moved in a light breeze, making the lights beyond them shift in the night. As she got closer, she saw a large structure, high in the middle and sprawling out on each side.

Lights were everywhere, white outlining the fascia of a wide porch that fronted the building. Red and blue lights wrapped the rails from side to side, but it was what was on the roof that held her attention: a life-size metal horse sculpture on the highest part of the middle section.

She slowed as she neared a turnout for passenger pickup and drop-off near a sweep of stairs that led up to double entry doors. It was all impressive in the way it seemed to belong in its surroundings, with the lights celebrating it being there. Caleb had left enough mature trees at strategic spots that they gave character and a sense of welcoming to the area.

But it was the roof sculpture that was incredible, the inanimate horse looking for all the world as it if was racing across the roof, its mane and tail flowing out behind it, with flames licking its back hooves. Simple white floodlights highlighted the extraordinary piece of art perfectly, so anyone who came here wouldn't forget it easily.

There was a sign to the right of a wide walkway to the stairs that said, This Is The Place! Come On In. She looked farther along the front of the building and saw a simple sign lit with a red arrow pointing toward the end of the parking area and to a delivery area in the back. She drove toward it, turned to her right to go around the end of the building and pulled onto a large area covered in concrete that was big enough to accommodate more than one eighteen-wheeler truck.

Caleb's directions, which he had given to Louise, were to go around the back to double brown metal doors marked Deliveries at the far end of the building. The floodlights that lined the sides of the parking area weren't lit, so all she could see was what the beams of her SUV swept over. First, she saw a huge silver pickup parked by the doors. She pulled in next to the truck, flipped up the hoodie attached to her suede jacket, then got out. She couldn't resist pressing her hand to the hood of the truck: it was warm, very warm in the middle of a very cold evening. So, the driver was inside the building. Either Caleb was that aggressive driver from earlier on the highway, or someone else inside was guilty.

She reached in the SUV for her large shoulder bag that acted as her briefcase and held all her notes, photos and lists of every service that she'd ever used for the business. She inhaled the frigid air, and she caught the scent of new lumber, freshness and something else she'd never been able to identify when she'd lived around the area. She still couldn't, but she liked it.

She approached the doors and reached for the latch on the closest one. It clicked then swung outward, giving her access to a fully lit storage room with dry goods, canned goods and paper goods lining shelves by a massive walk-in freezer. A door across the space stood open and gave access to what she thought must be the main part of Pure Rodeo. She stepped through it out onto wide plank flooring, with heavy beams high overhead that held large light fixtures lit with bare bulbs inside metal cages. She'd seen them a lot in livestock buildings. A staircase to her left was off center and led up to a partial second story.

She was anxious to look around on the main level, but it would have to wait until she found Caleb. She felt nervous as she climbed the stairs up to a walkway on the second level that seemed to give access to two doors, one on each end of it. Eight-foot-tall Plexiglas panels gave a full view of the bottom level. She glanced from that to the night view seen through the multi-paned windows that were straight ahead.

Staring out at a land that looked different than when she'd been there years ago, Harmony could see no shadows of old buildings that had been abandoned and rusted ranch equipment growing weeds between the wheels and plowing forks. That had all been taken away, and the pasture was empty. Then she looked farther and swallowed hard when she saw the silhouette of a massive ponderosa pine with a backdrop of shadowy trees and smaller evergreens rimming it. Even at a distance, she felt the power of it, now twice as tall as it had been before. It was her tree, her wishing tree. She had come across it her first week riding Duke. It had become almost magical for her, making her feel safe under its spreading boughs, as if she finally belonged somewhere. It was so strong, and she'd lie under it and make wishes. Sunlight played on the flat side of the needles and when a breeze ruffled them, it looked as if there were twinkling lights threaded through the branches. She'd thought it was magic, so she'd wished for things. Going there had gotten her through that last horrible summer at the ranch.

She wished she could walk out to it before she left, and despite bone-chilling cold in the air, she wanted to lie down under the big tree to look up through its branches as the sun reflected off the needles. Mostly, she wished she could lie under the tree on a summer's day with Joy and show her the magic of the tree's lights.

CALEB WAS IN his office anticipating the arrival of Louise Fletcher, who had five more minutes before she'd be late. He'd barely made it himself because of problems at C.D.'s in Cody, but he was here, sitting at the old wooden desk that he'd had for years in his room at the ranch house. Then he'd brought it over to Pure Rodeo until he found a new one he wanted. Now, he didn't want a new one. He felt as if the desk was meant to be in his office, and he especially liked the initials that friends had carved into the dark wood over the years. It wouldn't win a beauty contest for desks.

But the chair he was sitting in was another thing altogether. It was new, expensive and it was the only one he'd found that didn't make his bad leg ache after less than five minutes sitting at the desk doing his work.

He also enjoyed how easy it was to swivel around and look out the windows to the view of Donovan land rolling off toward the mountains in the distance. That happened more than it should lately and taking off for a ride didn't get things done. No wonder he couldn't put together the party. Once Louise was here, he'd show her around, and then leave for the main ranch house to get some rest and see his parents. An early-morning ride tomorrow sounded too good to pass up. Now that he had the party covered, he could ride up to the old adobe house on the original ranch that sat high above the valley, and he wouldn't feel guilty.

He'd left the office door slightly ajar, and the sound of someone clearing their throat jerked him back to why he was there. He eased himself out of the chair and stood to wait for Louise to come to the door. With the security monitors not hooked up yet, he had no idea if Louise had arrived or if someone else was paying him a visit.

He flexed his leg before he started across to the door and peeked outside. A lady was standing with her back to him looking out the windows. Dressed in a thigh-length dark suede jacket with its own hoodie, slim jeans and low-heeled boots, she seemed fascinated by the night view. He couldn't fault her for that. He'd done the same thing more times than he could remember. But the stranger wasn't Louise Fletcher. The woman he'd met had been heavyset, and maybe shorter than the person at the window. "Hello," he said, staying in the open doorway. "Can I help you?"

She jumped slightly at the sound of his voice, and then turned toward him. He didn't know her, but she had the deepest blue eyes he'd ever seen, and they dominated a finely boned face. "I'm so sorry," she said a bit breathlessly, staying where she was by the windows. "I was enjoying the view. This is all so amazing."

The minute she spoke, he knew the woman was Harmony Gabriel. Her voice gave her away. "Ms. Gabriel, what are you doing here? Where's Ms. Fletcher?"

She shook her head. "Something came up that was very unexpected, and I came to apologize and to explain the situation to you."

The idea of the party being dumped back in his lap could've made him panic, but he'd hear her out, and then decide what to do next. He motioned her into the office.

"Come on inside. Let's sit down and talk about this."

As she silently went by, the air stirred around him carrying a faint scent of flowers—roses or something delicate like that. "I'm sorry for the mess in here, but I haven't had time to set up my office yet." He went to get a folding chair he'd left by a stack of boxes that held office supplies.

He took it over by the desk and set it up for her. Harmony looked around the space and then met his eyes. "I understand. We've been at our new location for a few months and it's barely organized. All we've been able to do is put up a few holiday decorations and the brass plaque on the entry door. We haven't even set up a playlist for the background music."

He knew that beyond his desk with his printer, computer and phone setup, his office was a space filled with quiet chaos. Unopened boxes were stacked along the far wall with several cowhide-covered bar stools lying sideways on top of them. Still-packaged light fixtures left in front of the stools were destined to be installed in the office and along the walkway that went over to his private quarters. More boxes were sitting on the floor against the wall below the monitors. It would be this way up here until the downstairs business area was perfect.

"Please have a seat," he said and went around to sit behind the desk.

Harmony quietly put her bag on the floor by her feet, then slipped off the suede jacket and hung it over the back of the chair. A pink shirt emphasized the creamy tone of her skin, and with the hoodie gone, he saw her short blond hair. She used her fingers to comb through it and it framed her face looking for all the world as if she'd planned it to settle that way. Finally, she sat in the chair, on the edge of the seat, and spoke before he had a chance to say anything.

"First I have to explain why *I'm* here." She touched a delicate silver locket at her throat briefly then sat straighter, clasping her hands in her lap.

"You're canceling the contract?" he asked, not wanting to prolong the discussion if he was right.

"Oh, gosh, no," she said, her face touched with a blush of color that showed faint freckles dusting across her nose. "Not at all."

"Then why would you come all this way?"

Her tongue darted to touch her lipstick free lips, then she cleared her throat with a slight cough. "I'm here because Louise had a family emergency. Her father's in the hospital. I didn't have any other planner available to take over for her, so I came myself to do it."

His relief almost made him dizzy. "You'll be here for the whole time?"

She nodded. "I'll see it through to the end, if that's okay with you."

"That's fine with me. I'm sorry Ms. Fletcher's father's hurt, but thank you for stepping in."

"The thing is, there's one condition for me to stay and do the job." She spoke as if she needed to get that out as quickly as she could.

"What's that?" he asked cautiously, waiting for a gotcha moment.

He watched her, a slight frown drawing a fine line between those blue eyes and a certain nervousness in the way she kept her hands clasped tightly. He didn't have any idea what the condition could be. Then he made a wild guess. "Snow, is that it? If there's snow, you'll cancel everything? The party will be off?"

"What? Oh, no, but it could be a concern if it snows, and the party would have to be postponed or canceled. Down south we get our share, believe me. But I've heard up here it's not unusual to be snowed in with the roads shut down completely for days this time of year. I talked to a customer who had to climb out of their second-story window and dive into a head-high snow pile to get to their tractor and blade to clear a way to the barn and stables so they could take care of their stock."

She was right. He'd gone through winters even worse than that but had an answer for her. "We're in a serious drought up here, and we've been getting direct meteorological reports since June. This dry spell's expected to last until well into next year. That's why we've been getting irrigation systems together with other ranchers in the northern section. We need rain or snow badly, and to be honest with you, I wouldn't have thought of having the party this time of year if snow was likely."

He was done talking about snow because he was pretty sure that didn't have anything to do with her condition. "Tell me what the condition is."

CHAPTER FIVE

When Harmony had turned to see Caleb standing in the doorway to his office, it had almost knocked the air out of her lungs. She'd thought she'd know what he'd look like and was prepared to meet him in person. She'd seen pictures of an adult Coop. But she'd been wrong thinking she could come face-to-face with Caleb and not feel anything but the urgency to keep the job if that was at all possible.

When Caleb had smiled, all those years that had passed became irrelevant and it felt as if nothing had changed. The crush she'd had on him reared into the present. She'd felt her heart start to beat faster, and that uncertainty of what to do when she'd been twelve had come back with a vengeance. She'd tried to be calm, to talk evenly, to keep it all business, and she thought she was managing that as much as she could.

But he'd asked a question—one she'd expected, one she'd rehearsed her response to on her flight up to Cody.

Now her mouth felt dry, and she was clasping her hands so tightly in her lap that they were starting to tingle. She exhaled, forced herself to open her hands and press them to her thighs. She made herself keep eye contact with the adult Caleb, who had morphed into a tall, broad-shouldered man who seemed to emanate a sense of strength.

His dark hair was combed straight back from his strong features. Instead of the T-shirts and worn jeans she'd always seen him in years ago, he was in black jeans, a black Henley shirt and pretty fancy boots. He looked the part of the boss of Pure Rodeo. And all of his attention was on her.

He smiled at her, a slightly crooked and boyishly appealing grin. "Is this condition top secret?"

"No, no, of course not," she managed to say as his expression sent her back to when she'd been twelve and could barely breathe when Caleb had been around. It had been a childish crush, something that she'd made wishes about. A simple wish had been for

Caleb to smile at her like that just one time and mean it. Now he was trying to do business; it was a polite expression, one that she was certain he used in his work to his advantage. She remembered Dash charming people—a calm, likable big man. Caleb seemed a lot like his father. His smile was charming. It was her problem that she let it affect her, so she wouldn't let it affect her. That was a simple goal, and she'd make that happen.

"It's something that we have to agree on before I can go any further."

"Is this condition a huge problem for one of us?" Caleb asked, the smile gone now.

She felt a bit of relief that he was studying her seriously now. "Maybe for one of us, or possibly both," she said, surprised that her voice sounded pretty normal.

"Okay, let's get to the bottom line," he said, his dark eyes narrowing on her and not touched with any humor now.

Mandy had struck pay dirt finding a caregiver close to the Flaming Sky Ranch. The woman knew the Donovans and had known about the party. If Caleb didn't cancel, the woman, Raven Graystone, was very happy to help with Joy. Harmony braced herself, and then laid out what she considered a very viable plan to make things work for both of them. "I have a daughter, Joy, who's twenty months old, and I can't be away from her for Christmas."

He looked almost puzzled. "You mean on Christmas Day?"

"I mean from tomorrow until the day after Christmas Day."

The first thing he said was something else she'd planned a response to. "I don't see how you can do your job with a child along for the ride. No offense meant, and I may be wrong. I have no children and I'm seldom around them, but it sounds impossible to me."

She was so thankful for Mandy's find. "I wouldn't have brought it up if I thought I couldn't do a good job for you and your family. I made plans to make sure that I can give you and your family the very best celebration."

"What plans?" he asked, still interested, but with obvious caution.

"Mandy, who you met at our office, found a caregiver in this area with excellent references. She works out of her home, is fully licensed and impressed Mandy. Joy will stay with her at her home, and she can bring Joy here after work, or I can go to see Joy on my breaks."

He swiveled slowly from side to side without looking away from Harmony. He didn't look impressed, but he didn't argue, either. He asked, "Where does she live?"

"Five miles south of here. That would be close enough for me to be there for Joy in an emergency."

"What's her name, the babysitter?"

"Raven Graystone."

That brought that smile again. "You should have said that at the first." He sat forward. "I've known Raven for years. Their ranch is down off Leaping Deer Trail. So, she'll keep your daughter at her place, and you'll visit when you can?"

That wasn't exactly what she thought she'd do. "Pretty much."

"Five miles is very close." He nodded, seeming satisfied. "Where's your daughter now?"

"In Cheyenne with Mandy and her family. I want to get her up here by tomorrow. I promised Joy that we'd have Christmas together, and I keep my promises." He looked skeptical, probably about her promising a baby something and thinking they understood. But he wouldn't understand if she said she'd really made that promise for herself, to put a time limit on how long they'd be separated. "Are you still offering me your quarters to use while I'm here?"

"I planned on Ms. Fletcher staying in my private quarters, and I'd stay at the main ranch house with my family. It's yours as long as it's just you sleeping here. There's only one bed, although it's big, and I don't think any part of this place is safe for a child."

She nodded. "She wouldn't stay here, of course." Maybe Harmony could stay at Raven's some nights.

Before she could say anything else, a woman called up from the bottom level. "Hello! Caleb, hon, are you up there?"

"I'm here. Come on up!" he called back.

He looked pleased at the sudden arrival of the lady whose quick footsteps sounded first on the stairs, then on the walkway coming toward the open door. Maybe a girlfriend?

She was ready to leave the two alone and go to scout out the first level while they talked.

A woman came through the open door, and Harmony knew right away she wasn't Caleb's girlfriend. She recognized Ruby Donovan immediately. The lady hadn't changed a lot. There were errant streaks of gray in her long black hair she wore in a low ponytail, and her face had more lines. But she was still the attractive woman from Harmony's past. Even her clothes seemed familiar: work boots, jeans and a dark leather fringed jacket with turquoise buttons. The outfit echoed what she'd always worn in the past.

"The delivery doors were unlocked, so I came on in," she said. Her eyes flicked over to Harmony, and she hesitated. "Oh, I'm sorry. I didn't mean to intrude."

"You're not," Caleb said. "I'm glad you're here. I want you to meet Harmony."

Ruby came farther into the room. "So nice to meet you, Harmony. I'm Caleb's mother, Ruby Donovan."

"It's a pleasure, Mrs. Donovan." Harmony stood up. She remembered Ruby being tall, but now it seemed she wasn't more than a few inches shorter than the woman.

"That's a lovely name. And please, call me Ruby." She glanced at her son with a questioning look.

"Harmony's the owner of Perfect Harmony Events Planning in Cheyenne," Caleb said. "Her company's doing your party. I would have told you that if you'd been home when I stopped by before heading to Cody earlier. But I'm glad you're here now to meet her. She'll be here until after the party's over."

Ruby's smile came back quickly. "It's so good that Caleb hired you, Harmony. He's been going crazy trying to take care of everything and won't let me help at all. Honestly, I'm surprised that he admitted he needed help and handed it off to you instead of canceling. He's like that—in all the way or not at all. Even in his private life, he's—"

"Mom."

He just said that one word, and Ruby stopped midsentence. "Okay, I'm done. But I'm happy to see you found help. Otherwise I would have had to put on my own party."

"You just sit back and enjoy. Harmony

has it all under control. She's very good at what she does."

"Thank you, Harmony," Ruby said.

The last thing Harmony had wanted while being at the Flaming Sky Ranch was to come across other Donovans. She still felt that shame of being Les Randall's daughter. Even though Harriet was gone, that shame never seemed to lessen. The idea that they'd find out who she'd been was like a nightmare. But they saw Harmony Gabriel, a woman who was their equal, a woman who was actually helping the Donovan family. That's who she wanted them to see.

Despite that, she was almost happy to meet Ruby again after all the time that had passed. "It's my pleasure to be here, Mrs. Donovan. I'm very happy to make your celebration happen. Ask me for or about anything, no matter what. I'll make sure things are done your way. After forty years of marriage, you deserve the very best celebration ever."

"Thank you. I appreciate that."

A memory nudged at Harmony, not the horrible banishment from the ranch in the sheriff's squad car, but one of Ruby handing Harmony a pair of Western boots. She'd explained someone had forgotten them at a rodeo and had never come back to claim them. They had looked nearly new, and they were her size. She was thrilled to have them and threw away her only pair of shoes, which had their soles peeling off. That kindness toward a child who hadn't had much kindness in her life should never be forgotten. Harmony almost had, but she never would now.

"Mom," Caleb said. "I didn't hear you drive up."

"I didn't drive. It was so nice out that I walked over to give you a message from Heather Webster, who called me. She wanted me to tell you that she's sorry she missed you today and wants you to call her. She'll be around until after Christmas."

Harmony watched the two of them and could tell that strength of family they had before had survived over the years.

"You could have just called." Caleb shrugged. "In fact, Heather could have called me herself."

Ruby passed that off with a vague flick of her hand. "I wanted to take a walk."

"Thanks for passing on her message." He didn't look really pleased at the moment.

"Your dad's heading to Buffalo tomorrow early to pick up a saddle Turk repaired for him. He'd probably like some company on the trip if you could spare the time to go with him."

Caleb's expression turned to one tinged with concern. "You're saying he *needs* to *not* go alone?"

"No, that's not it, Caleb, he's fine. The doctor gave him a clean bill of health. He just mentioned how much he enjoyed going with you and Max to Two Horns last month. He misses his three boys being around. You're all so tied up in your work."

Caleb nodded. "Okay, I get the idea. I'll make a point of the three of us doing something with Dad after Christmas when Coop's here, too. Maybe we can go up to the old ranch."

Ruby looked pleased. "He'd like that a lot, but just don't tell him I mentioned it to you. He still kind of wishes you were all teens again and he was taking you boys to the junior rodeo competitions." She chuckled a bit unsteadily. "Life goes by so fast."

Caleb stood up and reached to give his mom a hug. The sight of them almost brought tears to Harmony. Her mother was gone before she'd even known her, and her father had always gotten rid of her every chance he could. In that moment, she knew it had never been the Donovans she'd avoided seeing again. It had been scenes like this. The mother and son caring about the father, and the dad wanting his sons around him. It hurt, but it wasn't them hurting her; it was her own memories of emptiness, with no one who really cared until Grandma Letty had come into her life.

"Mom, you know I want more time with Dad and you. That's a big part of why I chose to build the new place here, to be close to you two."

Ruby stood back and said, "Caleb Two-Hawks Donovan. You are a great son."

He shook his head. "Hey, don't get sloppy on me." But Harmony could see how touched he was by his mother's words.

Ruby turned to Harmony. "Sorry for the mush, but you know how families are."

No, she didn't, but that didn't stop her from wishing she did know what it was like to have a caring family. But Joy would know. She'd have everything Harmony never had. As Caleb turned to her, Harmony had a fleeting thought about him—that he'd make a perfect family man someday. He had the best example in his dad.

"Men are never great about showing emotions, are they?" Harmony said, trying to sound casual about her comment, as if she knew that from personal experience.

"Exactly. Now, no more mush. I'm heading back home. So nice to meet you, Harmony. What's your last name again?"

"Gabriel."

"I love that name, like the angel."

Harmony thought of something she needed to ask Ruby. "One other thing," Harmony said quickly before the woman could leave. "Pictures. I'd love to have some pictures of you and your husband, and the two of you with the family over the years. Wedding, birthdays, holidays and any rodeo pictures you might have."

Ruby smiled. "I've got lots of great photos. I'll go through them when I get back home tonight."

"Perfect. I'm kind of pressed for time."

"I understand," Ruby said.

Caleb spoke up and surprised Harmony by bringing up their discussion about Joy. "Mom, Harmony has a small daughter, and Raven Graystone is going to be taking care of the child at her house while Harmony's here."

Ruby grinned at his announcement. "How old is your daughter?" she asked.

"Twenty months, and I promised her I wouldn't leave her over Christmas. I didn't expect to be here, honestly, but the planner I had scheduled for this job had to drop out. So, I'm bringing Joy here to be close by, and I guess Raven's house isn't very far from here."

Ruby nodded. "It's very close and Raven's a lovely girl. She's gifted at dealing with children. She actually had a daycare center in Cody but had to shut it down over a year ago. I heard she was doing personal child-care out of her house. You're very lucky she's agreeing to working for you."

"I'll be here most of the time doing prep

for the party, and Caleb is letting me use his new quarters to stay in at night. Joy is going to be with Raven, and I'm hoping that works out. I've never really been away from her for very long before. But…you know Raven and you think it'll be good, right?"

"Yes, she's terrific, a nicer girl you couldn't find." Then Ruby frowned. "I know being away from your baby is hard and it'll be distracting for you, worrying and things like that. I might have an idea, maybe a better option for you."

"What is it?" Harmony asked.

"Our house is huge, and it's a half mile's walk from here. Why don't you and the baby stay there, and Raven could stay there while she's working for you? Then you'd be a lot closer to your daughter."

Harmony hoped her jaw hadn't dropped with surprise. Ruby Donovan was inviting her and Joy to her house, to live there for well over a week. "Oh, we're strangers to you, and it's the holidays. We can't intrude like that."

"My people have a saying that a stranger is just someone you haven't met yet." She laughed at herself. "I'm not sure *we* came up with it first, but it fits. You're not a stranger now. Besides, I haven't had a baby around since I can't remember when."

Harmony glanced at Caleb, who wasn't saying anything, just watching her and his mother. She couldn't tell if he was for or against Ruby's suggestion, but she was definitely all for it. "I think that would be pretty nice of you if we could do that. As long as Raven agrees to stay there with us, I'd love to accept your offer."

Ruby actually clapped her hands and said, "This is going to be fun."

Caleb finally spoke up. "Mom, Harmony's here to work. If she's up all night with a baby, that won't do. Originally her planner was going to stay here full time, and I thought that's what Harmony wanted while she's here." Caleb glanced at her.

"It's up to you, Harmony." Ruby looked at her, too. "I see the point of what Caleb said, but if that's not what you want…"

She made an instant decision to give Caleb a bit more assurance that things would be done his way while Joy was here. "I can stay here at night. But if that doesn't work out, I'll move over to your house. Is that okay with you, Caleb?"

She could see the reluctance in his expression, but he finally said, "We can try it, I guess." He wasn't smiling, and that made her uneasy.

"Thank you," she said.

"Now that's settled, I'll be heading home to dig out the pictures." Ruby hesitated. "Is your baby with Raven now?"

"Joy's with a dear friend in Cheyenne. The plan was, if Caleb agreed to Joy being here, that the family she's staying with will drive her up tomorrow. They have relatives north of Cody, and they're going there to visit for the holidays. So they can bring her here on their way."

"What time do you think they'd arrive?"

"Around noon. They aren't rushing it."

Ruby took out her cell phone and put in a call. "Raven, hello, it's Ruby Donovan." She smiled as she listened. "That's why I'm calling." She explained to Raven what they'd come up with and her smile didn't falter. "You're great. We can use the equipment, and you can stay with us." She nodded. "Exactly. She's coming at noon, so maybe you could come over to the house earlier with the equipment and help us get it set up?" Ruby looked at Harmony questioningly. "Is it okay to have them drive Joy to the main house, or would you prefer her coming here first?"

She didn't hesitate. "Your house. That way she won't have to take another ride right away to get over there."

"We'll all be at the house by noon tomorrow," she said into the phone. She nodded again. "Bless you."

She put her cell phone away. "Raven's right on top of it. She's got a crib, a high chair and safety gates all from her closed business. Everything we'll need for your stay."

"I don't know how to thank you," Harmony said. "I was worried about…" She passed that off. "All that matters is things are working out."

"They certainly are," Ruby said. She gave Caleb another hug, then smiled at Harmony. "See you tomorrow before noon."

With that, Ruby left, and neither she nor Caleb spoke until the sound of the delivery doors closing was heard. Caleb sat back down, and Harmony did the same thing. Her relief that it looked as if things were going to be okay after all was overwhelming. She wondered if Caleb felt the same way.

"I guess things are settled," he said, in an unreadable tone of voice.

"Thanks to Ruby. Goodness, she's so kind and thoughtful."

"She's the best," he said, still not giving away his thoughts about what she and Ruby had decided on.

"I'll just say this before we go any further. I promise you that I will do the best job possible for your celebration. And I always keep my word."

He looked at her hard for a moment, and then said, "I'll hold you to that."

"Please do," she replied.

CALEB WATCHED HARMONY call her friend and as she filled Mandy in, he knew the plan was going to work from the smile on her face. When she hung up, she exhaled in a rush. "They'll be here by noon. Now, I need to call a man named Dub. I don't even know his last name."

"What for?"

"He has a band, and he looks as if he's very good. He offered to play at the party."

"His name's Dub Bandy," Caleb said, "if his band is called The Silver Kickers."

"Mandy said he knew about us taking the job with you. You told him?"

"No, no, I didn't talk to Dub at all. But he's a friend of my older brother Max, and I bet that's who dropped that news on Dub."

"That's good that he know you all. I'll call him."

"This time of night, he's probably just starting his first set. Call and leave him a voice message, and he'll call you back or text you when he gets his break."

Harmony left the message, and then sat back in her chair. "I'm glad you brother told him. That's great to have him on board." She glanced around before looking back at him. "Where can I set up my laptop?"

"Anywhere you want to. In here or downstairs, although the manager's office down there isn't set up completely."

"I'll take anywhere as long as it has Wi-Fi."

He nodded. "There's free Wi-Fi downstairs for the customers, but it's not secure. Up here, I do my business on a secured line my tech guy put in. It's under the name Saferide3. The password is the hard part, and it'll cost you a hundred dollars to get it."

She started to agree. "Okay, I—" He could see the moment in her blue eyes when she realized he was kidding. Then a slight smile played around the corner of her lips. "Very funny."

That's what he'd tried for, to see if he could get her to really smile, and he'd almost done it. "Sorry, I couldn't resist."

"So, that's how you got rich?" Her comeback came smoothly, surprising him. "Charging for password usage?"

"You bet. But for you, it's free."

As her fine eyebrows lifted slightly, he thought he might be getting a glimpse of what Harmony would be like if he was around her more. "Okay, tell me what it is."

"I'll have to show you." He reached for the bottom right-side drawer of the desk, pulled it out, then turned the empty drawer upside down and held it out toward Harmony. "Twenty random uppercase and lowercase letters, along with haphazard numbers mixed with them and two special symbols. Oh, and you read them from right to left."

She squinted at the combination written in permanent ink and long enough to extend from side to side on the drawer bottom. "Your tech guy thought this up?"

"He had to. I couldn't memorize them, and he was wanting to do an automatic password change every twenty-four hours. I vetoed that." He slipped the empty drawer back into place, sat forward and rested his elbows on the desktop. "That's my idea of top security. I'm really the only one who will be using it up here in the office or in my private quarters, so it works for me."

Her smile grew a bit. "It works for me, too."

"If you want to work in here, you're welcome to."

She picked up her bag from the floor, unzipped it and took out a large white envelope. "Speaking of work, let's get to it. To start with, I've lined up a photographer, Royce Daniels. He's very good, and Mandy, my associate, is his sister. He didn't intend to work during the holidays this year, but she asked him for a favor. She told him about the party, and he agreed to do it, if you'll agree to his terms."

Caleb had met Royce when he'd been on the circuit, and later when he'd left, he'd been there for photo shoots at the big rodeo in Cheyenne when Coop had risen to the top. "What are his terms?"

"First, take a look at these two photos of his from within the last year." She opened the envelope and slipped out two eight-by-ten prints to pass over to Caleb. "They're both limited-number print runs. Royce has had gallery shows and both won picture of the year, one in sepia and one in color. He's also local from Cheyenne and truly understands all things rodeo."

He knew exactly where Royce lived, and he'd seen both photos before. But he kept quiet because Harmony looked very pleased to be presenting it all to him. He put them on the desk in front of him and studied them as if it was the first time he'd laid eyes on them.

One had been taken at a rodeo arena that

Caleb recognized and the other on deserted train tracks in the middle of nowhere.

The rodeo print done in sepia tones was of an older cowboy crouching over his fallen horse that had been injured during his ride. The man's strong hand rested on the animal's neck, while his other hand tugged at his hat as if to pull the brim lower and hide his face. Royce had caught that moment of raw grief between man and beast when they both knew it was over. Caleb had gone through something like that with a horse of his own about eight years ago. He knew that pain.

The train track photo was in color and showed a lanky cowboy holding the hand of a small boy with a bowl haircut. They were walking along the deserted tracks with weeds growing in between the rails, their backs to the photographer. No faces and no expressions were visible, and the land was shades of brown from the sand and the dried grasses. But Caleb could feel the emotions the photographer had caught.

Harmony had chosen two prints that touched him on a visceral level. "These are amazing," he said, thankful his voice didn't sound as tight as his throat felt then.

"He's very gifted," Harmony said in that soft tone that he'd heard over the phone.

He exhaled as he picked them up and passed them back to her. "I'll pay him whatever he wants to work the party."

"In fact it's not more money he's asking for."

"Then what is it?"

"His wife, Annie, she works with him, and he wants to make sure they can have some free time to dance and celebrate themselves. He promised he won't minimize what he's doing for you in any way. If you'd agree to that, I need to get back to him by tomorrow."

He'd heard Royce had married a woman from Montana maybe two years ago and lately Royce hadn't been working in the area. Caleb didn't hesitate. "Of course I'll agree to that."

"Oh, that's great," she said, a full smile coming so unexpectedly that it took Caleb off guard. That simple expression took her beyond pretty to stunning.

"Okay, that's settled," he said, wishing

he wasn't so aware of everything Harmony did. He picked up his cell phone and looked through his contacts to find the number he wanted. Then he held up a forefinger to Harmony. "This won't take a minute."

When she nodded, he put in the call and voice mail picked it up after one ring. "Hey, Caleb Donovan here. I just had a talk with Harmony Gabriel, your sister's boss. We all would be thrilled if you'd work the party, and I definitely agree to your terms. Harmony will be in touch with you tomorrow to work out details. Easy ride, and I'll be seeing you on Christmas Eve."

He stopped the call and looked at Harmony; her lips were slightly parted, and her blue eyes were on him. "Why didn't you just say you knew Royce as soon as I mentioned his name?" she asked. Her smile was gone. He wished it wasn't.

"Sorry for not telling you, but I didn't want to spoil your presentation. You did it very well, too. I've known Royce since just before I left the rodeo. He was starting up his business and covered a lot of the rodeos in the state. He and Coop keep in touch. I haven't seen him much since I left the rodeo circuit. I'm just glad that you got him to come on Christmas Eve."

She shrugged, a fluttery motion under her pink shirt. "I'm glad Mandy offered to ask him if he would do it. I haven't even met him."

"If I see Mandy again, remind me to thank her for her family connections."

"Sure," she said, not looking mad or annoyed at all, but he could tell he'd stolen a bit of her thunder getting Royce for a client's event.

He'd apologize, but he didn't figure that would go over well, either so he let it go. "Did you have a chance to look around on the main level when you came in?"

"I caught a glimpse of it before I came up the stairs." The smile that accompanied her words was just this side of being polite but not happy. "When you have a chance I'd appreciate a tour to get used to the layout and where you want things happening or spaces you don't want to use for the party. Maybe tomorrow morning first thing, if you'll be available."

"Sure. Glad to. Is there anything else?"

"I should have added that Mandy told me

Royce's wife is pregnant. Maybe that's why he wanted her to come with him."

"There goes his traveling all over for work."

"What does that mean?" she asked.

"Kids can tie you down. Royce travels so much, it seems it would be a problem sooner or later."

He hesitated, then decided he didn't know Harmony well enough to talk about his family with her. "It just makes sense. Royce will be working, and his wife will end up having to stay with their child, or children."

"Haven't you heard about asking for help?" she asked with just a flicker of humor in her blue eyes.

"Hey, I love my mother, but she…" He let that trail off on a shrug. "I get help when I need it. I got you, didn't I?"

"Yes, you did. Now, I need to go down and get my luggage out of the car."

Caleb stood, stretching his leg to ease the muscles. "Do you need help?"

"I could use some," she said. "See how easy that is?"

He made a scoffing sound. "You didn't ask. I offered. Big difference," he said. Harmony left her bag and jacket on the folding chair and Caleb let her go first out the door. Going down and out to the SUV to get her suitcases was quick because the air was cold and neither one of them had a jacket on. They were almost as fast coming back inside as they'd been going out. Once up the stairs, Caleb went toward his living quarters and when he got to the door carrying her luggage in each hand, Harmony leaned around him to push the door open for him.

Caleb took the suitcases to a settee positioned at the foot of the king-size bed that dominated his room. He'd only been in the suite a handful of times since it had been finished, and he liked it more each time. Once he'd put the suitcases down, he turned to look at Harmony, but she wasn't there. The next moment, she was coming through the open door with her jacket and leather shoulder bag.

She put her things on the red comforter that covered the bed and slowly looked around. "This is nice," she said in the soft voice he'd heard over the phone before. She motioned to the bed's headboard made out of rich dark wood with carvings in it from family friends down near Wind River. "Very, very nice," she murmured, and glanced over at him. "Did you have this custom-made?"

"Sort of. It's a long story. Maybe if we have time later on, I'll tell you the tale."

She nodded. "Now I'm curious."

"For now, get some sleep and in the morning we'll do the tour. Help yourself to anything you need."

"I'll be fine," she said.

"Good, then I'll take off. I'll see you around eight in the morning." He crossed to the door, then remembered something and turned back to Harmony by the bed. "I forgot to give you the directions for the alarm system." He went past her to a floating shelf by the headboard. "The code for the system is in here along with two ID words," he said as he pulled out a small, shallow drawer built into the side of the shelf.

He held it up for her to see the underside of it, and she came closer to read the printing. "Okay, that's easy. Which word is used for letting the operator know you need help, and which is everything's fine?" she asked.

"Number one, Bubba, means that all's

clear and you're okay. Number two, Bozo, means there's trouble and to send help."

"Your high-tech ability is really impressive," she said with a surprising touch of humorous sarcasm.

Dang, he'd never seen another woman who could be so businesslike one moment, then the next she was teasing. He liked that. "I aim to please, ma'am," he said, then did the smart thing and went back around her to the door. He wouldn't make an excuse to stay longer, even if he wanted to. "Pleasant dreams," he said then left, closing the door behind him.

CHAPTER SIX

WHEN HARMONY WOKE the next morning, it took her a moment to remember where she was. After calling Mandy again last night and talking to Joy on FaceTime, she'd showered and crawled into bed. She remembered lying there in the darkness looking out the windows and seeing the wishing tree under an almost full moon. She knew she'd been smiling as she lay there, but the next thing, it was morning and she remembered she was at the Flaming Sky Ranch. Caleb was coming over to show her around Pure Rodeo. It was like a dream, except she knew if she pinched herself, it would hurt.

She reached for her phone on the shelf beside her and saw it was eight thirty. That was sleeping in for her. Since Joy had come home with her, she was pretty much fully awake around six o'clock every morning.

Scooting to get out of bed, she headed into the bathroom to dress and when she stepped back out, she was ready for the day.

Dressed in comfortable jeans, low-heeled boots and a white turtleneck sweater, she went to the window and looked out. What an amazing thing for someone to own all this, wake up to this view every morning and know they belonged here. The closest she'd come to that was staying here for a handful of days before Christmas, but she'd never belong here. Still, she'd enjoy every minute of her stay.

As she was about to turn away and go to the office, she saw Caleb's silver truck come around the corner of the building and drive over to stop by her SUV. She kept watching, then the door opened, and Caleb got out. He was dressed as if he were a worker on the ranch, in a heavy denim fleece-collared jacket, jeans and boots. He reached back into the truck to take out his hat and put it on. Then he startled Harmony by suddenly looking up at the window and making eye contact with her. He grinned, waved and then stepped out of sight toward the delivery doors.

Right then she gave up the idea that his smile would just be part of his persona, that she'd see it and not react in any way. She accepted that and she'd deal with it by keeping her head down and doing the job she came here to do. She crossed to open the bedroom door and heard a beeping sound down below. Then it was gone and the door closed. Footsteps sounded on the wide plank flooring, and as she stepped out onto the walkway, she saw Caleb through the Plexiglas, striding toward the stairs, then he was coming up.

He spotted her. "Good morning." There was that smile again. "Ready to get busy?"

"I sure am," she said, going over to meet him at the top of the stairs.

"How'd you sleep?" he asked as he stepped up onto the walkway.

"I haven't slept that well in ages."

"That's good to hear." As he turned to walk toward his office, he tossed over his shoulder, "I'll be right back."

She took that time to go back in the bedroom and retrieve her small backpack she used when she was designing a floor plan and jotting down her ideas for a job. She hooked it over one shoulder to have easy access to it. Caleb came back wearing a faded red T-shirt with a logo that matched the horse statue on the roof. He seemed to notice her backpack and smiled at her. "We aren't going far enough to carry supplies with us."

She figured the Donovan charm must just be a constant when Caleb was around. If things were different, if she'd never been Harriet Randall, she wasn't so certain that she wouldn't enjoy it. She pushed that thought away. "I carry my work tools in it."

"Work tools?"

"You'll see," she said and fell in step with him to go down the stairs.

"Where do you want to start?" he asked as he stepped down onto the main floor.

They walked just far enough to go beyond the mechanical bull to their left and multiple pool tables to their right. The dance floor was dead ahead, and Harmony stopped just before they would have stepped into the dancing area. She faced Caleb. "Going from here to front to back, do you think this is about the center of this level?"

"Rough guess, maybe more like sixty percent front from here to the windows by the bar, and forty percent from here to the storage area."

She looked both ways and agreed on his estimate. "Are you planning on people riding the mechanical bull or using the pool table area?"

"No bull riding. There'll be way too many older men who can't resist showing they can still hold on for eight seconds, my dad included."

"What about the pool tables?"

"Yes, or no, whatever fits with what you think is the best thing for the party."

"That's a tough call. But maybe it's better to not have them available. I'm not trying to be sexist, but men seem drawn to pool tables like bees to honey. I don't think men in one space and women in another is a good idea."

"You're right. No playing pool."

"The way I see it, we don't want to put up solid barriers to keep the guests contained to the front. I've always thought that was rude. We can use this whole section to the windows, and keep the back area shut off, but not with hard barriers. Nothing that looks hard or intent on keeping the guests in this area."

"How could you do that without being obvious?"

She ignored the question for a moment as she headed over to the bar. "Do these swivel?" she asked as she reached for the nearest stool, the seat covered in cowhide and a brass rail around the legs near the bottom.

"Yes, they do. Why's that important?"

She wanted to have her idea firmly in mind before telling him about it, and she had a method to get the perspective she needed. Caleb came up beside her as she tried to pick up the stool. It was heavy. "Did you make these out of solid steel?"

"No, but they're reinforced to survive the customer sitting on them and make sure they can hold the weight and be comfortable, too." He reached for another stool, and she watched him turn it on its side, grab the brass rail and put the swivel seat's edge on the floor. "Where do you want it?"

She went over to what she thought was

the middle point of the sixty percent area. "Right here."

He rolled it over to her, using the swivel seat as a real wheel, then set it upright for her.

"How's this?" he asked.

"Perfect," she said, and she sat down on it.

Caleb didn't go to get another stool for himself, so Harmony just did what she needed to do. She slowly started to twirl around. "This party is about being together, and we want togetherness, not people wandering off into small groups all over the place."

CALEB FELT HARMONY had hit the nail on the head. She had some gift to figure out how to contain the party guests without making them feel penned in. "Okay, tell me the idea you have."

He watched her when she started to speak, and he liked the enthusiasm in her voice. "We can do it with the lighting. Lighting can be magical, and I think this is a case where that'll really work well."

Her blond hair feathered around her face as she talked. It only emphasized her features, especially her eyes. He'd thought he might have exaggerated how blue they'd been last night, but now they were every bit as pretty. "How do you do that with lighting?" he asked.

She stopped swiveling and tipped her head back to look up at the vaulted ceiling crisscrossed with heavy beams and the caged light fixtures. "Do they dim, and are they on a timer?"

"Yes and yes. They can be programmed to any pattern you want. All the lighting in the service areas is brighter."

"Good. We can do a program for each part of the party, and we'll add more festive lights to encourage people to stay away from the back sections. The lights beyond that can be turned off or be set to give off a very low glow."

"What other lighting would you add?"

"Christmas lights on beautiful Christmas trees that will be placed strategically to cut off natural paths to the back area."

"You think that would actually work?"

"Yes, it will. But I need to figure out where to get the trees we'll need, then decide on a decorating scheme so we can figure out the light colors and types of bulbs."

"Red and green works, I guess."

"Is it okay with you if we do the tree at the head table with ruby-colored twinkling lights for your mom, and gold ornaments that are individually handblown?"

That sounded nice, but he wasn't looking for nice. "I guess so."

She frowned slightly, then nodded. "Sorry, my bad. That sounds so generic, except for the handblown ornaments. I've seen them before, and they are beautiful. In fact, the same vendor does rodeo-themed ornaments. The lights, I think, should be rope lights woven all through the tree. Rope, as in rope." She chuckled at that. "That's rodeo, don't you think?"

"Absolutely, rodeo with Christmas mixed into it."

"How about a gold star on the top of the tree for your dad?" He nodded his approval, and she was off and running with ideas. "Maybe to make it truly Christmassy, we could alternate between the larger trees decorated with the ruby light ropes, and some smaller ones decked out in good old-fashioned red and green Christmas lights.

Sometimes simple is better, and the obvious is the best choice."

She was really something; she obviously loved her work and was very good at it. "I'm impressed by your ideas, but I'm starting to realize that the time to get this all done is really short."

She shook her head. "No, no, it's very doable. I can see it now the way it'll look when it's finished. Mandy's been filtering the vendors for me, and we're all set with them. She found some good rentals close by, but the best thing she found, in my opinion, was Raven Graystone. After I meet Raven today and make sure it's going to work, I can focus better. After Joy arrives and gets settled at your house, this will all go smoothly. What time is it?"

He checked his phone for the time. "Nine thirty."

"Okay, I need to find out how the drive's going and get some information from Mandy. I'll let you give me the rest of the tour later. Right now, I need your office for around half an hour before I go over to the main house to meet Raven and help your mom get things arranged."

"Sure. Go ahead. I'll put the stool back."

"I'll do it," she said as she slipped off the stool.

He could see how anxious she was to have noon come quickly so her daughter would be here. She hadn't even opened the backpack. "No, you go on up to the office."

"Thanks," she said and hurried upstairs.

Caleb had meant to be out of the way when the child arrived, but something in him wanted to see the toddler himself. Harmony hadn't been gushing about her daughter, but he could tell she was crazy about her. She hadn't mentioned the child's dad. He'd wondered if the father had just dropped out of sight. He headed to the kitchen, found some energy bars, put a few in his pocket, then went back upstairs, but didn't go into the office. The door was shut, and he wouldn't intrude.

He sat down on the top step, looking out over the emptiness of the bottom level and wished he could envision it after everything for the party was in place. About the only thing he could envision for his future was his next expansion after Pure Rodeo. He'd been seriously eyeing a property in the county seat, Twin Horns, about the size of C.D.'s. Maybe he'd get Harmony to plan the grand opening party for it. He chuckled to himself. By then, he had no idea where she'd be, but she'd definitely still be a mother who doted on her daughter.

"What's so funny?" he heard Harmony say.

He turned and she was coming toward him. "I was just thinking about life. I've been doing that a lot lately."

"Me, too," she said on a sigh as she sat down by him.

"You're fast," he said. "Did you get everything done?"

"Yes. Mandy said they're making good time and so far, the kids are having a ball. I'm going over to help your mom and Raven. If I have any questions, I'll call you."

"You do that. Do you have the code for the gates at the ranch entry?"

"No, I don't, actually."

He gave her the simple four-digit number, then said, "Take the main access road and look for the sign that says Private on your left. That leads right up to the house. It's the only one on that road, a large adobe."

She hesitated before she spoke. "Thanks, but I think I'll walk over. I won't be here that long, and I'd like to see as much as I can of the ranch."

"It's a pretty long walk."

"Then I guess I'll be going. I'll call you if I have any questions."

"You could get lost the first time."

"Oh, no, I won't," she said quickly.

"You know how to get there?"

"No, but I can figure it out."

She looked slightly embarrassed, a touch of color in her face that showed the freckles. In that split second he had the feeling he'd seen her somewhere before. But he couldn't find the where or the when. "I need to pick up something I forgot to bring with me this morning, so how about we walk over together?"

She stared at him for a moment, and then said, "Walk with me? Sure, of course. If you want to."

He did.

THE AIR WAS COLD, but the day bright and clear. Harmony pushed her hands down into her pockets as she and Caleb walked away

from Pure Rodeo and out onto the southern
pasture. They were angling to the northwest, crushing dried weeds and grass under
their boots with each step they took. And
they were moving fast. Harmony was anxious to get to the house and for Joy to arrive.

"Hey, can we slow down a bit?" Caleb
asked.

She stopped and turned to him. She'd noticed the slight limp he had when she saw
him yesterday, though she'd hardly noticed
it today, and she certainly hadn't thought
about him not being able to walk fast. "Oh,
gosh, I'm sorry. I forgot… Are you okay?"
She knew she'd said the wrong thing when
he frowned but didn't have a clue how to
take it back and not sound condescending
or too worried.

"I can walk just fine, or run, if you want
to run, but I thought you were taking the
walk to see the land around here."

"Of course. I'm just a bit anxious to get
to the house. Sorry."

"Don't be sorry. It's fine. I'm fine."

She was relieved to walk slower and
not talk about his limp. They didn't, but
Caleb brought up a question for her. "Can

I ask you why her father isn't taking care of your daughter for you, or why he didn't tag along?"

She'd had that question more than once, but it seemed different coming from Caleb. "Because there is no father."

"What?" he asked and stopped walking when he did.

She smiled ruefully. "It's not what you think. I adopted Joy. I saw her and fell in love with her."

"So there's no one else? It's just you and her?"

"At first I thought there might be someone else with us, but that didn't work out." She didn't want to go into all that. Her relationship with Garth had effectively been done the day she mentioned the idea of adoption. A week later, the relationship was officially over. "We don't need anyone else. We're doing fine on our own."

She started walking again, and Caleb fell in step beside her. "That has to be hard for you with your work and everything."

"It can be," she said, staring off into the distance, then over at the wishing tree, which was getting farther and farther away the closer they got to the main house. Wishes did come true, but sometimes they were almost forgotten before they happened. "But it's doable. Anything's doable if you want it bad enough."

"I agree," he said. "When I hurt my leg, I was riding a bull on the final night of a rodeo in Phoenix. My shinbone was shattered along with bones in my ankle. I've got enough metal in me to set off the scans at the airport."

She felt vaguely sick as he spoke, thinking of his leg being damaged, and what he must have gone through. "I'm sorry. That sounds awful."

"It was, but in the end, it all worked out for me."

"You went back to the rodeo?"

"No. I probably could have, but I was never better than good enough to win some minor recognition, anyway. So I changed direction, focused on what I really wanted and found a great compromise without actually being on the circuit. I'm still surrounded by the rodeo in a lot of different forms, and I love doing what I do. So, I make it work, and so far, I've been right on the mark."

"That's great. You were smart to leave."

"Honestly, I knew I didn't have what Coop has, despite being identical twins. Maybe I left so I wouldn't be embarrassed—or because I was smart enough to do it." He shrugged good-naturedly. "Either way, I'm in a good place. I've got things mapped out, and it's working. How about you? Is it working okay?"

"Better than okay. Way better. Not that I'm great at this parenting thing, but I sure am doing my best. I've never been happier." She didn't know why she added that, but it was a solid truth. She stopped and undid the top buttons of her jacket, then lifted the small heart locket she wore around her neck and opened it. "This is Joy," she said as she showed the small picture to Caleb. "That's the day she came home with me and could stay forever. The woman is my Grandma Letty. She saved me from a lot of things when I was young, and she's the closest I've had to a mother. My two most favorite people ever."

Caleb studied the tiny photos. "Joy kind of looks like you," he murmured.

"That was a happy coincidence." Harmony hadn't really noticed until Mandy pointed it out the first time she saw Joy.

They both started walking again, and Harmony felt a relief that Caleb knew about Joy. She wasn't hiding her adoption story, but talking about it was new to her; she held it close most of the time. Telling people Joy was adopted wasn't what she wanted to do. Adopted or biological, she loved her daughter so much. She wanted to change subjects, and she did. "How many TVs do you have on the bottom level?"

"Around fifteen. Why?"

"Are they all on the same feed?"

"They can be, or on multiple inputs."

"Royce said he's able to set up a live stream that runs old pictures mixed with live feed shots of what's going on at the party."

"Mom would like that," he said and flashed a smile. He had that down to a fine art. Harmony was pretty sure a lot of women would swoon if that smile was directed at them. She couldn't believe he wasn't married already.

"Do you have fun doing what you do with your business?" Caleb asked after a moment of silence between them.

She hadn't expected that but considered it. "I enjoy it most of the time. But it's hard work, too."

"I get that. My business is to help people have fun, and by osmosis, I do, too, usually. I have to go back up to Cody later. Saturdays are our biggest day of the week. We're closed on Sundays, except for special occasions."

In that case, she'd go by and see the wishing tree up close when she walked back to Pure Rodeo after settling Joy in. He'd never know. "The Christmas trees I was talking about, I'm going to need probably a dozen in different sizes. I was wondering if you knew a wholesaler around here. I can order them online if I have to, but I really want to see at least a sample before buying any. Sometimes supplies and deliveries are a problem, especially around Christmas. I might not have a great assortment to choose from."

"These Christmas trees are not going to be artificial, are they?"

She'd had no intention of using plastic-and-metal trees, but she didn't tell him that when she looked over at him. "If you don't want them to be fake, no, absolutely not."

His dark eyes held hers for a second. "I happen to know a place close by where you can pick out the trees and have them delivered same day."

"That's perfect, if they have the sizes I need in stock. Are they close?"

"Around half a mile from here."

"That's great. North or south?"

"West, actually," he said.

"Okay, what's their name?"

"The Flaming Sky Ranch." He beamed. "And no need to call ahead. I'm still here. The trees are grown at the start of the foothills, all different sizes, trimmed and healthy."

She never knew what to expect from Caleb. "You could have told me that earlier."

He smiled that smile and said, "I suppose so. Now, speaking of healthy, your cheeks are red from the cold. We need to walk faster."

She complied and picked up her pace so she wouldn't fall behind Caleb now. "You said they're grown specially for sale?"

"Partly," he said as they stepped out onto a hard dirt road that went north and south. "My uncle, the ranch manager, it's his project. He grooms them and generally takes care of them, then around the holidays, he sells a few, but mostly he donates trees to people who need them but can't afford to buy them."

"That's really lovely. How would it work for us to get some for the party? You'd be basically paying yourself for your own trees."

He chuckled roughly at that. "I'll figure that one out." She took one last glance at the wishing tree from a distance, and her memories of making wishes under that tree were as vivid as if they'd just happened. Harriet Randall had found a safe place to pretend she was anyone but a kid nobody noticed and without anyone who cared about what happened to her. Under the tree she'd imagined that she had a family, great parents and that she belonged in a place like the Flaming Sky Ranch. It had taken her almost seventeen years to get close to that fantasy and bring it into reality, all but the part of belonging on the ranch. At least she was visiting it for a short while. The wait had been worth it to have the life she lived now. She thought that if she really did live here, she'd make sure the wishing tree was lit up every Christmas so it could be seen from Eclipse to Cody.

She smiled to herself as she looked ahead of them and saw a curve in the road. She knew where she was from the times she'd ridden along that route to get to the wishing tree.

"I have an idea of how to get those trees you want quickly."

She stopped and looked at Caleb. "What's your idea?"

"I know Uncle Abel's going to agree to let you have them, so tomorrow morning, we'll get out to the planting area, and you can select them, and you'll have them by the evening."

"That sounds great."

"Do you ride?"

That stopped her. "I used to years ago."

"Then we'll ride out there tomorrow morning. It's Sunday, and like I said, we're closed in Cody, so I can help you with picking out the trees and tagging them."

He'd offered the answer to another wish

she'd made so long ago. She loved the idea of a ride with him to pick out the trees, but then it struck her that Joy would already be here tomorrow, and she couldn't just take off. "I'm sorry, but I don't think I can do that."

He frowned at her. "Why not?"

She hated to answer that, especially since she'd promised him that Joy's coming wouldn't make any problems. "I'm just not sure I can leave tomorrow to do that." She wanted to say she had other things she had to do for the party, but she couldn't lie about it.

"Why?"

He asked, so she finally told him exactly why she couldn't go tomorrow. "It's too soon for me to not be here for Joy in a strange place. I can't do that to her."

"I thought that's what Raven was for, to keep your daughter entertained and cared for."

"I'm her mother, not Raven. Raven's my backup. Joy is mine in every way, and I need Raven's help. But that doesn't mean I'm tossing my responsibilities aside."

"What time does she wake up in the morning?"

"Depends. She's been known to be awake for good at four in the morning, or to sleep in until noon, but that doesn't happen often. If I'm not going to work, I let her sleep."

He seemed to consider that. "How about we leave at dawn, if she's still sleeping? We won't be more than an hour and a half, two hours tops, and we'd be back around eight o'clock."

Harmony didn't know about that. "What if she wakes early?"

"Does she nap?"

"Of course. She takes long naps."

"When she naps, we can go and take care of the trees."

She envied his ability to arrange his time to do what he wanted to do. "I guess that could work. Do you have cell reception in the foothills?"

"Mostly, but there's backup with a satellite radio system. I can take that with us, and we'll be covered. We could get back pretty fast from anywhere we'd be on the ranch. What do you do when you're working? Is she there with you all the time?"

"Most of the time, but I have arrangements with my staff to help out when needed. Mandy's great with Joy. My neighbor was a good friend of my grandmother's and she's watched Joy some. It all works out. I'm flexible, and Joy's getting to be, too. But there's times when I don't have an option."

"Okay, I get it. It's up to you. The trees are there, so when you can go to see them, call me," he said.

They were getting close to the house, and it looked almost like it had years ago, except the trees were taller, and a whole wing had been built on the southern end since she'd seen it last. It was rough adobe with clay tile roofing, and open land around it with grass that was more brown than green. The portico at the double-door entrance at the top of a semicircle driveway had the same wooden beams as the roof at Pure Rodeo. A small red truck was parked under it.

Caleb stopped and Harmony turned to him before she went up to the doors. "I'll hunt down Uncle Abel, so tell Mom I'll be back before I head up to Cody."

"Sure," she said. "Thanks for showing me

the way over here." She'd enjoyed the walk, surprised at how easily the two of them could talk, even about Joy's imminent arrival and her adoption. She seldom talked to anyone about that unless it was Mandy. Now she was going with Caleb to pick out Christmas trees. She felt like an equal, and she'd do anything she could to make sure Caleb and the others would never know who she'd been before Harmony Gabriel had started her new life. Never.

"I'll let you know what Uncle Abel says," Caleb told her before he headed farther down the road in the direction of the arena and stables. It was the main area of the ranch where they held rodeos. It had been beautifully developed with great care by Dash and Ruby, so it seemed almost like a rodeo amusement park to a twelve-year-old. Riding, roping, barrel racing, horses and cattle grazing in the pastures. Junior rodeos were the local entertainment. The summer night rodeos under the arena lights had been the best. Even though she'd watched them from underneath the bleacher seats so no one would know she'd sneaked in, she still enjoyed them all, especially when Caleb had been competing.

WHEN CALEB WENT back to the house before heading to Cody, he'd ended up helping Raven install a monitoring system in the guest room while Harmony and his mom had put together a crib and set up safety gates. His dad had left to go to town to pick up some groceries. Caleb figured if his dad played it smart, he wouldn't come back until the baby was here and down for a nap. He'd pretty much decided to get clear of the house before Harmony's kid showed up. But when he was leaving around eleven thirty and stepped outside under the portico that rose at least twelve feet above the flat-brick U-shaped drive, a white king-cab pickup truck swung off the hard-packed dirt road and onto the driveway. It stopped within a few feet of Raven's small red pickup.

He heard his mom call from inside, "They're here!"

Yes, they were here, and a full half hour early. A thin, tall man dressed in khakis got out of the truck on the driver's side, while Harmony's associate, Mandy, opened the passenger door and stepped down and out. The man opened the second door and leaned inside. When he moved back and stood straight, he was holding a little girl with pale blond curls, dressed all in pastel blue and rubbing her eyes as if she'd been sleeping. The man grinned when Harmony almost flew past Caleb to get to him and Joy.

"Special delivery," the man said as the baby spotted her mother, let out a squeal and almost twisted out of his arms. Harmony was there, catching her and pulling her into her arms. She went around to hug everyone, including two preteen girls who had come out of the truck. Then Ruby was with them, followed by Raven. The two girls were running around and laughing. They looked as if getting free from the truck was the most exciting thing in the world.

Caleb stayed back, keeping out of the way, watching the happy chaos in front of him. Then Harmony turned, and her smile was radiant. He wasn't certain he'd ever seen someone so joyous before. She wasn't married. He'd thought about that a lot after she'd told him on the walk it was just her and the child.

He watched as Harmony made introductions. "Ruby, this is Mandy, my best friend and my better half in the business." The two girls were next as they whizzed past the adults. "Her daughters, Milly and Missy."

Mandy spoke up as she took the tall man's hand in hers. "And this is my husband, Eric."

Raven Graystone, a tiny woman with braided black hair and a huge smile, dressed in jeans and a white T-shirt, approached the group and slowly got close to Harmony and the baby. She leaned in and said something. Harmony nodded, then Raven took a small toy out of her jeans pocket. Joy eyed it, then slowly reached for it. Once her little hand closed over what looked like a tiny stuffed unicorn, the baby pulled it to herself, and a smile lit up her face.

His mom was waving them all toward the open front door, seemingly almost as happy as Harmony was to see Joy. "Come on inside. It's cold out here."

Mandy and Eric rounded up their daughters, then walked with Ruby into the house. Raven stayed near Harmony, whose eyes looked overly bright as if she was fighting tears. They came toward Caleb, and Harmony stopped in front of him. "This is Joy," she said, and the baby looked uncertainly at Caleb. She was every bit as pretty as her picture in Harmony's locket, and she did look a lot like her mother.

"Hello there, little one," he said, feeling just a bit awkward. He always did around tiny human beings that could barely talk, cried when they wanted to, spit out their food and seemed to control the schedule of every adult around them. At least it had seemed that way when he'd been around the children of friends.

Joy was very still, her eyes never leaving Caleb. "Joy, this is Caleb."

The baby studied him with wide blue eyes. Then she looked at Raven and back at her mother. "Bo-bo," she said softly, and Harmony took a pacifier out of her pocket.

Joy grabbed it and started to suck on it, her eyes returning to Caleb.

"I'll keep my promise to you," Harmony said.

"What's that?"

"That she won't cause any disruptions to my work while she's here."

Ruby was back at the door. "Hey, Caleb, let them get inside. It's too cold to talk out there."

Joy turned at the sound of Ruby's voice, and then nestled against Harmony's chest, her blue eyes on Caleb again. She was frowning at him, and for some crazy reason, he felt offended that the child almost looked mad now. She might be cute, but it looked as if she had made up her mind about him. "I won't bite," he said to her.

Harmony laughed softly at that. "I sure hope you won't."

Caleb shrugged. "Let's just say I haven't so far," he murmured and then spoke to his mother. "I'm going to work. I'll see you later on." With a wave, he turned and went back to the trail that led to the southern pastures to walk to Pure Rodeo. He heard a tiny voice say, "Bye-bye," and he turned to look back over his shoulder. He was surprised to see Joy waving at him solemnly. He waved back before he even thought about doing it, and then walked off by himself.

CHAPTER SEVEN

HARMONY DIDN'T GET back to Pure Rodeo until eight o'clock that evening after Joy had fallen asleep in the guest room with Raven sitting alongside her crib. Joy had slowly taken to both Ruby and Raven, probably because they didn't force anything. They let Joy come to them, one offering a toy, the other a cracker, until the three were on the floor together clapping hands and making a stuffed horse whinny when you squeezed its sides. Joy had loved the attention and the fun, but she'd finally run out of steam and fallen asleep sitting on Raven's lap.

Harmony felt good about the way things went, and when Ruby had offered to drive her back to Pure Rodeo, she'd accepted and planned to walk to the big tree later. She'd been okay leaving, too. Things looked good and she was pretty sure the baby would sleep late if she wasn't disturbed. She talked it over with Raven, and then told her she'd be going for the trees early the next day, but all she had to do was call her and she'd be back in a flash if needed. She went inside after Ruby had driven off, reset the alarm and headed upstairs.

She tried to call Caleb, but his phone kept going directly to voice mail. She hoped he could still take her to pick out the trees early in the morning, so she could get back to Pure Rodeo and do as much work as she could before Joy needed her. Joy had been through so many foster homes; she was sort of used to new people showing up and others disappearing. Harmony wasn't going to disappear, and she wanted Joy to know that more than anything.

She sat down on the top step and waited for Caleb, hoping he'd come by before he went to the main house for the night. Her phone chimed, and she glanced at the screen. Caleb. "Hello?"

"Hey, it's Caleb. I saw you called a few times. Is anything wrong?"

"No, nothing's wrong. I think I can go to

the trees with you in the morning, but it has to be early."

"How do you feel about waking up at dawn?"

She'd done that a lot after Joy had come home with her. "I can do it."

"You're sure?"

"Yes, I am. Joy's settled at the house, sleeping, and Raven's with her. She took to your mom and Raven, and she didn't nap today, so she'll sleep in tomorrow. I think we can get the trees tagged and get back before she wakes up."

"Good, okay. Do you want to ride or drive?"

She hesitated. Just the passing mention of riding brought back her memories of riding Duke, and she wanted to do that on this land one more time. This time she wouldn't have to worry about getting back late and her dad leaving her to walk the two miles at night alone to where they parked their truck and trailer. And she'd finally get the chance to ride with Caleb. "I'd rather ride."

"I was hoping you'd say that. I look for every chance I can get to ride around here.

Do you have any boots or clothes for riding with you?"

"I have jeans and boots. I can layer a sweater over my shirt and with that under my jacket, I should be okay."

"How about a hat?"

"The hood on the jacket I wore here. Since I came to work, I didn't pack for a vacation."

"I think you'll survive," he said, a touch of humor in his tone. "You survived the cold walk today."

"I'll be warm enough," she said, and hoped that proved to be a fact, not wishful thinking. "So, I'll be up waiting for you at dawn."

"Okay, dawn it is. I'll see you then," he said and ended the call.

She closed her eyes and sighed. She was going riding on Flaming Sky land with Caleb Donovan. Just the two of them, and this time she wouldn't be left to watch Caleb take off with his friends. She'd never expected that wish to come true, that she'd do that with Caleb, and now it had. Even if it was just business, she'd take it.

DAYLIGHT WAS FAINT by the time Caleb went back to Pure Rodeo the next day. He tied the two horses—one he'd rode and one he'd led—to a hitching post. Nearby was a corral connected to a small stable designed to look like a much smaller version of the main building. Then he took a very conspicuous floral tote bag off the saddle clip and went in the delivery doors, disarmed the alarm and stepped into warmth and silence in the main lower level. He crossed to the stairs, went up and looked in the office. Empty. He turned and crossed to the closed door on the other end of the walkway.

He listened, but he couldn't hear anything behind the barrier. He waited for a moment before knocking on the wood. Nothing. He rapped on it again and finally heard a voice say, "Just a minute." There was stirring, then the latch clicked, and the door swung back. Harmony was there, dressed in pajama bottoms and an oversize blue T-shirt, her feet bare and her hair tangled around her face. She'd obviously just woken up. "I'm sorry, I… I overslept." She combed her fingers through her hair, and her eyes were still heavy with the last remnants of sleep. "That bed is so comfortable."

"Blaming the bed?"

She almost rolled her eyes at that. "If I could, I would, but it's all on me. I should have set my phone alarm to wake me up."

"It's just coming on dawn, so we need to get going."

"Oh, yes, sure, um, I'll... I'll get dressed." She glanced at the large bag he'd hung over his shoulder.

"Oh, Mom sent you a few things. She was worried about you being out in the cold and not being dressed warmly enough." He held the bag out to her. "She's like that. She worries a lot. She even put a hat in there for you."

She was gathering herself and standing a bit straighter as she took the bag. "I'll hurry," she said and turned, heading in the direction of the bathroom.

He'd been looking forward to the ride since last night and was impatient to get going. He crossed to the back windows and looked out at the pale pastels of dawn creeping into the sky, and in the distance he could see the line of trees clear over by the beginning of the foothills. He sat down on the leather settee that faced the window and just enjoyed the view of the shadows being gradually overtaken by the first light of day.

He heard Harmony moving around the bathroom. Then the door opened, and she came out. He stood and turned to see her wide awake and dressed for serious cold. She had on a green plaid flannel shirt with jeans and red boots. Her hair was tamed, and she was carrying a bright red jacket. "Wow, that all fits you," he said.

"Yes, it does, even the boots." She slipped on the jacket and zipped it up. "I forgot the hat," she said, and went back into the bathroom. When she came out, she had the hat on. She looked good in it and smiled at him. "Does this look Western enough, so I won't stand out like a sore thumb?"

"It sure does," he said. "Uncle Abel was happy to let us take whatever trees we want. The tallest is twelve feet, but he doesn't want that one touched. Every other tree is fair game."

"That's really nice of him," she said. Then her phone chimed, and she picked it up off the floating shelf. She frowned at the screen before she answered it. "Raven?" He watched her listen, then her expression eased. "Good, okay. That's fine. Call me if you need me." She ended the call.

"Bad news?"

"No, Raven was just checking in. Joy woke up for a few minutes, then went back to sleep. She's okay for now."

Caleb was relieved the child was sleeping, but he could feel the tension in Harmony. He wanted this ride to get out on the land, but he also didn't want her to go with him if she'd worry the whole time. "If you can't go, I understand. You can tell me what you need, and I'll go out there to tag the trees."

He'd thought she'd be relieved not to go, but instead, she looked bothered. "I don't know..." Her voice trailed off, and she looked away from him. "I can go."

That took him aback, but he didn't want her to spend the ride regretting her decision. "No, I'll do it. Just give me a list of what you want."

He stood there, anxious to get away and stop this growing feeling of wanting to make things right for Harmony. But he had no way to do that except to go without her. She looked right at him. "I'm sorry. Everyone's being so great, but I keep thinking that Joy's with strangers."

He exhaled. He couldn't change that. They were all strangers, or near strangers, and he saw a hint of fear in her eyes. That was something he didn't want to see. "How long ago did you adopt her?"

"It…was finalized three weeks ago." She hugged her arms around herself. "I know, I know, I'm being silly about this. I don't want to be. I do trust your mother and she trusts Raven, and I should, too. I really should. And I want to ride. I'm just…"

As she closed her eyes, he watched her simply breathe in and breathe out. She was trying to calm herself, and he wished he could help her. But he didn't have a clue what to say next, or what to do, if anything. This was all because of a tiny person who had all the power. Kids confused a person's life and altered what they wanted. It was always about the child. He'd seen that in his own life. His father had walked away from the rodeo, something he loved doing, and put his children first.

Caleb had never truly understood exactly why his dad had given it all up. He'd told his sons, "I want to be here for you three boys, not somewhere on the circuit when you need me, and when your mother needs me. I'm home for good." Caleb had loved the idea of his dad being there, but it bothered him to see how much his dad had given up. He still felt a sense of guilt for that, stupid as it sounded, but it was there. His dad had settled instead for bringing as much rodeo to Flaming Sky as he could.

"Harmony?" he said.

At first, she didn't even seem to have heard him say her name, then she opened her eyes and looked at him. "I'm sorry. I made a promise to you, and I'm going to keep it. Joy's close by, and I know she'll be okay. I'll be back, not like the others in her life who were there one day, then gone forever the next."

He'd had a gut feeling that it wouldn't be easy to have her child on-site, but he couldn't do a thing about it now. "Of course, you'll be back. She'll figure that out sooner or later." As soon as he said that, he knew he'd probably made things worse.

"Yes, she will, but in the meantime, she'll be looking for me and not seeing me. I've heard that kids love playing peek-a-boo, because they really think the person disappears when they put their hands over their eyes, then the person reappears when they take their hands down. I was told to never play a joke and quickly hide before the child takes their hands away. It scares them."

He shrugged. "I can see that happening, so don't ever do that with your daughter."

She grimaced and shook her head. "I won't," she said. "Can we leave now?"

He'd made things worse, but he kept any apology to himself. "We sure can."

He was more than ready to get out of there and keep his mouth shut. None of what happened in her life was any of his business. Things could get messy, and all he wanted was a great party. This wasn't a relationship; it was a business deal. Whatever scrambled feelings this woman stirred up in him didn't mean anything. They couldn't.

When her phone chimed, Harmony

quickly took it out and opened a text. She scrolled through it, and Caleb could see the relief it brought to her as she read it. When she was done, she put her phone in her jacket pocket and looked at him. "Are we walking over to get the horses?" she asked.

"No. They're waiting out back, saddled and ready to go."

He wanted to ask what the text was about, but it wasn't any of his business. It definitely hadn't been bad news. He hoped the baby was sleeping soundly so her mother could do her job. He walked down the stairs with Harmony following quietly until they stepped out into the crystal-clear air of early morning. He loved this time of day, especially when he was going on a ride.

HARMONY SAW THE two horses as they neared the end of the building. They were tied to a hitching rail by a corral. "Oh, wow," Harmony said and hurried ahead of Caleb to get over to the horses.

One was a big horse, maybe over sixteen hands, and the other was a bit shorter. The big one was beautiful, his coloring what

Les had called a steel gray. His sleek coat had hints of blue in it, and his midnight-black mane and tail set it off perfectly. He was tall and strong. "What's his name?"

"Blue Knight, as in Knights of the Round Table. I just call him Blue," Caleb said as he came up beside her.

"That's a strong name, and it fits him. How long have you had him?"

"Six years. He was born and bred on the ranch."

"He kind of reminds me of the sculpture on the roof here."

"I tend to ride bigger horses, and when I commissioned the first sculpture for the opening of C.D.'s Place, it was fashioned after my horse back then, Shadow."

"Shadow was real?" she said.

"Yeah, he was with me on the circuit and when I left, he came home with me. He was big and black as night—coat, mane and tail—and strong and game for anything. He'd disappear racing into the shadows of the pasture on a moonless night, then suddenly he'd come out of the darkness flying past and disappearing again. I think everyone who's around horses has a Shadow in their memories, that single animal that just becomes a part of who you are. You never forget them."

She'd had only one: Duke. Caleb was right; she'd never forget him. "Is he still on the ranch?"

"He was until three years after I opened C.D.'s Place. It was a freak accident. He caught his leg in a sinkhole up near the original ranch, and..." He shook his head. "He ran with abandonment." Harmony could hear the regret in his voice. "I shouldn't have let him run up at the old place, but he loved it there. There was no preventing it except to keep him confined on a fenced pasture. But he loved the speed and freedom."

"I'm sorry," she murmured. "But what a wonderful way to remember him. He lights up the sky at night, and he's running free."

Caleb was very still before he spoke again in a low, slightly rough voice. "You've been there, haven't you?"

She hugged herself to try and not shiver, partly from the cold her jacket couldn't quite keep out and partly from thinking about Duke. "Not the way you have. But there was a horse when I was about twelve. For one summer, I rode him everywhere. He understood me. I know some would call that crazy, but I know he did. He was there for me. Then I...we had to move on, and that meant leaving him behind. I still think about him." She felt certain the Donovans gave Duke a good life and would have cared for him to the end. "He was a good horse."

She chanced a look at Caleb and saw his breath misting up into the cold air. "I'm so grateful to your mom for lending me the warm clothes and boots."

"They're yours," he said and undid the horses reins. He offered her the set for the second horse. "He's called Runt," he said.

She turned. "Runt? That's an awful name for a horse when he's not a runt." He was a sturdy animal, nothing showy, with a chestnut coat, a slightly lighter mane and tail along with a blur of white on his muzzle. He stood patiently; his big brown eyes focused on her. There was something about his demeanor that felt familiar, and she knew what it was: he looked a lot like Duke.

"Don't blame me. It was my brother's idea," he said.

"Runt, is it okay if I ride you?" she asked the horse in a low voice as she brushed her hand over his strong neck. "I want you to know, I would have never named you Runt." She moved to put her left foot in the stirrup and surprised herself by how easily she mounted him. "You deserve a good name, maybe even a noble name."

Caleb got on Blue and looked over at Harmony. "What would you have called him if you'd been the one to name him?"

"I'd have to think on that," she said.

"Let me know when you come up with the name," he said.

"Okay, what's his bloodline?" she asked. "Maybe he has some royalty in that lineage."

Caleb nudged his horse and started off to the west. She came up alongside him. "Sorry, no royalty. His dam was a quarter horse, with no registered breeding line, and his sire was older but had a terrific temperament. Runt has the same personality, which makes him a great horse for inexperienced riders and children. Calm, not easily riled and a smooth ride."

She could tell Runt had that smooth way of moving. "What's Blue's bloodline?"

"We never knew exactly. His sire came from a trade Dad made through a horseman who worked for us at the ranch off and on. He had no paperwork, no history, but Dad liked the horse and bought him off of the guy. He called him Peak. Dad's a big man, and Peak was about Blue's size. Dad rode him for years. Blue's dam was a quarter horse, dark from what I remember."

As Harmony listened, she realized she knew the horse Caleb was telling her about. She'd been there when Les had sold Peak to Dash. He'd thought he was working Dash, but she had a feeling he hadn't fooled the big man at all. Les had made enough money from that sale to stay drunk for a month. She felt light-headed and made herself breathe evenly.

"Are you okay?" Caleb asked.

"I… I'm not…" She drew the horse to a stop and stared straight ahead.

Caleb turned Blue toward her, then came close enough to reach out and touch her hand where it gripped the saddle horn. "Hey, what's wrong?"

She felt vaguely sick with the memory hitting her so hard. Les never truly went away. Caleb's hand over hers gave her some much-needed warmth and she forced herself to sit up straight and keep breathing. "It's been a long time since I've been in the saddle."

"Do you want to keep going or head back and see your daughter? I'll take care of the trees."

She was missing Joy, but he'd read her wrong. None of this had to do with Joy not being with her. She shook her head. "Oh, no, I'm going."

He drew his hand back and his dark eyes studied her intently. "If you say so," he murmured. Then he turned Blue toward the west and started off at an easy gait.

Harmony nudged Runt to get going, and rode beside Caleb, but kept her eyes ahead. "This hat your mother sent, I can't take it. I shouldn't even be wearing it now. I saw the branding inside it, and I've heard how much your brother's merch sells for." It was beautiful, done in brushed leather.

Its brim was slightly rolled, and a silver star was held at the front by a band around the crown made from a chain of smaller stars. "It's lovely."

"It's yours," he said. "She gifted it to you, and you'd better take it with a smile or Mom will be crushed. So will Coop. It's one of his top sellers in his women's line."

"I can't take this. If I ruin it because I'm foraging through Christmas trees, I'll never forgive myself."

"You've never learned to take a gift with a smile and a thank-you, have you?" He wasn't smiling or frowning, and she couldn't read him at all.

"You're right, and I apologize," Harmony said. "I'll take it off while I tree shop."

He nodded and pointed ahead. "We'll cut through those trees up there."

Harmony was pacing Runt to stay side by side with Caleb and Blue. It was obvious she knew a lot about horses, even if she hadn't been riding for a long time. "Can I ask you something?" she said.

He glanced at her and saw her breath misting into the air. He nodded. "Sure."

"How did you get your name?"

"Caleb and Cooper were the names of my grandfather's twin brothers. Twins run in the family."

"I meant Two-Hawks."

She must've caught his mom calling him that. "My mother's grandfather's legal name was Egan, Joseph Elder Egan, but he was given Two-Hawks by his father's tribe, the Arapaho. His mother was French. Mom didn't want his heritage to be forgotten. It's her way to remember family. Who were you named after?"

"My grandmother, Leticia Rose Gabriel. She went by Letty."

"How about Harmony?"

"That was all my doing. I loved that name, and when I was given a chance to change my name, I did."

"How did that work? Did your parents let you name yourself when you got old enough to do it?"

"No, my parents were gone when I changed my name. I was thirteen, and I was living with my grandmother. She petitioned to adopt me and told me I could choose any name I wanted. I took her surname and used Leticia for my middle name, and I… I always liked Harmony. The judge signed off on it."

So she'd been adopted, and now she'd adopted her daughter. Her doing that on her own made a little more sense to him now. "What was your name before?" he asked, and he could see her tense as they kept riding.

She looked at him, her blue eyes narrow as she squinted in the brilliance of the morning light. "I don't even think about that name anymore. That name is not me. This is me, Harmony Leticia Gabriel. Joy was already named when I adopted her, and I had the right to change it. I left Joy because I loved it, gave her Leticia as a middle name, and changed her last name from Woodson to Gabriel. When she's old enough, she might want to change her name." Her expression took on an edge of sadness. "I hope she doesn't, but she could. I really do want a sibling for her, maybe just one, or maybe five. I don't know, but I hope they'll all keep the name Gabriel."

Caleb had never thought of changing his name. There was no nickname for it—at least, he thought there wasn't until Coop came up with C.D. That stuck and he didn't mind it. "How did you adopt her?"

"I first spotted Joy at a foster home in Cheyenne about a year ago. One of our planners was staging a party to celebrate the foster system, and I went to check on its progress and saw this tiny little girl sitting in a high chair. She looked so sad, so alone. I could almost feel it myself.

"I talked to her and picked her up, but she just stared at me. I couldn't tell what was going on with her. No smiles, no talking, and her foster mother said she was like that all the time, that her development was very slow, but they weren't sure how permanent her problems were."

She drew Runt to a halt, and Caleb stopped Blue by them. "I left but I couldn't forget about her. I contacted Joy's social worker, and the lady was very open about her problems and delayed development. It took me a month before I called and asked what I had to do to foster Joy while I tried to adopt her."

He remembered the child, the way she studied him, the way she was around strangers. "She seems pretty good," he said.

That brought a grin from Harmony. "That's the best thing. Since Joy's been home with me, she's smiling. Believe me, we celebrated that. She's talking—single words repeated most of the time—and she started walking almost as soon as she came to live with me. So far, her testing has improved, and she's in the normal range."

He didn't know if Harmony was waiting for him to say, *Wow! That's great!* but he couldn't do that. All he could think of was how much responsibility that must be for her, running her business and raising her daughter on her own. "You're a determined person, aren't you?"

She shrugged at that. "Is that a good thing or a bad thing?"

"I'd say if you get what you want, it's a good thing, but if you fail, it could be a bad thing."

She looped her reins around the saddle horn and rubbed her hands briskly together. "I'm cautious, and that means I don't usually start anything that I know I might not be able to finish."

"That sounds like it should work," he murmured, then remembered something as she rubbed her hands together again. "Mom said to let you know there's gloves in the pocket of that jacket."

Harmony quickly checked and pulled out a pair of white knit gloves. "Oh, these are so great," she said, putting them on.

"Let's keep moving. This cold sneaks up on you." As they started off again, he said, "Sorry I forgot to tell you about the gloves earlier."

"I have them now," she said. "Your mom thinks of everything."

"Yes, she does," he agreed.

"I'll have to remember to thank her."

"She'd appreciate that," he said.

"See, I'm not too old to learn."

"I guess not," he murmured, keeping his eyes on the distance.

Harmony rode on, looking straight ahead. The day was beautiful, and she was riding Donovan land with Caleb. She would have given anything as a kid to be in this position. But now, this adult version of Caleb kept her off balance. She'd never known what a life with balance was for her first twelve years, and once she found it, she'd guarded it with a vengeance. She still did.

They rode side by side not talking until they were nearing the big pine. Harmony felt her heartbeat increasing. She'd thought she would see it as they passed by, but she wanted to get closer to it and stop. She wanted to look up through the branches and see if the sunlight would sparkle off the needles' flat sides or if she'd just imagined it before.

"About your hat," Caleb said, and Harmony could feel him looking over at her.

"I *will* thank your mother for it," she said, her eyes fixed on the wishing tree ahead of them.

"I didn't mean that. I thought you should know why Mom gave you that hat."

"Oh, I… I thought it was hers and she didn't want it anymore." She glanced away from the towering tree and over to Caleb.

"The ladies' hats are her favorites of Coop's merchandise," he said. "I was going to explain what that hat means."

"What *does it* mean?"

He drew Blue to a stop about fifty feet from the trees and she reined in Runt beside him. "The company that manufactures the merchandise for the Flaming Coop line didn't have a special line of hats for women. Mom complained to Coop, and he talked to their designers, and they started a women's line. It launched two years ago, and it's been an amazing success. Mom gets samples all the time, and she gifts them to women she feels deserve something special. She said that she wanted you to have the hat because she felt you were special."

Harmony shifted in the saddle to face him. "Why would she think that?"

"Simply put, she's met you. She likes you. She admires you running an impressive business and being a single mother. She remembers her struggles when we boys were small, and Mom was working the ranch a lot without Dad around. He wasn't always able to be there for her to lean on, and she knows that some people don't have anyone who's always there for them. Bottom line, she wanted to share something with you. She also wanted me to tell you that you're no longer a stranger, and you'll be welcome at the ranch any time after you go back to Cheyenne."

Harmony felt overwhelmed. "I… I don't

know what to say," she murmured. She'd treasure the hat.

He took his phone out of his jacket pocket. "Is it okay if I take a picture of you wearing it? She'd like that."

She nodded, and Caleb lifted his phone toward her and took the shot. He looked down at the screen and smiled. "Nice," he said in a low voice.

"You have a pretty terrific mother," she said.

His smile came without warning, and she felt a lurch in her chest. "She's the best. She's kind and caring and generous. But she can be determined and tough when she needs to be."

That described the Ruby that Harmony had known, the woman who had given her boots when she needed them and let her eat at the table with the ranch hands but didn't take any nonsense from anyone. Maybe she was the reason her sons weren't married. Maybe they held her up as the role model for what a woman should be and had been unable to find a match.

He pointed to their right. "We'll ride along this tree line and find the bladed access road that cuts through the trees. Dad keeps it open for when he's running cattle on the west side, grazing land. It cuts off some time. Those pastures run a long way back to the foothills and the switchback that leads up to the original ranch on top. That's where my grandpa Donovan first built until he could afford to come down into the valley."

She'd never been invited when the boys took their friends up there to swim in a natural lake on the higher property. She'd almost gone up to the old ranch once on her own, but she'd been uneasy about being so far away because her father wasn't above driving off and leaving her when he'd finished working if she wasn't around.

She'd learned that when she'd fallen asleep under the wishing tree once, and Les had been long gone before she'd taken Duke back to the stables. She'd had to walk a couple of miles through the dusk to get to where he'd found an out-of-the-way place to park the truck and trailer. At least the walk back had been mostly downhill, and Les had been passed out by the time she'd arrived.

They were within fifty feet of the trees, and Harmony looked away from Caleb to tip her head back far enough to see all the way to the top of the pine. She knew the tree was just a tree, and that it didn't make the display of sunlight glinting off its needles just for her to see. But there was a connection there, one she'd valued so much that last summer. She wished she could bring Joy here and lie under its boughs on a balmy day to make wishes for them both.

CHAPTER EIGHT

"WOULD IT BE okay if we stop so I can go take a closer look at that giant pine?" Harmony asked impulsively, not wanting to be this close to the tree without going all the way.

Caleb shrugged. "Sure, if you want to."

That was all it took for her to dismount and jog the distance over to the tree. As she stepped under its lower branches, she had a feeling of homecoming, along with a sense of security and peace that she really hadn't felt since her last time there. The scent of pine was all around, and she wanted to lie on the ground and look up through the boughs to see if the sunlight really would reflect off the needles the way she remembered.

"You're fast," Caleb said, and she turned to find him walking toward her, his limp more noticeable as he led the horses behind him.

Harmony grimaced. "I'm sorry. I didn't mean—"

"That's all right." Caleb stopped when he would have had to duck under the branches to get to where she stood. His dark eyes narrowed on her. "I know what I can and can't do, Harmony. Walking fast is a 'can do' until it's not. Don't worry about me."

He looked so strong, his wide shoulders testing the denim of his jacket. Having a weakness had to be hard on Caleb. "How long ago did you hurt your leg?"

"I can give you the exact date and hour it happened, but who's counting?" he said with more than a hint of sarcasm. "Have you seen enough?"

"Another minute?"

"Sure. This was one of the first pines my grandpa put in when he moved down here from the high foothills, and it's thrived here."

"It sure has," she murmured. "I mean, it's way taller than any of the other trees around."

She kept her eyes on the tree while Caleb spoke. "My brothers and I would climb it to put on the decorations at Christmas."

That brought her attention back to him. "Decorations?"

He pushed the brim of his hat back on his head a bit with his forefinger and she could see his eyes better. "Mom decided when Coop and I were around sixteen and my brother Max had just gone on the circuit that she wanted to have a tree lighting on our land the week before Christmas, but the tree had to be visible from the highway, the house, the rodeo areas, the barns and stables. She even wanted it to be seen from up at the old ranch. When I was deciding on the spot for Pure Rodeo, I had to make sure it wouldn't block any sight lines when the tree was lit."

Her wishing tree had its own lights at Christmas, and everyone around could see the display. Knowing that gave her a pure sense of happiness. "That sounds wonderful. But how do you light it up way out here?"

"It was Mom's Christmas present from Dad that year. He did all the work on it. We have a backup generator for the ranch near the rodeo area in case there's a power outage. Dad put a smaller one out here so the tree could be lit up from dusk until dawn for five days before Christmas until after midnight on New Year's Day. Mom always said it was her best present ever."

Ruby seemed to have an innate sense of things that could make a difference in a person's life—from her family to a stranger passing by on the highway and a lonely twelve-year-old child. "But how do you get the lights up there and a star on top?"

"We used to do it ourselves, but when people around the area heard about it, they started volunteering to help, and the energy company eventually stepped in. They offered their equipment they use to work on power lines to make it safe to decorate right to the top of the tree. They've done that every year since."

She felt a breeze come on and looked up through the limbs. There was nothing at first, and then it came: the twinkling light from the morning sun seemed to be everywhere. A moment later it was gone, as the air stilled. On impulse, Harmony turned to get close to the thick trunk and reached out her arms, circling it as far as she could.

"Thank you. I missed you so much," she whispered.

"What are you doing?" Caleb asked.

She stepped back, embarrassed to have done that in front of him. She'd forgotten he was there when the lights twinkled. She couldn't tell him she was thanking an old friend for still being there for her, so she said something sensible and sane. "I was trying to measure the circumference," she said as she kept her eyes down and walked past Caleb to get over to Runt.

Her heart felt so light as she got back in the saddle. Something seemed complete in her, and the day brighter. "Thank you for letting me do that," she said as Caleb mounted Blue.

"I think I just saw my first tree hugger," he said.

She smiled at that. "As big as life and twice as natural."

He blinked. "Say what?"

"Nothing. Just an old saying from my grandma."

He shrugged. "Let's find the shortcut and get to the Christmas trees."

Moments later, they were riding along

the outer edge of the thick stand of trees watching for the access road. Harmony was still smiling.

It hadn't been a child's wishful thinking that the "lights" were there. The sunlight still filtered through the tree boughs like it always had to catch the needles just right to make the lights. It was very real and very beautiful. She was so glad she'd come.

Runt was making her happy, too. He was steady, smooth and responsive. He had a temperament very much like Duke's. If she could, she'd buy him from the Donovans. Then it hit her: she *could* buy him if they'd sell him to her. Letty's house in Cheyenne was hers now and it sat on four acres. Not very much land, but enough for zoning of large animals. Maybe she could take Runt to Cheyenne. She'd love Joy to grow up with her own horse.

CALEB HAD NO idea what had happened at the tree, but Harmony had walked away with a smile on her face, and she was still smiling as they neared the access path. Ever since he'd heard her voice over the phone, he'd been intrigued. Then he'd met her, and intrigue had turned to real interest, which he'd tried to minimize and keep away from. Finding out she wasn't married had encouraged him to maybe try to see what his feelings might be about, but she had a child. That bothered him. He was so stretched with his businesses, he had to take personal time wherever he could find it. With a child involved, that would be almost impossible.

But for today, he was going to enjoy this ride and play it all by ear. He wouldn't expect anything, but he wouldn't turn anything down, either. None of it had to be forever. While it worked, it could work. When it didn't, that would be that.

To bring himself back to the present, he asked, "So what are you doing when we get back from the tree hunt?"

"Maybe go to see Joy, then find dark green linens for the dining area. You'd think at Christmas, dark green would be everywhere, in every form."

She hesitated then said, "I talked to Raven about possibly bringing Joy over to Pure Rodeo for visits. She has some child gates, and she'll come over and help put them at the top and bottom of the stairs. The Plexiglas makes it pretty safe up there. I wanted to make sure that was okay with you before we did it."

What could he say and not look like a heartless heel? "I guess once in a while, that would probably work."

"Thank you. That's great. I'll let Raven know when I check on Joy."

Just like that, things were changing, and work was being planned around the kid's schedule. It had to be that way; he knew that, but when he'd hired Harmony's company for this job, he hadn't expected a child to factor into the party planning. She'd probably stop and see Joy on the way back, then ride back to Pure Rodeo with him when she was satisfied everything was okay. Or maybe she wouldn't. He blew out air and was glad to find the path to cut through the dense stand of trees.

As they headed onto the bladed ground, they kept riding side by side. Sunlight filtered through the mostly bare tree branches overheard.

Harmony asked, "Do you know anything

about therapy for troubled kids where they use horses to help?"

"I've heard of it. My brother Coop sponsored something like that a few years ago for kids associated with the rodeo by family or work. He seemed to think it was a really good option for some people."

"I'd love to get Joy interested in horses while she's young."

"Well, I was on a horse when I was about three, according to my mother. I don't remember when I wasn't on a horse. Now I ride a computer chair." He laughed roughly. "What a change."

His voice echoed in the silence around them, bouncing off the dense trees. As they neared the opening onto the western pastures straight ahead, Harmony glanced at Caleb, and he motioned to the foothills in the distance where the land began its gradual incline. "That's where we're going," he told her. "That dark line cutting across north to south is pretty much all different kinds of pine trees," he said and they rode in that direction.

"I really like the way Runt rides, and his temperament is really good. Do you think he would make a good first horse for a child?"

He knew where she was going. "For your daughter, no. She's way too young."

"I know that, but I was thinking I'd try to get a horse and have her get used to it long before she'd be riding."

"I guess a horse like Runt would be a good choice if you don't want to mess around with a pony first. He's not overly big, and he's very calm. Do you live on a ranch near Cheyenne?"

"No, just four acres, but it's zoned for animals. The number's limited, but while it's just me and Joy, a horse would be legal. If I had more kids, I guess I'd have to think about getting more land so each child could have their own horse. I was just wondering if you'd ever consider selling Runt to me."

"I've never considered selling him, and I don't think anyone else in the family has. But if you did buy him, you could give him that noble name you were talking about before."

"I think I'd call him Runt until Joy was old enough to give him a name herself."

"I guess you could. Although to be honest with you, I had a guy at the ranch who really understood horses tell my dad that renaming an adult horse can cause trust issues further down the road."

"Really?"

"That's what he said, but he said a lot of things when he was drunk and did a lot of things, too. Old Les was a genius with horses, but miserable with everything else when he wasn't sober."

Caleb turned a moment later when he realized Harmony wasn't riding beside him anymore. He looked back and saw her standing by Runt, her head down, and a hand pressed to her stomach. He turned around and rode back to her. Dismounting quickly, he said, "What's going on?"

She didn't move for a minute, then looked at him. "A…a cramp." Her hand went to her thigh. "It just came out of nowhere," she said, her voice sounding tight. "I'll walk it off. Go ahead."

He went closer. "No, I'll walk with you."

HARMONY FOUGHT NAUSEA that had flooded over her when Caleb had named the drunk at the ranch. It had crushed her, and she'd wanted to turn and ride away from everything. But Caleb was there, concern in his eyes, and she'd lied about having a leg cramp. She hated herself for that, but she never, ever wanted to be remembered as the daughter of drunken Les Randall. She held Runt's reins and actually faked a limp as she started to walk. "I'm okay," she said, another lie. They were piling up.

The dried dead grass underfoot crunched with each step they and the horses took. "You sure?" Caleb asked.

"I'm fine. You should be riding," she said.

"Don't worry about me. It's good to stretch my legs."

She stared straight ahead as they kept going. "It's beautiful here, isn't it?"

"It never disappoints me," he said. "How's the jacket working for you?"

"It's a lot better than my jacket would have been."

He cocked his head slightly to his right, nodded and said, "Fun fact for a diversion. Never put butter on a burn, no matter who tells you to do it."

"Why would you tell me—?"

He cut her off with a smile. "Just kidding. I couldn't resist. FYI, that's really true."

She sighed. "My grandma Letty told me that's what her mother did when she burned her hand on the stove. I guess they really did do that back in the day."

He adjusted his hat, pulling the brim down a bit more. "I guess the diversion worked. You look as if the cramp isn't bothering you much anymore."

She'd actually forgotten to keep up the ruse. "Oh…no, it's okay. The walking helped." She pulled the reins to stop Runt, and then swung back up into the saddle.

"How far is it to the trees?" she asked when they were both riding again.

"Half a mile or so."

She felt better. "You know, I don't think I'd change Runt's name. I don't want issues with him if I can buy him from you or your parents. Do you think they might sell him?"

"That would be their choice. I can ask Dad, if you're serious about it."

She didn't hesitate. "I am serious about it."

He nudged Blue to a faster pace and Runt kept up. Finally, they were at the trees, and he stopped by four hitching posts at a central point where a path was cut for walking through the stand. They dismounted. Harmony secured Runt next to Blue, then she looked around. Lines of different pine trees went in both directions. She could see the progressive pattern of the trees going from two or three feet tall all the way up to what had to be the biggest tree, the one Caleb's uncle didn't want tagged. "Wow, I had no idea there were this many."

"Uncle Abel dotes on them, believe me. He also takes trees to shelters and families who might not otherwise be able to get one."

"I feel kind of guilty cutting trees for the party. I mean, if others really need them."

He gestured to an aisle among the six-footers. "Uncle Abel was happy to do this. It's for his sister, and family's everything to him. Donating them for the party will make him very happy, and Mom will really appreciate them."

"Okay," she said and took off her hat to hang it on the saddle horn, then took out her list. "Should I start with the main tree I wanted, the tallest one?"

He took strips of bright yellow tape out of his jacket pocket and gave them to her. "Let's start big. When you find a tree that you want, tie one of these halfway up on the front and another on the back. Ready?"

"Absolutely."

Half an hour later, there were tags on twelve trees, and Harmony was very happy with her choices. On the way back to the horses, she spotted two smaller trees near where they'd entered the plot. They weren't perfect, maybe three feet tall, with one leaning to the left and the other with random-sized branches, but she took out her ties and put them on both trees.

"That should do it," she said and walked toward the horses with Caleb following her.

She paused by a single ponderosa pine his uncle had planted a few years back. She ran her hand over the needles, then lifted her fingertips to her nose and inhaled. "They smell so good," she murmured.

Their scent was in the air around them, too. "You made some good selections," Caleb said.

"The important one was for the honors table. I love Fraser firs for statement trees.

That touch of silver on their needles is almost a decoration of its own."

"It's impressive. But what about the two small ones? If you leave them for another year, Uncle Abel will work his magic on the them and they'll be perfect."

She cast him a sideways glance. "I thought we'd decided that nothing's ever really perfect. No one marries someone because they believe they're perfect. They get married despite the flaws. It's called love. If someone expects perfection, they're in for a rude awakening. Do you think your parents saw each other as perfect and that's why they got married?"

They were at the horses and Caleb put the last of the yellow tape in his jacket pocket before he got up on Blue. Harmony looked up at him, and he said, "I don't know if they saw each other as perfect, but I'm sure love is blind sometimes."

She didn't respond, just got on Runt, and they started back the way they'd come. She knew she should say something, but she didn't know what.

"My parents love each other and look how long it's lasted. They've seldom been apart except when my Dad was on the circuit. But he finally quit. He wanted to be home with us and Mom. But he kept rodeo all around him. Mom, too."

"I've noticed that," she said.

"Dad had multiple championships for bull riding, lots of buckles and trophies and saddles and some money. My mother was pretty good at barrel racing, and my brothers and I joined the circuit right out of high school. Three of us started, and only one stayed, my brother Coop. He's a real star in bareback bronc riding, a five-time world champion, and he's also done bull riding and steer roping. My dad didn't have to retire, but he did it for Mom. I know that was mostly it. She'd be alone a lot and have to keep the ranch going. She would have never asked him to quit, but he did...for her, and for us boys, I guess, too."

"You left after your injury, but why did your older brother leave?"

He shrugged. "Well, Max never rode a bull with the stupid name Buttercup, and got his leg shattered." He gave her a wry grin and she smiled. "He simply realized it wasn't his passion, the way it was Coop's.

Max just said goodbye and went on with his life elsewhere. It wasn't to please anyone. He did it for himself. He joined the Army, was accepted into the Army Rangers, then came home after two tours. He was elected sheriff and he's doing a great job. He likes it."

She nodded. They'd all grown and changed since the last time she'd seen them.

"Even if I'm not in the rodeo anymore, I'm surrounded by it at work and at home. I like that. Both businesses are centered on the rodeo, and our family life is dead in the center of that. It's in the Donovan genes. My parents met at a rodeo down by the Wind River Rez. They got married the day before my dad won his first championship."

"He must have been very good."

"The best." Their pace was slow and easy. He wasn't in any real hurry to get back.

"And he just walked away?"

"Yes, but he's still involved in rodeos locally. We have Junior Rodeos all summer at our ranch and a big one in July before the Cheyenne show."

She asked something she'd never had the

nerve to ask when she was younger. "Your father's called Dash. Is that a nickname?"

"His real name is Dashiell Maxim Donovan. Dashiell became Dash, and it fit him. He was quick back then."

"A very grand name," she murmured.

"Dad's always hated it, and he made Mom promise that none of their kids would carry that name. She settled for Max being Maxim, but no Dashiell. He kids her about saving his full name for a grandson." He chuckled. "I don't see that happening, unless Coop or Max oblige her."

"And you?"

"Oh, me, I've got a lot of things to do with my life. I'm not sure I'll ever be ready for kids, no matter what they might be called."

Harmony was oddly unsettled by Caleb's honesty. She didn't know why. He knew what he wanted, and it was none of her business. "If you never want kids, that's a pretty simple way to avoid a dispute about what to name them."

"I didn't say never, I just—" He stopped himself. Why should he be defensive about what he wanted to do with his life? Her approval or disapproval shouldn't mean a thing to him. "It's where I am now, and I can't see far enough into the future to think it's going to change anytime soon."

She nodded. "That's your choice."

"Nothing else to add from your well of wisdom?" he asked, slightly irritated.

She shook her head. "No."

He rode along beside her, keeping his thoughts to himself until he couldn't. "Maybe you should remember your own words—that nothing is perfect and that includes people."

Harmony said one word, "Obviously."

Nudging Runt to a faster pace, she moved ahead of him, and he was happy to stay behind her all the way back to the stable. That was when he remembered Harmony had gone to the main house to see Joy. "You changed your mind about going to see Joy and Raven?"

He saw her remember, but she just shrugged, not admitting she'd probably forgotten too. "I'll call and have Raven bring Joy over here."

Caleb was ready to leave as soon as possible. He'd be polite, and he'd thank Harmony for all she'd done then take off for Cody for a couple of days. He was surprised to see a familiar truck parked by the corral: a totally restored green Chevy pickup from the fifties. It was his uncle's pride and joy.

"Hey, boy," Uncle Abel called as he came out of the stable. "Glad you got back before I left." His uncle was medium height with gray hair cropped short, deeply tanned skin and the sharp bone structure of his Native American ancestors. He was solidly built and wearing work clothes, all denim, all faded, with work boots and a plain beige Stetson. His dark eyes went to Harmony as she stopped Runt and dismounted. "Hello, there. You must be the party girl."

"Uncle, no," Caleb said, barely keeping a straight face. Uncle Abel spoke good English, but he tended to use the wrong words from time to time. Caleb never figured out if he meant to do that for shock value or fun, or if it was unintentional.

"What'd I say, boy?" he asked as if he didn't know.

"Harmony is a party planner. She's here for the party for my folks. Harmony, meet my uncle Abel, Mom's brother and our ranch manger. He's also one of the best at horse breeding of anyone in this state."

"Ah, boy," Abel said. "You embarrass me. But I am good." Then he spoke to Harmony. "Pleased meeting you, ma'am."

"It's nice to meet you, too," she said.

While Abel smiled charmingly at Harmony, Caleb filled him in. "The trees are marked with yellow tape. Oh, there's two in section three with tape, also."

He nodded. "Got it," he said, finally turning to Caleb. "I'll trim the small ones before Cam and Joe B. bring them down here. They'll be here before the sun goes down today."

"Oh, no, don't trim them, please," Harmony said. "I like them the way they are. They have personality."

Abel chuckled. "I understand, ma'am. Most people don't see the personality of trees like I do."

"I sure did in the smaller ones," Harmony said with a smile. "All the trees were beautiful."

Caleb was watching the two of them.

A seventy-year-old horse breeder and a twentysomething party planner agreeing good-naturedly that trees had personalities. He cut in on the discussion. "How about bringing them down tomorrow sometime?"

"Okay, they'll be here." Abel held out his hands to take the reins from Caleb and Harmony. "I'll put the horses away for you two. No problem. Get going in where it's warm," he said with a flick of his free hand.

If they stuck around, Abel was apt to start talking again and there was no way to predict what the subject would be. "Let's do that. I need to get my things, then head out."

She waved to Abel, then went with Caleb inside through the delivery doors and toward the stairs. She stopped before going up, tugged off her gloves and pushed them into her pockets. "Thank you for going with me. Your uncle's very nice."

"He agreed with you about trees having personalities."

She chuckled at that, and he liked the sound in the otherwise empty space. It kind of helped him forget about their conversation just before they came back to Pure Rodeo. "Yes, he did. He has a good imagination."

"You should hear the stories he tells sometimes."

"I bet he's a good storyteller," she said, then asked, "Are you leaving now?"

"Yes, I am. I have some loose ends to tie up in Cody. I might be gone a few days."

"Is it okay if Raven brings Joy over and we kid-proof your private quarters? Nothing permanent, just making sure she can't get into anything."

It had gone this far; he wasn't going to argue over safety measures. "Sure, fine."

"I'll spend tonight here, if Joy's doing okay, if not, I'll leave you a message and let you know what's going on." Harmony stood very still, then said, "That huge pine? When do they put the lights on it?"

"Pretty soon. Mom should know. She takes care of getting the crew here on time."

"I don't want to miss that, so I have to get down to work and get my crew ready to come here and do their job. I'll be here most of the time, and people will be going in and out. My insurance agent is getting the temporary liability coverage for the party, and he mentioned you'll need to agree to it by signature."

"Yeah, I know all about insurance in my business. Let me know when you need me to sign."

"I will. Thanks." Without warning, her stomach growled. "Oh, excuse me," she said.

"You haven't eaten yet today," he said.

She didn't realize until he asked that she hadn't eaten since yesterday when Ruby had offered her a sandwich while they'd been putting the baby's stuff together. "No, I haven't."

"I had coffee this morning, and I'm hungry. Why don't you call Raven and see when she'll be coming over here, and I'll look in the kitchen and see what there is to eat?"

"Oh, no. I can just have one of the energy bars I brought with me."

He countered that with, "Tell you what, why don't we both go to the kitchen? I should eat before I head out for the day."

She was pretty sure he wasn't going to give up, so she agreed. Real food did appeal to her. "Okay."

CHAPTER NINE

THEY WENT INTO the kitchen, which was well set up with impressive appliances, a huge prep area and a service island in the middle. It was as good as any fancy restaurant Harmony had ever seen. "Give me your jacket," Caleb said. "I'll hang it up."

She slipped it off and handed it to him with her hat, too. After he'd put it with his jacket and hat in a small side office, he came back to her and motioned to some backless stools along the island. "Take your pick, and I'll get the food started. How do you like your eggs?"

"Not burnt."

"I can do that," he said with a smile as he crossed to the huge built-in refrigerator that could have held enough food for a small country.

While Caleb cooked, Harmony touched base with Raven. The news was all good.

Her daughter had slept until seven o'clock and was now out with Ruby and Dash to see a donkey named Morris. Everything was going well. Raven agreed to bring Joy over after she got back from her donkey visit and had some lunch.

When the food was ready and Caleb had put two plates on the island, both loaded with bacon, eggs and home fries, Harmony actually felt hungry. "If you need anything else, let me know," Caleb said as he nudged a knife and fork in her direction across the island with his forefinger.

She bit her lip as she noticed how strong his hands looked. Despite his being a white-collar businessman, they were the hands of a man who was used to hard work.

"How's your tiny person doing?" he asked as he sat down.

She told him and liked the way he smiled when she mentioned Morris. "Kids love that donkey. He's a real favorite around the place."

"Dash and Ruby took her to visit him."

"She'll be in love right away," he said. "Can I ask you something?" He passed a couple of napkins over to her.

"Sure."

"Do you want a different horse if you take another ride around here?"

That took her aback. "Why would you ask that?"

"I thought maybe I made Runt sound more suited to children. I didn't mean that, not at all."

"Of course you didn't, and I'd love to ride Runt again if I can spare the time."

"Good, now eat up and get some food in your stomach."

She didn't have to be told twice. She tried the home fries and eggs, they were good. After washing them down with coffee Caleb had brewed, she said, "You cook a good breakfast."

"I'm glad. This is pretty much all I can cook in terms of things that don't require barbeques and sauce."

"I used to eat my eggs scrambled with hot sauce on them."

"That sounds good to me, but I don't know where I'd find hot sauce."

"I don't use it anymore because Joy always wants a bite of anything I'm eating. She has a varied palate, but when it comes spicy hot, that's off the menu. Period. She's fast when she wants something, and one time she had some of my eggs off my plate and into her mouth before I could stop her. Let's say that didn't end well."

"My mother makes great tamales and unbelievable salsa, which is very hot. Maybe she'll make some while you're here."

"I'd love that. As long as Joy's not around," she said and tried the bacon.

When Harmony had almost cleaned her plate, she sat back and sighed. "Thank you so much for this. Now I'll have the energy to get things done around here."

Caleb ate a couple of home fries and finished his coffee before he said, "That's why I hired you. I was losing time in every aspect of my life—family, business and personal. It made sense to get help. I'm sure you understand that."

She understood, but a social life didn't even enter her mind as something she wanted to cultivate anytime soon. "We all have to figure out our priorities," she said.

"I can tell you've got your priorities in place."

"You can?" she asked, ignoring what she'd left on her plate. "How?"

"It wouldn't take a mind reader to figure out your daughter is your first priority. I'd say your business comes in second."

He was spot on, but she sobered when she realized she was looking up at a man whose simple phone call had tipped her world off balance three days ago. She'd been forced to face a past she'd blown all out of proportion, and she'd realized she should have taken another look at it a long time ago. Caleb had put that in perspective for her without any knowledge that he'd helped her. He'd never know, but she would. He'd turned out to be a decent person—caring, family oriented and a hard worker. She never would've realized that if he hadn't made that single call to her business. "I wouldn't put it that way," she said.

"Maybe that's just an empty guess by me." He grinned at that, and the expression almost stunned Harmony. The man had something more than just a smile, and she wasn't certain if she could define it. But in that moment, she wondered what would happen if she let herself act on what the Donovan charm did to her. Thankfully, she didn't have to worry about that. When she finished here, she'd go home without the past chasing her.

CALEB LOOKED ACROSS the island at Harmony. She'd used ketchup, not hot sauce, on her eggs and home fries. Now she had a speck of ketchup on her chin. He wanted to reach over and wipe it off for her with his napkin, but he didn't have that right. "Ketchup," he said, touching his chin with his forefinger.

"Oh, thanks." She wiped at the spot with the napkin. "This was really good."

"Food always helps, doesn't it?" he asked.

"Absolutely, it helps," she said, nibbling on the last bit of bacon on her plate.

Harmony just plain looked good to him; with her feathery blond hair and those blue eyes, she amazed him. Her smile when it showed up lit up the room and made her all the more appealing. She popped the last piece of bacon into her mouth. "You'll make a woman happy someday."

He exhaled. "You sound like my mother. She's on a one-person campaign to get all three of her sons married." He shrugged. "Which is okay, because it keeps her busy."

Harmony smiled at him after swiping at her face with her napkin again. "I guess she's hopeful because she and your dad seem to have a great marriage, and she'd like her sons to have the same thing."

"You're probably right, but I've never really seen many people have marriages like Mom and Dad do."

"Have you never thought about getting married?"

"Once. I almost did, but the operative word is *almost*."

She pushed her plate away. "Why almost?"

"I realized, before it was too late, that we were riding on separate paths. Mine wasn't hers to take and hers really wasn't mine to take, so we walked away."

"Hmm," she said as she rested her hands on the stainless-steel island top. "I'm sorry."

"It wasn't what either one of us wanted." He could look back and see it so clearly now that he and Kim never would have made a go of it, but back then, it was hard to give up. "I always figured if I ever did get married, I'd marry who I wanted, not who was pushed at me until I thought she was what I wanted. She wasn't, and that wasn't her fault."

"Oh, your mother set you up?" she asked.

"Actually, my dad. He meant well, but what worked for him and mom when they met, didn't work as well for me." He drained the last of his coffee, then put the mug down by his plate. "We were both in the rodeo, on the circuit, and I figured that wasn't a bad foundation for being together. But it didn't work out. How about you? You ever get close to marrying?"

Her blue eyes met his, but barely made contact before she shifted to look down at her almost empty mug. "Well," she said on a soft exhale. "Once I thought I might want to get married, but it didn't work out. Sort of what you had—we weren't on the same page about something very important, and he suggested that we needed to take a break, then regroup and see what happened." Her chuckle was not terribly humorous. "It's been almost a year, and we've never regrouped."

He tried not to wince at that. "I'm sorry."

"Oh, no, it was the right thing to do. We never would have agreed on a compromise. I didn't want the compromise he offered, and I know he wouldn't have ever agreed to what I asked of him. So, we went our own ways, and that was that." She shrugged. "Besides, I like my life the way it is now, and I know I wouldn't have had it if we'd stayed together."

He thought the guy must have been stupid, but simply said, "Whoever the guy was, he was the loser."

He liked that soft smile of hers. "Yes, he doesn't know what he's missed. But then again, he wouldn't have cared. He's doing what he wants, and he's very successful. I'm happy with where I am."

"Then it's all good, I guess." He stood and started gathering up the plates and mugs. "That's all you can ask for."

Harmony was on her feet. "I don't know. You make that sound as if I'm settling instead of getting what I really want."

He stopped and looked across at her. "I didn't mean that, but do you think you're settling?"

She turned away and came around the

island toward the row of sinks on the back wall beside a commercial dishwasher. Caleb stepped over to her, scraped the plates clean, then opened the dishwasher. "I know I'm not settling in most things," Harmony said. "But I guess everyone does in some parts of their lives."

"You're right," he admitted as he closed the dishwasher and hit a rinse-and-hold cycle. Turning, he found Harmony right by him. "I guess it's part of life, maybe the smart part."

"How do you figure that?" she asked as she washed her hands.

"Haven't you heard the old saying, 'Be careful what you wish for…you might just get it'?" He knew that was true. "I've been there, done that."

She reached for a dish towel and dried her hands. "When did…? Oh, you're talking about when you almost got married?"

"I was doing it because I thought I should. Kim was great. She did barrel racing and was great at roping. She was fun to be with. We both understood the rodeo life and liked it. We seemed to fit, the way my parents had."

She frowned slightly. "You thought that was a basis for marrying someone?"

"Back then, yeah, I guess I did."

"Do you think that's all your folks have in common?"

That took him aback. "No, but back then, maybe."

She looked around the large food prep area before glancing back at Caleb. "How did you figure out you were wrong?"

"When I hurt my leg. At first Kim was all over me, doing everything she could for me, even driving me to and from therapy sessions."

"That sounds good," she murmured.

"It was, until it all changed."

She shook her head. "I don't get it."

"It's not worth talking about," he said and started for the door. He could feel Harmony close behind him, but he didn't look back. Why had he even told her about Kim? The past was the past, and he hadn't thought about that part of his life for an awful long time.

He took the stairs up to the second level, then paused at the top to look down at Harmony, who'd stopped two steps below him.

"I'm sorry if I was prying," she said. "That wasn't any of my business."

He didn't care about his history with Kim, but he liked talking to Harmony. He liked listening to her voice and watching her facial expressions. "There's not much more to say about what happened."

He'd thought they'd sit in the office, but he changed his mind and sat down on the top step. "How about sitting here?" He patted the stair beside him.

She sat down, and he liked her being there. He liked the soft fragrance that seemed to cling to her, and he liked not being alone at the moment. "Talking about the past doesn't change anything. But it can help you see where you went wrong and hopefully you won't make that mistake again." He exhaled. "That has real value."

"You're right. It can give you some perspective, help you adjust your priorities. Hopefully you won't make the same mistake again." Harmony spoke in that soft voice, sounding as if she was almost thinking out loud. "A shake-up in life can actually make things better down the road," she said.

He wondered what shake-up she'd had in her life that left her with that knowledge. She was intriguing, but not really knowing her put a limit on what he could ask her, and he wished it didn't. He'd still like to know more about her, even though he knew it wouldn't go anywhere. But he'd live in the moment, and sitting there with her seemed like a good moment to him.

"So…you're happy with your life."

"I am. Very happy with it. I mean, there's always trade-offs, and sometimes I feel as if I'm flying blind. But I'm learning as I go, and sometimes I get it right, sometimes I don't. But I'm a quick study." That brought the hint of a smile from her. "At least I try to be."

"That's when family really helps."

"I bet it does, but I don't have much family. There's just the two of us."

He decided to just ask the question he wanted to know the answer to. "You said you weren't married and you have your daughter. That's it?"

"Yes, it's just me and her."

"Do you know much about her biological parents?"

"I just know her mother was very young, and the father disappeared, abandoning her. When the adoption was final, they gave me a sealed envelope with any information they could offer about her lineage. It's a painfully thin envelope. I'm thinking I'll keep it and when she's old enough, I'll let her decide to open it or not."

"How old is she again?"

"Twenty months. She'll be two on April 11."

"Well, that's the beginning of a family," he said for something to say, but she actually looked pleased at his offhanded comment.

"Exactly! I really would like Joy to have a sibling or siblings."

"Maybe you should wait until she's old enough to tell you if she wants one or ten siblings, or none," he threw out as a slightly sarcastic joke.

It didn't bring any laughter, not even a polite chuckle from Harmony. Just a serious statement. "I was an only child, and I wished so many times that I'd had a brother or sister or both."

He shrugged. "I used to wish it was just

me from time to time as a kid, but the truth is, I don't know what I would have done without Max and Coop."

Talking about his past love life, and then talking about her daughter, had shifted everything for Caleb. He liked Harmony, and that was where it would end. If he thought he could be simply a friend to her, he might have tried for that status, but he doubted he'd ever look at her and think, *Wow, what a great friend*, and not think about what having more with her would be like. He didn't see himself doing that. "Mom always wanted a daughter, but that never happened. We boys weren't too disappointed about that."

"Maybe one of you will have three daughters to sort of balance things out."

"Don't hold your breath for that. I mean, it could happen if my brothers wanted to settle down and do the whole family thing."

"They might surprise you," she said. "Or you might surprise them."

He doubted that. He was pretty okay with his life and what he saw in the near future, the plans he had. "Who knows? But I'm doing fine, better than fine." He was dragging his feet and he knew he needed to stop that and leave. As he stood, she tipped her head back to look up at him. "I'll be going," he said.

A buzzer sounded, and then a door whooshed open. "We're here," someone called, then Raven came out of the storage room carrying Joy. Harmony hurried down the stairs, and when Raven put the child down, Caleb watched the baby run to her and wrap her arms around her mother's leg. "Mama, Mama," the child said. "Gee-Gee." He had no idea what that meant. He went down the stairs, nodded to Raven and looked at Harmony. She reached down, and when the child let go, she gathered her up in her arms.

"Did you see a donkey?" she asked the toddler, who nodded emphatically, which was probably a coincidence and not a real answer. He was quite certain she was too young to understand what she'd been asked.

"She loves Morris," Raven said. "She sat on his back and patted him." She took out her phone and opened it, then held it out for Harmony to see a picture.

Caleb could see a photo of the child sitting on Morris's back, smiling up at the phone. Cute. That word always popped into his mind when he saw the kid or even a picture of her. "Hee-Hee," Joy said, poking at the screen of Raven's phone.

"Dash was telling her that the donkey spoke donkey and that it said, 'Hee-haw.' She got the *hee* part right."

He looked at Harmony and the softness in her expression as she looked at the baby was indescribable. She was so in love with that little person. "I'll be going," he repeated. "If you need anything, call me. Otherwise, I'll be back in a couple of days."

"Thanks, I will," Harmony said.

Caleb headed back to the kitchen and came out wearing his jacket and hat and carrying hers. He put her jacket over the stair railing and the hat on the first newel post. He nodded to her as he crossed to the open door to the storage space, then left.

THE DAY THAT had started out with riding in the early morning with Caleb, hugging the wishing tree and choosing beautiful Christmas trees for the party, had such bad moments woven into it, all of them leading back to Les. She had to push that all away. It was done. He didn't exist for her, but she was allowing him to take up space in her emotions. She had to get rid of that. Harriet didn't exist anymore, either. Harmony existed, and that was what mattered.

Late in the afternoon three days later with Caleb still gone, Harmony was in his office working out the logistics for the catering service when Raven came to the door and looked inside. "Should I take Joy back with me, or are you going to bring her with you when you come for dinner?"

Ruby had insisted that Harmony, Joy and Raven share the last meal of the day with them. Harmony had loved doing it. A family meal, where only two people were related—Dash and Ruby—but Raven, Joy and Harmony were treated as family. She wanted that for Joy, and she wanted that for herself, too. "What's she doing?"

"Watching a cartoon on my laptop. She's really absorbed in it."

Raven stepped to one side, and Harmony had an unobstructed view into the bedroom from the desk through both open doors.

Joy was sitting on pillows on the floor, intent on the screen of the laptop. Harmony stood and stretched to ease the tightness in her shoulders from spending too much time hunched over, working on the seating arrangements she'd drawn up. "Why don't you head over to the main house while I take Joy out to see the horse on the roof light up? Take a hot bath, relax and we'll see you at dinner."

"You had me at hot bath," Raven said with a smile. "Joy hardly touched her juice, and she ate two of the teething cookies you got her. Last diaper change was about an hour ago."

She went over to where Raven stood in the doorway. "You don't have any idea how grateful I am that Mandy found you?"

Raven looked a bit embarrassed. "I have to say, this is the best job I've had in a very long time."

"Then we both win big-time," Harmony said.

"Yes, we sure do."

They walked together across to the bedroom and Joy looked up at the two of them.

The baby blue jeans Ruby had gifted her, along with the pink plaid shirt Joy was wearing, fit her perfectly. Raven crouched by the baby. "I'm going bye-bye, and I'll see you soon."

"Bye-bye," Joy said and waved at Raven.

Harmony loved the way Joy waved, more flapping her hand than a royal wave, but it was so cute. As Raven grabbed her jacket and left, Harmony smiled at Joy. "Gee-Gee?"

The baby knew right away what was going to happen. She scrambled to her feet and ran at her mother. Harmony scooped her up and said, "Let's get you in that new warm jumpsuit Ruby bought you and get out there to see the lights come on."

"Yites, yites." Joy had added an *s* to the word a day ago. Another small step that made Harmony smile.

When they both had warm outer clothing on, they stepped out of the bedroom with Joy leading the way to the stairs. She waited for Harmony to catch up, then put out her hands. Picking her up, Harmony glanced through the Plexiglas and smiled at the scene below.

The Christmas trees were in the building, yet to be decorated, but the scent of pine hung in the air. What would look like confusion and disorder to most others looked beautiful to Harmony. Packages were stacked in each designated section of the area, along with multiple round dining tables laden with folded green linens, boxes of ornaments by the bare trees and raw lumber piled on the dance floor with a table saw in its midst. Soon the stage would be extended to accommodate an upright piano for Dub's band. It looked like great progress to her.

After opening the gate, she carried Joy down to the bottom level. Stopping to unlock the second gate, she stepped out onto the plank floor. Everyone had left an hour or so ago, but things were going very well. "This is going to be great," she said, and Joy responded with, "Mama, go, go!"

That was Joy talk for, "Put me down!" She'd learned it from Raven, whom she called Ray-Ray.

"Not just yet," she said as she carried Joy across to the reception area, not about to put her down near the boxes of gold and red decorations for the windows, the bar and the stage in the dance floor area. As soon as they were by the entry door, Joy was adamant. "Go, go!" She squirmed to get down. She was ready to go outside and watch the horse on the roof come to life with lights.

Harmony had kept the reception space clear of any deliveries. The whole area was rodeo oriented. The wall behind a long wooden desk that must have once sat in a hotel lobby a hundred years ago and had been restored perfectly, held dozens of framed pictures. They were all rodeo shots: riders on bulls, on bucking horses, men and women showing off their championship winnings. Right in the middle was a large picture of a big man on a massive bull. Harmony hadn't needed to read the plaque below the picture giving the rider's name and the date. She recognized Dash Donovan when he had won his first world championship.

She held Joy's hand and glanced at the open merch store, which had been fully stocked the day before. When she saw the display of Western hats on the far wall of the space, she remembered she'd forgotten her hat. Despite it being a beautiful hat that she had come to love wearing, she'd left it upstairs.

She didn't want to go back up to retrieve it from the bedroom, but she could find an alternative in the store. She wouldn't use one of the good hats, but she spotted a white knit beanie on a revolving rack by the wide entry. "Perfect," she whispered, making a mental note to pay for it when she saw Caleb again. She took Joy by the hand over to get it, and then let go of the baby to check the tag. Twenty dollars. A tad expensive but worth it right then. She pulled it on, glanced at the mirror mounted on the top of the rack, then turned.

"Let's go and—" She stopped dead. Joy was nowhere in sight. She couldn't have been in the store for more than a minute, two tops, and her daughter was gone. She ran back toward the main area and was stopped in her tracks when she tripped over her own feet and lost her balance. She pitched forward and fell to the floor. The next thing she knew, she was looking up at Joy being held by Caleb. The child was grinning, and Caleb was frowning.

CHAPTER TEN

HARMONY SCRAMBLED TO her feet as quickly as she could and faced Caleb, dressed in a thigh-length leather coat, black jeans and fancy tooled boots. The surprise of him being there almost overwhelmed her. She reached for Joy, who fell toward her into her arms to hug her around her neck. "Where was she?" Harmony asked.

"On the second stair up."

She knew the blood must have drained from her face. "Oh, gosh, no." She'd left the gates open when they'd come down without even thinking about it. "Thank you for stopping her. She's so quick." Joy twisted around to look at him. "I stepped into the store to get a hat." His dark eyes flicked up at her hat, then back at her. "How could she go that far so fast?"

"That doesn't matter. What matters is, she did," Caleb said evenly.

Ouch. Joy wanted down again, and Harmony couldn't make herself do it. She held on to her. "I'm sorry, very sorry, and it won't happen again."

He ignored her apology. "Why were you getting a hat out of the store?"

"Oh, I'll pay for it," she said right away. Then, "I got down here with Joy and realized I'd left my hat—the one your mom gave me—upstairs, and I..." She exhaled. "It doesn't matter. I should have just let the whole hat thing go."

"Were you going to take her back to the house?"

"No, not yet. I was taking Joy out to see the horse on the roof. She loves it, the lights and everything, and every night I take her out to see it. She has a thing for pretty lights."

He glanced around the space, then back at her. "You're getting things done, it seems."

"It's all going to come together, but it's going to look like chaos until the day before the party."

"The trees look good, if bare," he murmured.

"I can't do the main tree until I get the

special ornaments for it, but I have a team coming in tomorrow to decorate the others." When Joy jerked back, Harmony almost lost her hold on her. She needed to get the horse viewing over with and get back to the ranch house for the night.

"Hey," Caleb said, and Harmony realized he was speaking to Joy. "If you keep that up, you can't see the horse."

That caught Joy's attention and she turned to look up at the man. "Gee-Gee?"

"Whatever, no horse. He's my horse and I say who sees him and who doesn't."

Joy was very still. "Gee-Gee," she said in a half whisper, although Harmony doubted the child understood exactly what he was saying to her. It had to be his matter-of-fact tone of voice.

"I wish you hadn't told her that," Harmony said as calmly as she could.

"It worked, didn't it?"

Everything he said was true, but Joy was pushing herself back against Harmony now. "She's upset." She shook her head. "I know you don't—" She stopped short of saying he wouldn't understand, but apparently he knew what she was going to say.

"I could see she was fighting you, and she stopped. Just because I can't build a truck doesn't mean I couldn't drive one safely."

That stopped her dead. "What kind of metaphor is that, if that's what you were going for?"

"One that I should have thought through before saying," he said and let out a long breath. "Forget it. Take her to see the horse and I'm going to clean up. Set the alarm when you leave."

She'd been sleeping at the main house with Joy since Caleb had left but using his private space during the day because it made it so much easier when Raven brought Joy over to be with her in the afternoon. It had been a perfect setup until right then. "I'm sorry, I need to pick up a few things in there. I didn't know exactly when you were coming back."

He looked at Joy, who was silently watching him now. "Be a good girl for your mother so you don't force her to break her promise again." With that, he walked away.

She turned to go back into the entryway and over to the door. "Let's get this over with," she said, and took Joy out to see the horse on the roof. It was already lit up.

"Gee-Gee," she squealed when she saw it. When they went back inside, Joy was acting clingy, meaning she was either hungry or tired. Harmony figured it was both. Making sure to close the safety gates behind her, she carried Joy up to the second level. As she passed by the office, she saw that Caleb wasn't there. She hadn't expected he'd go into his quarters, but he must have needed something. She found she was right when she crossed to knock on the door.

It opened almost immediately, and Caleb was standing in front of her, not carrying clothes with him, but now he was dressed in regular jeans and an untucked and unbuttoned chambray shirt with its sleeves rolled up. He was wearing socks instead of boots. "I did a quick change since my clothes were here."

"Sure, of course," she said.

"So, did you get to see the horse?" he asked.

Harmony wasn't sure if he was asking her or Joy but answered for both of them. "Yes, we did, and now she's hungry and tired." Her phone chimed and she awkwardly took it out of her pocket. She recognized the number from the main house and tapped the speaker icon so she didn't have to put Joy down to talk. "Yes, hello?" she said.

"Harmony, Dash has been delayed," Ruby said. "We'll be eating a bit later tonight, around seven. Raven's here and she said she can come for Joy if you want to work a bit later."

She looked at Caleb. "If she could, that would be great." Caleb was watching her, but didn't say anything, so she spoke up. "Caleb just got back."

"Tell him about dinner, okay?"

"Sure, I will."

"Raven said she'll be coming over in fifteen minutes."

When she hung up, Caleb asked, "So, how's Raven working out?"

"She's wonderful, and your mom's great, too. This is like a minivacation for Joy, and she's really enjoying it."

He smiled, and Harmony realized how much she'd missed him being around. "I bet she is," he said.

"Oh, the utility company was here yesterday and put up the lights and ornaments, even the huge star on top of the big pine. I watched them from here. I was impressed. I can't wait for them to light it up tomorrow night."

"It's quite a sight," he said. "You're going, right? You aren't going to watch from here?"

"Of course I'll go down to see it up close. I can hardly wait."

"It should be fun. You're doing a remarkable job, but you need a break."

She wouldn't argue about that. "You're going to stay around for it?"

His smile grew. "Absolutely."

From the way he was dressed when he came back, she'd wondered if he was just stopping by to check on the party preparations then taking off again. "Good. Ruby and Dash will be happy you're back." She wouldn't say she was, too, but the fact was, she liked him being here again.

There was a pounding coming from the back of the building, and Caleb stepped out onto the walkway to look through the back window. "It's Max," he said turning to Harmony. His eyes flicked over Joy, who was definitely asleep now. "Hey, put her down on the bed in there until Raven gets here."

Her arm was almost numb, so she didn't argue with him. "Thank you," she said and hurried into the bedroom.

The baby sighed softly when Harmony laid her down on the red comforter , leaving her dressed so she could get her things together, then go to the main house. Joy opened her eyes and looked up at Harmony. "Mama loves you, baby," she said. The child's eyes slowly closed. Then she curled on her side and went back to sleep.

Harmony sat there just watching Joy for a moment, and then she heard voices downstairs. One was Caleb, and the other had to be Max. She couldn't quite make out what they were saying, but there was some laughter blended in. She'd told Caleb she'd wished she had a sibling, and the two men below just cemented that fact. She wouldn't let Joy be an only child if she could help it. She needed a brother or sister to laugh with and count on in her life.

She bent to kiss her daughter, before carefully shifting off the bed and going to the door. Leaving it wide open, she crossed to the office and pulled the door there fully open, so it was against the wall, to keep Joy in view while she sat at the desk.

Before she settled down to work, she checked the lock on the top child's gate. Of course, Caleb had secured it. She went to the back window behind the desk and looked down at the parking area. A large white SUV was there with a swash of green along the driver's side that held a large gold-on-black circle: Clayton County Sheriff Protect & Serve. More laughter came up from below. Harmony crossed to sit at the desk and heard the gate below being opened and shut. Then the top gate was opened and closed, and a moment later Caleb walked into the office carrying a large white envelope.

"Max just left," he said, approaching the desk and gave her a quizzical look. "Why are you sitting there in that horrible folding chair?"

She'd used the folding chair because the good chair was too big to position at the angle she needed for a clear view of Joy through the open doors. "I can see Joy from here."

"Oh." He held the envelope out to her. "Max got this from Kyle Reed today in Eclipse. Kyle asked him to give it to you as quickly as possible, but to make sure Mom and Dad weren't around."

"Thanks." She took the envelope as Caleb went to sit in his chair. She opened the envelope and slid out some eight-by-ten proofs of old newspaper clips. Kyle had nailed it.

"I didn't know Kyle Reed did photography. His main skills have always been bull breeding for competition," Caleb said.

"This isn't photography per se. His hobby is being a newspaper archivist, and he's really good. He did a search for me to see what he could find on the old rodeo performers who were invited to the party." She sorted through the photos, saying each name on each print. Kyle had supplied the dates and names for each picture. "'Rio Daily, Bart Conner, Judge Boyd, T-bone Weston…'" she read aloud and kept going until she'd recited all ten names, the tenth one being Dash Donovan.

Kyle had found a write-up about Caleb's

dad in the newspaper, and the accompanying picture showed Dash in the center of a packed arena, a fancy saddle in front of him. He held a large belt buckle over his head and grinned into the camera. Ruby was off to one side with her three young boys, and they were clapping and smiling. Pride radiated from them all.

Caleb took the photograph from her and looked at it with an unreadable expression on his face. "I remember this. Dad had set a new points record with the win. The next day we had to come back to the ranch, and Dad went on to a rodeo in New Mexico. Weeks later, he called Mom, and I overhead her saying, 'Do it only if *you* want to do it. We'll always love you and be proud of you, no matter what you decide.' I didn't know they were talking about him retiring until he came home three months later and announced he was home for good. That was the best day."

Oddly, Caleb wasn't smiling at the memory of his best day. "But…?"

"What?"

"You look as if it bothers you that he quit."

"No, not at all. We had a big party and

barbeque, and Dad started laying out the plans for the main arena so we could all practice in there and host junior rodeos." He exhaled. "I asked him once why he retired, and he said he married Mom to be with her, not to be away from her more than he was here. He said he didn't have sons so they could be 'the men of the family.' He had sons so he could be there for them no matter what."

"From what I've seen of Dash, he still feels that way, despite you three being grown and living your own lives. And it's obvious that he meant that about being with Ruby. I've never seen a couple more complete when they're together than Ruby and Dash. When the other one's gone, they look a bit lost. I have very little experience when it comes to family life, but I really am touched by the way they are. I know I'm a stranger, or at least close to being a stranger and I've only been here a handful of days, but what they have is really incredible."

"A stranger." Caleb looked at Harmony, then said something that almost took her breath away. "You know, I've had this

weird idea for a while that we've met somewhere before."

Just when Harmony thought she'd make
it through the ten days with Caleb Donovan and was actually starting to feel good
about things, her heart plummeted. Surely
he didn't recognize her. He couldn't. That
would be impossible, unless she was wearing a huge sign that said, I Am Harriet
Randall. The girl he'd last seen had been
known among the ranch hands as "that
skinny, ragamuffin Randall kid." It had
been a pretty accurate description, too. No
way—he couldn't possibly be remember-
ing her.

"You think you've met me before?" she
asked, answering a question with a question
to buy time to try and figure out how to get
him out of the office or how she could leave
so she could breathe again.

Caleb tilted his head to one side, his dark
eyes still narrowed on her. "I'm probably
wrong. I thought I remembered you from
somewhere in the past."

The best response she could come up with
was probably the most overused response.

"I must have one of those faces people think they've seen before."

"I don't know about that." He shook his head slightly. "The truth is, I can't imagine I could have actually met you, then not remembered where and when. So, I guess I'm just mistaking you for someone else."

"That happens," she tossed out, then changed the subject. "I've been sleeping over at the main house since you left. It just seemed easier. But it's up to you if want your bedroom back or if you want to stay at the house."

"You choose. I'm good either way."

"Okay, I'll sleep over at your folks' place tonight, but tomorrow night, if you'll agree, I'd love to sleep here. The tree lighting's tomorrow, and you said the lights stay on until after the New Year, right?"

"Yes, they do."

"The bedroom has a perfect view of the big pine, and I'd really like to fall asleep looking at it."

His dark eyes held hers, and then he asked another question. "What is it about you and the big pine? It's impressive, but it's a tree."

She thought about passing that off without saying too much but decided she didn't want to. "When I was young, I was going through a pretty bad time. I was out riding one day, and I came across a Ponderosa pine, maybe half the size of the one out there. Did you know that Ponderosa pines have a flat side on each needle, and when the sun hits that side and there's a breeze, if you lie under the tree and look up through the branches, the reflected sunlight on the needles makes it look as if the tree has a million twinkling lights?"

"I never knew that. I didn't even know that the big tree is a Ponderosa pine."

"Well, I thought it was a magical tree, and I started making wishes on it. The special horse I told you about before, I rode him that summer, and he was the only one who knew I was going to the wishing tree. And you know what? He never snitched on me. Not once. Then we had to leave, and I never saw the tree again or the horse. That tree was the only place I felt safe that year or any year before that. I know, kids get crazy ideas, but I think that crazy idea probably saved my life on some level."

Caleb was quiet as he found out one

more thing about Harmony Gabriel: she'd had a bad childhood, maybe worse than bad. "No, it doesn't sound crazy, because I've done the same thing." He rubbed at his right thigh. "Not because my childhood was bad, or I didn't have anywhere else to turn, but I had times when I'd take off alone for the old ranch at the top of the switchback and just breathe. I remember when I found out about Dad retiring, I headed up there and stayed until Max and Coop found me and rode back down with me."

"I thought you said it was the best day of your life when your dad retired. Now it sounds as if you got upset and ran away."

"No, I wouldn't use the word *upset* for what I felt. It was more that I saw it as a loss for us boys, and for Dad and Mom, too. I was happy he was going to be home more often, but the rodeo had been our life for as long as I remembered." He pushed hard on his thigh muscle as he kept speaking. "When I got back, that's when Dad explained we were going to bring the rodeo home, make a place for smaller shows and junior rodeo events. It was the beginning of a new part of our lives. And, honestly, as good as the past had been, the new life was maybe even better."

She looked toward the bed to check on her daughter, and then said to Caleb, "He never regretted leaving the circuit?"

"He says he doesn't."

Harmony looked down at the photo of Dash that Caleb was still holding in his hand.

Caleb hadn't seen that photo for years, and it had brought back that night so clearly to him. The pride, the excitement, the crowds chanting, "Dash! Dash! Dash!" during his father's victory ride. His dad was a hero, at the top of the mountain, and it was only three months later when he retired.

He could feel Harmony watching him, and he passed the photo back to her. "That's a great picture," he murmured.

"I was looking for one special picture to enlarge and put in the entry area when the guests come in. I think I found it. It sort of sums up the whole idea of celebrating their time together and the family they formed. This shows it all—a father who was a true hero to you all, a mother who obviously loved you and their father so much and a strong family unit. It's a wonderful picture."

He nodded and realized his leg was throbbing. He stretched it out to try and ease it. "You're doing a great job."

"Thank you." She stood. "Raven should have been here by now to get Joy."

There was knocking on the rear doors, and Caleb shifted to look out and saw the red short-bed pickup truck. "She's here. I'll go down and let her in."

"No, I'll go," Harmony said after he'd only taken a couple of steps. "You stay here and watch Joy. I'll be right back."

She brushed past him and was out of sight. With a shrug, he went across the walkway to the bedroom and stood leaning against the doorjamb, watching the baby. She was sleeping, but in a blink of an eye, she was rubbing her eyes, and the next instant, she pushed herself to her feet and scrambled toward the edge of the bed. As quick as he was to get to her, he barely caught her from falling off onto the floor. Her blue eyes widened, and then she started to cry. He instinctively pulled her into a hug and tried patting her back. "It's okay, it's okay," he said. "You could have fallen on the floor." She wasn't interested in any explanations he could give her, but her crying started to change into more of a whimper.

Then Harmony was there. "What's wrong?" she asked, and the baby jerked at the sound of her mother's voice, twisting away from Caleb. She all but fell into her mother's arms.

She was quiet now, resting her head on Harmony's shoulder, but her blue eyes in her tear-streaked face were on him. He didn't know a child that age was capable of giving someone the stink eye, but this kid sure was.

"What happened?" Harmony asked.

"She woke up, sat up and darted toward the edge of the bed and I caught her just before she fell off the bed. That's when she started crying."

Harmony patted Joy softly on her back, but the child was still frowning at him. "She's okay now. She probably wasn't fully awake and thought she was with a strange man."

Raven was there, wedging herself between Harmony and Caleb to get directly to Joy. She put out her hands, and the baby let Raven take her. Again, she cuddled in easily.

"Yeah, I guess so," he muttered.

"Raven, can you take Joy over to the house? I have to figure out the seating before I leave here."

"Sure, but what about dinner?"

Harmony hesitated. "You know, I'll just get something here. I'll be over in a couple of hours, maybe sooner if things work out."

Caleb's phone rang and he picked up the call from his tech guy. "Hey, Gus, what's up?" he asked, stepping out of the room onto the walkway.

"I wanted to tell you that your video security system is up and running. I did a full test on it before I left and told the lady who was there to let you know."

"Thanks." He looked at the blank screens and thought they weren't on, then he saw a blue tinge to them. "How do I get it going?"

"It's in sleep mode. Go on your computer, and you'll see the icon for the system.

Double tap and put in your password—g.o.t.t.c.h.a.—but end it with a capital *A*."

Caleb went into the office, sat down at the computer and did what Gus said. One by one, the monitors lit up. The pictures were full color, crisp and clean, and his eyes roamed over the images. "It's great, Gus. Beautiful resolution."

"You got the best. You can split screens if you want and blank what you don't need. They'll be on 24/7 unless you manually shut them down, one or all fifteen."

"Okay, got it. You did a great job, as always."

"I aim to please," Gus said, and the call ended.

It was a beautiful setup, and he scanned each monitor to see how the visuals worked. There was no camera in the office, and certainly not in his sleeping quarters, but only one on the second level that showed a panoramic view from the office door to the door to his bedroom. Every corner of the bottom level was covered.

There was no sight of Harmony, the baby or Raven for a few minutes, and then the single camera showed motion. Raven came out of the bedroom first carrying Joy, with Harmony following behind them and closing the bedroom door. She walked with them to the top of the stairs, unlocked the gate to let them go down, then hurried ahead of them to undo the bottom gate.

They exited through the delivery doors and Caleb caught them on an outside camera, where Harmony hugged Raven and kissed the baby on her cheek. Without a jacket on, she stood there, hugging herself against the cold, until they were out of sight.

He watched her come inside, reappear at the bottom of the steps—leaving the gate undone—and take the steps quickly to the top. She paused there and he had a clear view of her face on the camera. She looked puzzled, then turned, and he saw she was going to knock on the office door a second before she did.

"Come in," he called.

Then she was there. "Joy's gone, and your bed's all yours. I left a few things in the corner by the window, so they won't be in your way." She bit her bottom lip. "Thank you for catching her before she could fall off the bed."

"I've had females cry because of me before, so it's no big deal." His attempt at humor fell flat, the way it usually did with Harmony. He had to stop doing that around her.

"She's a baby, and she's been moved around a lot, and she can't go abruptly from one thing to another. I'd put her down and then a strange man was picking her up. That's a second rescue you've made. First, the stairs, then the bed. I apologize for that but thank you for being there."

"So, you aren't going to have dinner at the house?"

"No. I forgot I'm losing time tomorrow to go to the tree lighting, so I need to do a few things tonight. I won't get in your way, and I'll set the alarm when I leave."

"Do you need help?"

"No, I'm figuring out the seating plan. Ruby gave me a list of names of people who can and can't be seated at the same table. I have to double-check that. Now that I have Kyle's printouts, I want to make sure all those men are seated either at the head table with the family or adjacent to it."

She stepped inside and crossed to the papers Kyle had put together. "I need these," she said. "Oh, the bling that you're giving to each guest is being packaged in some really cool pewter holders that look like feeding bags for horses. The guests' names will be etched on them, so they'll act as place cards, too."

He sat back in his chair. "I remember you texted me about what I wanted as gifts for the guests. I didn't have a clue, but I see you took care of it. What did you decide on?"

"It was hard. They're all adults, and pretty, shiny things don't really get their attention. You told me to just pick what I thought was best, and I did. Each person will get a special pass for Cheyenne Frontier Days that lets them pick and choose any event they want to attend during that time—or all of them—and it includes VIP tickets for every day of the rodeo, with special seating and free food and beverage service."

He stared at her. "How much did that cost?"

"You said money was no object, didn't you?" He had said that, but he hadn't expected all this. "And you want a great party that they won't forget, right?"

"Yes, and yes," he agreed.

"Don't look so bothered. I got a great deal on all of it because you told me that you and your family are always there when Coop rides. I checked and your family is in the VIP area and Coop is on the schedule for every day performing or doing PR events, and when he's not, he'll be in the VIP box with you and your family. He's a huge draw, and they decided to make a special edition, all-encompassing ticket for your guests, and whatever money they might lose doing it, it'll be made up for in box-office sales, and extra money generated by general sales."

"Bottom line?" he asked.

She quoted the figure with a pretty smug smile. "How does that sound?"

He was impressed. "More than reasonable," he admitted.

"I thought the people who could afford to pay would like a freebie. Most wealthy people do for some reason I've never figured out. The guests who couldn't afford to attend every day of the rodeo can finally do it all with VIP treatment. It'll be great for everyone."

She'd hit the mark again. "You have a gift for what you do…and I am deliberately making a pun."

Her smile turned pleased now. "Thank you. I like doing it. I love seeing people's faces when they open a gift and it's something that they never thought of having but are thrilled that it was given to them. Kids are the best. But adults are the worst criers! Happy tears, you know, but even the men cry sometimes."

"Yeah, I've seen that," he said.

It looked as if she'd just noticed the monitors were working, and she turned to scan them. "Oh, gosh, I forgot to give you his message," she said, and a blush spread across her face, exposing a hint of freckles. "I'm sorry. I got distracted."

"That was him calling me about it."

"I hope it didn't cause any trouble."

"It's all good. I meant to ask you if you'd gone riding again."

"No, I haven't had time. Things here are gearing up, and the days before the event are the most frenzied and the most demanding." She put the papers in the envelope and looked at Caleb. "Enjoy your monitors and have a good night."

"You get some rest," he said.

As Harmony left the office, he kept her in sight on the monitors, feeling a bit like a voyeur. He watched her near the front part of the building where one chair and one table had been set up in what she'd determined to be the middle spot when she'd done her first tour. She looked around, wrote something in a folder, unrolled what looked like a blueprint of some kind and started putting stickers on it.

Caleb checked his emails and when he looked up a half an hour later, Harmony was still there looking over what appeared to be a diagram of the floor plan below. Then she sat back, stretched her arms over her head before she rolled up the paper in front of her. She combed her fly away hair with her fingers and stood, looking around at the upper part of the room, and he could tell when she spotted one of the cameras Gus had activated. She stared into it and waved before she walked toward the storage area. She ignored her jacket and hat on the newel post and looked around for another camera, then she did something he didn't expect. She did a quick two-step—a real two-step without music—then ended it with a curtsy toward the camera. There was a smile and a wave, before she disappeared into the storage room. She came into view again on the next monitor walking across the open space to the double back doors.

She reached for the door but hesitated a moment before facing the camera across from her, waving again and finally walking out. Gus had activated the security lights in the back, and they flashed on when they detected Harmony's movements. When she got to her SUV, she reached inside and took out a box of something, then turned and hurried back inside.

He was smiling when she came into view again heading to the table where she'd been working. She veered off before she reached the table and went into the kitchen, the door shutting behind her. The silliness of her actions had been totally unexpected, but he'd enjoyed them. Especially the dance steps. He got up and went out onto the walkway, then sat down on the top step waiting for her to come out of the kitchen.

When time passed and she hadn't appeared again, he realized the space had expanded around him since Harmony was out of sight. He got up and went back into the office and saw her immediately on the monitor from the kitchen. She was stacking goblets and folding napkins. His impulse was to go down and join her, help her out if he could, but he wouldn't.

He grabbed his jacket and hat and left to go down to the bottom level, then out to the back door. He paused to set the alarm since Harmony would be there alone, then went into the night. As he walked across the cement and headed toward the main house, he impulsively called Harmony on her cell phone.

He stopped walking when she answered. "Hi, there."

He didn't even know why he called, so he made it count. "I just wanted to tell you how impressed I am by your dancing. Very good. Better with music, but still very nice."

For the first time when he made a joke aimed at Harmony she laughed, a sound that ran riot over his nerves. "I thought you might notice that I'd been carried away."

"I noticed," he responded and hit a brick wall of ideas of where to go with the conversation. Then he knew he was playing a game, wanting to talk to her all the way to the house. She was working, and he was intruding. "I'll let you go so you can get over to Mom and Dad's for late dinner."

"You'll be there?" she asked.

"No, I'm walking over there now to get my truck. I need to make a run into town, then get some rest."

"Good night," she said.

"Pleasant dreams," he murmured before he hung up.

The minute she wasn't on the other end of the line, it was like any other night in his past when he'd walk to the house instead of driving. He usually enjoyed walking the

land alone, but right then he felt the vast-
ness of it all around him. A sense of lone-
liness he hadn't expected washed over him
as he walked through the night.

CHAPTER ELEVEN

AT DAWN, Caleb saddled up Blue and rode out to the huge pine, which looked regal with its boughs heavy with ornaments and lights. No one was there, but everything had arrived for setup for the gathering to light the tree. He'd help his dad later with that, but right then, he dismounted and walked over to the tree. He took off his hat to clear the branches as he walked under them to where Harmony had been before. He reached for a low branch and pulled it down to eye level and saw the needles close up. They did have a flat side, and he wondered if they really did reflect the sunlight and give the illusion of twinkling lights. Or if maybe that had all been wishful thinking of a sad and lonely child.

He let go of the branch then tipped his head back to look up through the boughs of the huge tree. Nothing happened. A tree was a tree. Then he heard a rustling sound and felt a cold breeze on his face. He looked up again, and he saw the magic lights, white and twinkling as far up as he could see. Then the air stilled, and the lights were gone. She'd been right. Harmony hadn't imagined it. He could see how a small girl would have been comforted by the phenomenon and even thought it might be magic just for her so she could make her wishes. She'd implied that she'd wished for the impossible back then, but seeing Harmony now, he wondered if some of those wishes had come true.

He didn't know how long he was there before he went back to Blue. He hesitated then pulled out his phone and put in a call. It rang twice before his dad answered with, "We're gonna have a great time tonight! And you're invited!"

Caleb laughed at that. "I hope so," he said. "I know you're busy, but do you have a minute to talk?"

"For you, Caleb, I've got all the time in the world."

Even though he'd laughed at what his dad

said, he could tell Dash knew this was important to him. "I've been wondering something for a long time, and I wanted to ask you about it. I need a real honest answer, okay?"

"Yes," was all Dash said.

"When you retired early and came home, I need to know, did you ever regret it?"

"Wow, I did not expect that. Okay, here goes…" He exhaled. "Yes."

Caleb's stomach sank. "Thank you for being honest."

"Son, what's going on?"

"Nothing." That was the basic truth. "I always wondered how you'd walked away so easily from the life I know you loved. It was your life, Dad."

"I answered your question, now let me explain why that answer never stuck."

"I don't get it."

"I was ready to stay with the circuit until I retired, maybe ten years longer. I wanted a sixth championship. Boy, I wanted that, then the night you all left to go home after my win, and I was in my hotel room packing to head off to New Mexico. It hit me

like a kick from Old Morris that I was totally alone. I started crying. The loves of
my life were gone, and I just started to cry."

"Dad, I'm sorry, I…"

"No, don't be. It took me a while to figure things out, but when I did, I knew what
I valued most the world. I could get ten
more buckles and still worry about getting another one. I mean, I loved the rodeo,
being there, having close friends ride with
me, and testing myself every time I did a
ride, but what I loved and still love a whole
lot more is you boys and your mom. So, to
give you a straight answer, yes, I regretted
it…once…when I actually packed up my
things after my last ride. But by the time I
was in the truck coming home to you all,
I never regretted it again."

Caleb had closed his eyes as he listened
to his dad. "Thank you," he said, not knowing at all what he was thanking him for.
Maybe for everything good in his own life.

"Son, I should add a PS to that. When
I told your mom I was finished, she cried
because she thought you kids and her had
forced my hand. You all didn't. I told her

that. She said she'd go along with me retiring, but if I ever felt I had to go back, I had to tell her. She said she'd let me go."

Caleb opened his eyes to the bright light of the early morning. There was so much about his parents that he didn't know. "Dad, I'll be by the house soon to help with the setup for tonight."

"Good, I can use the help. Can we keep our talk between us?"

"Of course," he said.

He heard something in the background, and then his mother calling. "Dash, breakfast's ready. Come on in. The baby's not waiting any longer for you to get to the table."

"I'm here, I'm here. And tell the little lady it's time to eat." Then he spoke back into the phone to Caleb. "See you soon, son."

"Thanks, Dad," he said and wished he had it in him to be more like the man his dad was. He glanced up at the pine and exhaled before nudging Blue to ride along the edge of the thick stand of trees. He hesitated going directly to the main house and when he came to the bladed pass-through, he took it and rode out onto the west pastures. When he'd cleared the outbuilding, he angled to the northwest and the switchback private access to the old adobe on the high ranchland. This time he wasn't going there because he was angry or confused, but because he wanted the peace he found there. He needed to get himself in order, get through the next few days until after the party and honestly wish all the best for Harmony and her daughter when they left.

WHEN HARMONY GOT back to Pure Rodeo to open up for vendor deliveries around eight o'clock the next morning, she was tired. Joy had been especially clingy before going to bed, and she'd slept with Harmony all night. Then this morning, she was happy as could be to stay with Ruby and Dash and go and see Morris, her donkey friend, Hee-Hee. That made Harmony smile as she got out. Then, instead of going directly inside, she crossed to the stable to see Runt.

Neither Ruby nor Dash had mentioned anything about her wanting to buy the horse. She slid the doors back and Runt was there with a flake of fresh hay in the crib.

But Blue was gone. Caleb must have gone on an early ride. She wished she could, but someone had to be there to accept the deliveries and oversee early setups.

She went straight up to the office and picked up two files for which she needed to fill in the log and make the receipts. When the phone rang around ten o'clock, it was Ruby calling. "Hello? Ruby?"

"Hi, Harmony. I was just wondering if you'd heard from Caleb this morning or if he was there with you. His phone's going straight to voice mail."

"No, I haven't seen him since I got here, but Blue's not in the stable. I assumed he went on a ride. I thought he'd be back by now. I have some things he has to sign off on."

She heard Dash in the background. "He'll show up, Ruby. He's coming to help with the setup for the lighting. He probably just needed time alone. Things are going crazy around here, you know. In a good way."

Ruby sighed. "Dash is right. He's probably just holed up somewhere relaxing. But if he shows up there, please have him call me."

"Of course."

She handed the receipt to the worker who had finished the stage extension. "Great job," she told the middle-aged man with sawdust clinging to his jeans and T-shirt.

"Thanks, ma'am. If you ever need help with carpentry again, you call us up."

"I certainly will," she said and meant it. His work was really nice, and the stage didn't stand out from the rest of the room like a sore thumb.

When he was gone, she looked around. Both deliveries had been signed for, and she needed to check her calendar for the remaining time leading up to the final day before the party. She went up to the office, got her laptop and took it out to sit on the top step while she went over the calendar. That was when she realized Caleb's door had been shut since she got there. What if Uncle Abel had picked up Blue for something, and Caleb was sleeping inside and hadn't heard what was going on in the rest of the building? He'd mentioned soundproofing his office and his quarters. She walked over to the door, rapped on it and nothing happened. She knocked again. Nothing. Just to be sure, she tested the latch and it clicked open. The door swung back, and she called out, "Sorry to disturb you, but…" Her voice trailed off. The bed was mussed, pillows were on the ground at its foot, and no one was sleeping in it. The bathroom door was open, and she could see it was empty.

She went back out and sat down on the top step to go over her schedule. No more than ten minutes had passed when she heard the delivery door open then close. The alarm had been off all morning, and she hadn't reset it. "Hello?" she called.

"It's me," Caleb called back, then appeared down below, approaching the stairs. "Sorry if I scared you."

He took the steps slowly, maybe favoring his right leg, then he was standing over her taking off his denim jacket and tossing it onto the walkway behind her. His hat followed and landed on the jacket. He was wearing a red flannel shirt, jeans and boots, and she noticed the belt buckle she'd seen him wear before.

She must have stared at it too long, because he said, "My first buckle I ever won." He sat down by her. "Not for my last ride, either."

"It's impressive," she said.

"I got a saddle, too. I still have it."

She looked at him and thought he seemed tired as he sat down by her. "You have to call your mother and let her know you're here."

He gave that crooked smile that she liked. "Done. My phone lost signal when I was riding, and as soon as I got it back, I had messages from Mom and Dad, and Max. The only one who didn't call was you."

"Honestly, I thought about it, but realized Ruby would know better where you'd be riding Blue."

"She called right when my signal came back. She was lucky."

"Good. You're going to help your dad do the setup at the tree lighting?"

"This family spreads all the news, don't they?"

She couldn't read his expression beyond getting the vibe that he was tired. "I heard

Dash talking in the background when Ruby called to see if you were here. He mentioned you'd be back to help out."

"That's why I came here first. I need a shower and clean clothes before I head over there."

"It's all yours," she said.

He didn't move but glanced at her laptop open to her calendar. "You're working?"

"Always. I'm trying to make up for the time I'll lose tonight."

"You already told me that."

"Sorry. Did I ask you about the limited liability insurance for the party?"

"Yes."

"You need to sign because it's on your premises, and I have to sign because I'm on your premises doing it."

"A neat little package," he said. "Just let me know when. I'll be leaving right after the tree lighting, and I'm not sure when I'll get back. One of the voice mails I got just now was from Brick, my manager at C.D.'s. They had a bit of excitement last night. Someone broke in and did some damage. Probably a couple of drunks who wanted to get even drunker after they closed the place."

"Oh, my gosh. Did they do a lot of damage?"

"Not a lot, but they smashed two original windows and destroyed the bull ride. Probably thought they could beat it and make it work. Little did they know, it wasn't turned on. Now I wish it had been and they'd broken their necks and not destroyed it."

"Wow," she said.

"Just kidding. My sense of humor seems to have taken the day off. I have to go up there to deal with the police and the insurance company and try to ID the two men on camera. I don't know how long I'll be gone, but I'll be here for the party, of course."

"Good luck. I'm sorry you have to deal with all of that."

"Look at you. You're doing everything around here and doing it well. You're getting snowed under by your work and still doing it." He chuckled at that. "I didn't mean to use that saying. I don't want snow, and so far, it looks as if there won't be any.

That's a very good thing," he said, and eased himself to his feet. "I'll see you at the tree lighting."

He smiled again and she was starting to believe that smile would never not affect her in some way. This time, she just felt badly for him, wishing she could do more to help him. "Yes, I'll be there."

"Almost forgot. Uncle Abel wants the horses back to him today. He's got the farrier coming in to check their shoes, and he needs Blue and Runt there this afternoon. I told him I'd ride Blue and trail Runt. So, if you go out and they're gone, you'll know who took them."

"Thanks, I probably would have panicked and thought you had horse thieves around here."

"Then I did a good thing that you can remember me by sometime in the future." His dark eyes held hers. For a moment, she thought he was being serious, then he added, "And I will remember your wishing tree. I rode past it today and I saw the lights. I'd thought you might have imagined them, but the breeze came and so did the lights."

"You went back there by yourself?"

He nodded.

She smiled up at him. "I kind of wondered if I actually saw what I saw, but you saw them, too."

"I sure did. They're real. I understand why you'd lie there when it isn't freezing and just let them shine."

That meant so much to her, but she didn't say that to him. "I'm glad you saw them," she said instead. Then she added, "Maybe we're both unstable."

At the same moment, the two of them laughed, and she liked it very much.

Caleb reached down to pick up his jacket and hat, then looked at her. "I'll straighten out the bedroom so it's ready for you after the tree lighting."

"Good, thank you. I'll get back to work."

He fingered the brim of hat with his strong fingers as he looked down at her. "I'll see you when I see you," he said. Then he went into the bedroom and closed the door.

He'd seen the magic lights. That was

something for him to tell her that. Maybe he'd be riding over there in the summer and watching the lights from under the tree's limbs. She didn't know why but she almost cried imagining Caleb there.

Perhaps she really was a touch unstable.

THE CHRISTMAS TREE lighting seemed to be a bigger event to Caleb than it had been any of the prior years. But maybe that was because he was looking for Harmony as soon as he turned the corner and stepped off the private road and onto the main access road. He'd chosen to walk from the house and thought he might pick up Blue to ride out to the tree lighting. Approaching the parking lot of the outdoor arena where everyone was gathering, he could tell more people had come to watch this year.

As he got closer, he saw people milling around, greeting each other, smiles and goodwill everywhere. But he was too nervous to engage with them beyond a smile or nod as he made his way past them. When he finally arrived at the open doors to the inside show arena, he spotted Harmony.

She was talking to Raven and holding her kid. The fading sunlight picked up the streaks of gold in her hair. He stopped and waited until Raven took the baby and walked over to where his mom was standing with old friends. People were drinking something steaming out of paper cups— coffee or hot chocolate, most likely—and the kids had at least one cookie in their hand along with a candy cane. Caleb just wanted to get to Harmony before everyone started the trip out to the southern pasture.

As he made his way over to her, he could tell she was zeroed in on watching her daughter, whom his mom was now holding while she talked to friends. "She does like some strangers, doesn't she?"

Harmony turned to him, a slight frown between her blue eyes. "Pardon me?" she said obviously surprised by him being there.

"I was just…" He let that fade away. "I was hoping you were here already."

"We all walked down from the house about a half hour ago," she said. "Joy loved that Dash gave her a shoulder ride. She calls him Gee-Gee now."

"What's Gee-Gee mean?" he asked cautiously, not about to guess and hope he was right.

"Oh, it's a word she's picked up for horses, and Dash said he was a horse. He also said something like 'Gee-up.' She got the first half and made him—"

He had this one. "Gee-Gee because she doubles her words."

"Exactly."

"She's safe if Mom's with her, so don't worry about her."

She met his gaze and nodded. "I know. Ruby's fantastic with her. I really trust her, and your dad, too. Joy adores Dash. I thought with him being so big and…" She stopped herself and gave him an *I'm not going to say it* look.

"Dad's big and rough, but trust me, under that tough cowboy exterior, he's pretty much mush, unless it's business."

"He's been incredibly good to Joy and me. We're strangers, but he's made us feel so welcome, both him and your mother. I'm really in their debt."

"A suggestion?" When she nodded, he

said, "Never say that to my parents. They don't do anything with payback in mind. Except in business. They're good at business, but even so Dad's been known to let some things go because he's always thinking about helping, not breaking, people."

"How about you? Did you inherit his patience?"

"Good question," he said as people moved around them. "No, I inherited more impatience, wanting to get things going, expanding into a franchise. The accident stopped me from staying involved in the physical side of the rodeo, but I'm all for spreading it into unexpected places."

"Really?"

"For now, I'm focused on getting Pure Rodeo up and going. Then I'm thinking about Colorado. Big rodeo following there."

"I guess patience wouldn't be your first virtue on a list, would it?"

He could laugh at that. "I wouldn't bet on it being in the top five. I can have it when it's warranted, but I'm not the most patient person around. How about you?"

"I'm patient, I think."

"Do you want to expand your business?"

He wasn't surprised that she hesitated before saying, "I don't think so. I kind of like the situation the way it is. It's balanced now, and that's important to me. It's good for Joy, too." She looked around, and then back at him. "I didn't have a lot of patience when I was trying to adopt Joy. It drove me nuts, but now I realize whatever pain I went through was worth it for the outcome."

"Hey, they're getting ready to head to the south pasture, better known as Ponderosa pine tree territory. Funny...last year I didn't even know what the tree was called."

That softened her features, only making her more attractive. "You're never too old to learn," she said.

"You think I'm old?" he asked, falling into the conversation easily.

"You're older than I am. You're probably about..." She stared hard at him. "Let me think. I bet you're about five years older than me. Right or wrong?"

He chuckled. "I can't tell you that unless you tell me how old you are."

"Oh darn it, you're right. Never mind,"

she said with a mock grimace. "I don't need to know how old you are."

His mom showed up carrying Joy, and Raven was nowhere in sight. "Harmony, you and Joy can ride in the number one wagon with us. Dash is driving it, so we'll have a front row seat. I was thinking we ought to get going."

"Oh, yes, of course."

Joy looked at her mom and reached for her. "Mama, Mama."

"That's me," Harmony said as Ruby gave Joy back to her. "Let's go see the lights, okay?"

She clapped. "Yites, yites."

"That's it. Pretty lights." Ruby led the way to the wagon labeled #1, which had been decorated with garlands all up the sides and along the back. Red Christmas bells were hung on each support post of the wooden safety rails.

It was already to the point where dusk was shifting into night, and the safety lights for the arena were flashing on. Ruby got in and Harmony handed Joy up to her. Dash arrived right then. He was dressed in a bright red jacket and wore a Santa hat. "Hey," he said. "Let's take a ride." He looked back at the trailer. "Darn, I think the load's about where it can handle the ride fine, but any more weight might make it too heavy."

"Dash, what are you talking about?" Ruby asked.

Caleb could see the bales of hay used for sitting were all taken, and there wouldn't be enough space for him and Harmony to sit on the flat front seat with his mom and dad.

"Just that it could do damage," Dash said. "We don't want a broken axle." He looked at Caleb and Harmony standing by the wagon. "How would you two feel about riding out to the lights? Abel had your horses checked out and they're right inside the stable doors with their tack along the rail. We really should have set up one more wagon."

Caleb saw what his father, the failed matchmaker, was doing and he tried to go along with it as smoothly as possible. "As long as Harmony's okay with it, sure, we can ride. How about it, Harmony?"

He could see the conflict in her eyes and expression—not wanting to be separated from her daughter, but also not wanting to cause a problem. "I guess that's okay. We'll be there right after the wagons get there." Harmony looked at Joy. She seemed happy in Ruby's lap.

"I'll be careful with her," Ruby said, "And I promise the lights won't be turned on until you're right there with Joy. Then everything will be magical and wonderful."

"Okay, good. We'll be there as quickly as we can."

"We'll save a space right by the wagon for your horses," Dash said.

"Thanks, Dad," Caleb said, then touched Harmony's arm. "Come on. We need to get the horses ready."

She turned and started off ahead of him. She was stepping inside the stable when he caught up to her. Runt was there, tied to a hitching post just feet away from the door. Blue was beside him. For some reason, both were already saddled. Harmony was up on Runt right away, and Caleb did the same with Blue. "Ready to go?"

"You bet I am," she said as she rode forward and out the through the stable doors.

It was colder now, and Caleb put on his leather gloves and saw Harmony putting on white wool gloves. He came up beside her and kept pace as they cleared the parking area and rode out onto the main entry road. When they neared the private drive to the house, Caleb said, "Turn here. We'll go straight over to the south pasture this way."

She slowed. "I thought Ruby said they were going to go on the frontage road that runs inside the fencing along the highway."

"They have to go that way with the wagons, but we'll manage just fine and maybe get there before them if we take this path. It's a bit shorter."

She looked a touch skeptical but seemed to choose to go along with his explanation and not argue. "Okay."

"It's a better ride for a horse than the frontage road."

They were side by side, not talking, as they neared the turnoff for the house and went past it onto a lane framed by leafless trees. It was the same path they'd come out on when they'd walked over from Pure Rodeo. "Do you think I could hold Joy with me on Runt during the ceremony?" she asked.

"Of course. I think she should sit with you, either on the horse or on the wagon."

"I know I'm overreacting, but I don't want to miss her reactions. I missed the first time she danced. That was the first night I was up here. I have a video of her, but that's not the same." She shook her head. "I'm sorry. Just ignore me."

That stopped him, and he shifted in the saddle to look right at her. The brim of her hat shadowed her eyes, but he could see the unsteadiness of her chin. He couldn't ignore her if he tried. "You're her mother. You're supposed to want to share milestones with your child. My mom sure did and still does. Don't beat yourself up when you think you might have missed the mark. That doesn't change how important she is to you. Let's keep going. They're going to hold the whole thing up until you're there."

They started off again, and he wondered where all those words had come from. He'd never even thought about any of that until he saw how uncertain Harmony was and all he wanted to do was make her feel okay.

"Thank you," she said. "I needed that. I know kids aren't a priority for you, but you're being nice. I like nice."

He chuckled. "Nice?"

He chanced a glance over at her and saw she was smiling now. "Yes, very nice," she said, and he felt good that she was smiling. She'd get to be with her daughter for the lighting of the tree, which meant a lot to her. He was happy for her.

"I don't know much about kids, but I fully expect a parent to favor theirs and find the smallest thing they do incredibly important. My parents are like that. That's what I'm used to, even now at my age."

He knew she was feeling better when she said, "So, how old did you say you are?"

"Nice try," he responded easily. "Tell me your age first, then I'll tell you mine."

"I've never known a man to be so worried about telling someone his age. I'll guess your age and that'll be that."

"Go for it."

"Okay, thirty-four."

"So, you're twenty-nine. Now I can rest easy knowing that."

"How did—"

He looked at her and grinned. "You told me you were five years younger than me. I've always been good at math."

She waved her hand dismissively. "So am I."

He stopped Blue just before they reached the pastureland and looked over at Harmony. "If you want to sit in the wagon with your daughter, go for it. Mom can sit on Runt. She wouldn't mind."

"Thanks, but no, I'd like her on Runt with me. I like to feel her close. I want her to know she's wanted. No kid should feel they're a mistake or a burden or a nuisance. Every child needs security. Joy's mother didn't want her, and her dad left both of them. Then she was in the system. I think it's amazing that she's so good and sweet."

He reached out impulsively and covered her gloved hand with his where she gripped the saddle horn. "I'm not good with mushy things, but I want to say that I think what you did and are doing for Joy is pretty amazing."

She stared at him, then smiled. "That's the first time you called her by her name. Wow."

"No, it's not."

"Yes, it is. I noticed you always called her a kid, a baby, my daughter—everything but Joy. Thank you."

CHAPTER TWELVE

HARMONY WAS STARTLED to hear an announcement over the loudspeaker. "Ten minutes to countdown!" She was pretty certain the voice belonged to Dash.

"We made it," Caleb said as he drew back his hand. "We need to find Mom and Dad."

They rode toward the gathering, a wide half circle about fifty feet back from the big pine. Ruby and Dash were easy to find, and they wove through those already there to make their way to the #1 hay wagon, center front. Dash was standing on the seat facing the crowd with a wireless megaphone in his hand.

Joy was there, looking up at Dash, but not afraid, despite how loud the megaphone must have been that close to her. Then she scrambled to her feet, and Ruby had her arm around her protectively. Harmony was thankful for Ruby's concern when Joy spotted her coming on the horse and started bouncing and clapping.

Harmony approached the wagon to get close to Ruby. "Thank goodness," Ruby said. "I was ready to send out a scouting party to find you two. Did you have trouble?"

"No, we didn't," Harmony said, and Ruby lifted Joy up so Harmony could take her.

"When Dash makes the big announcement, put your hands over Joy's ears. She didn't get really upset, but I could tell she didn't like the loud noise."

"Thanks, I will."

When Dash looked over at Harmony, she'd managed to sit Joy on the saddle in front of her. Caleb was right beside them. Then Dash lifted the megaphone up to his mouth and Harmony covered the baby's ears. "Friends and neighbors, it's time to light up our beautiful tree so we can share Christmas with y'all."

Joy didn't fight having her ears covered. Instead, she was watching Dash intently as he kept speaking. "Merry Christmas to y'all and a fervent wish that we see the end of this drought soon."

Cheers rose from the gathering, and Dash held up his hand. When it had quieted down, he added, "Whatever happens, we start our New Year knowing we aren't alone and we'll get through it together!"

People clapped and cheered until Dash lifted the megaphone again. "Okay, folks, it's time for the countdown."

While "O Christmas Tree" played on the outdoor speakers, the countdown began, and everyone clapped and chanted in time with the numbers as they got closer to one. Then the wishing tree came alive with lights and oversize ornaments on the branches. The tree topper, a huge gold star, lit up with the Flaming Sky Ranch logo on it in red and black. Harmony had taken her hands off Joy's ears and the baby was clapping wildly, pushing to stand up, and Harmony obliged.

"Yites, yites, Mama!" Joy announced with glee.

"Beautiful lights, sweetheart. Just beautiful."

Dash waved to Joy. "Do you like the tree, pretty girl?"

Harmony answered for her. "She loves the tree!"

"It looks like you do, too," he said as he finally sat down. People came up to the wagon to talk to Ruby and Dash and take pictures of the tree and their friends. The Donovans were thanked over and over again for having the tree lighting and sharing it with everyone.

Joy became quiet, sitting down again, then she turned and rested her head against Harmony's chest.

She looked at Caleb, who was talking to a blonde woman in her early twenties, and then Raven came around to speak to Harmony. "Looks like she's ready to sleep," she said about Joy.

"I think so, but she loved it."

"It was great. Dash always knows what to say to make the holidays brighter, despite the drought. He's wonderful."

Ruby spoke up and agreed. "He's very, very wonderful."

Dash heard her and said, "Aw, shucks. My wife's a bit biased." Then he looked the wagon over. "Is everyone accounted for?"

he asked. When everyone agreed they were all there, Dash sat down and gave the other wagons a thumbs-up.

"Harmony," Ruby said, "we're going back by the house, and Dash can let Joy and me off there, if you want. You and Caleb could ride your horses back to Pure Rodeo or take them to the stables. Joy will be fine. When Raven comes back, she can take Joy over to see you for a while. You said you're sleeping at Pure Rodeo tonight?"

"Yes," Harmony said. "Okay, she can go with you and I'll either come back to see her before she goes to bed tonight, or Raven can bring her over."

Ruby got up and reached for Joy, who stirred but went right back to sleep once her head rested on her shoulder. "We'll have hot drinks waiting for you if you want to stop by the house, then go back to Pure Rodeo."

Enough wagons had already left to allow Dash to swing a simple U-turn and go the way Caleb and Harmony had entered the south pasture earlier. Caleb looked at her, seemed as if he was going to say something, but didn't. Instead, she said, "You don't have to go back with me to the house or to Pure Rodeo. You can go wherever you want."

"I want to see if Uncle Abel needs help cleaning up."

"Sure. I'll see you later."

He dismounted, and then led Blue back toward the trees where a group of men were picking up markers and scattered trash. She recognized one as his uncle. She turned and rode over to the way they'd come and onto the packed dirt road. By the time she got close to the house, the wagon Dash had been using was out of sight. As Harmony went past the house on the way to the stables, she called Ruby on her phone to check on Joy and let her know she'd be back before heading to Pure Rodeo for the night. Ruby assured her that Joy was asleep, and that she and Raven were going to play poker with Dash. That made Harmony smile. She felt okay staying away a bit longer to make sure Runt got settled in the main stable.

After brushing him down, Harmony put

the horse away with fresh hay and water. The stall beside Runt, marked for Blue, was empty. She sat on the closest hay bale and watched Runt taking care of a hay flake. Then Caleb arrived, leading Blue behind him, and saw her.

"I just put Runt in his stall," she said. She watched while Caleb brushed his horse until the animal's coat was a sleek gray blue. "Blue is a beautiful animal," she commented.

He was checking Blue's feet. "He's eye-catching, that's for sure," he said as he put Blue in his stall. He came over to her. "Are you ready to head back to go to bed and watch the lights through the window? Or maybe you'd rather stay here and camp out in the stables?"

"I'd only sleep here if there was a litter of new pups. Then I'd consider it."

"Sorry, it's too late for that this year." He took off his hat, raked his fingers through his hair and then put his hat back on. "Was the Christmas tree lighting everything you thought it would be?"

"More than I'd imagined. I guess I should get back to the house."

"Wait a minute," Caleb said and sat down on the large hay bale next to her. "I'm going up to the old ranch tomorrow around dawn, then I'm heading to Cody. I wanted to ask you if you'd be interested in coming with me to the ranch."

There was a time when she would have jumped at the chance to finally go up to the original ranch with Caleb Donovan. She'd wished so often during that last summer she'd spent on the Donovan ranch that Caleb would ask her to go there with him. Now he had asked her, and she couldn't go. She'd decided early on to never tell him about being Les Randall's daughter, but this went beyond that. She liked him, she really liked him, and it had slowly dawned on her that she could probably fall in love with him if she let herself. A ride up there, just the two of them, was too risky. She had to protect herself and Joy. He'd never be what they needed, and when she left, she was leaving everything here behind.

"Thanks, but I can't. I have so many people coming in tomorrow to prep, and I have to be there for deliveries. There's also the short-term insurance for the event, and I have to be there to digitally sign it when they email it to me."

"The work never stops, does it?"

She shook her head.

"Well, then I probably won't see you tomorrow. I've got my date with the sheriff about the break-in, and I'll be busy fixing what I can."

She got up, went over to Runt and stroked his muzzle. She'd taken off her gloves and liked the way his breath warmed her bare hand. "Thanks for the ride, Duke. I probably won't see you again unless I get to take you home with me when I leave." His soft brown eyes looked right at her, and she leaned forward to kiss him on the irregular white marking on his muzzle. "Sleep well."

She turned and Caleb was staring at her. "So, you decided on a name?"

"Pardon me?"

"What did you just call Runt?"

She went closer to him. "I guess I called him… Pal." She'd hoped he hadn't heard her slip and now she tried to brush it off. "I kind of like that. Nothing too pretentious, and easy to say. Joy could call him Pal-Pal. I might, too. I told you I had a horse years ago who happened to be my friend, my only friend, actually. I had a habit of calling him Pal. He was patient and gentle and, if a horse could be kind, he was kind. What do you think about it?"

"I think Pal should be with you."

She blinked. "What?"

"I'll let Mom and Dad know that he's going to a new home in Cheyenne when you have things set up for him at your place."

She felt a burst of happiness like she'd felt when she touched the wishing tree just days ago. "You mean that? Really, honestly?"

"Absolutely."

She did a modified fist pump and killed the impulse to do a happy dance right then and there. "Thank you, thank you!" she said. "That's so great. I mean, that's terrific."

"Pal. I like that."

She kind of wished she could be friends

with Caleb, but the break when she went home had to be clean. She would be worried all the time that sooner or later he wouldn't ask if he'd ever met her; he'd *know* he had—and when and how and why.

You can't outride your past. She never wanted him to match her with her father. Never. "I like it, too."

"Then it's a done deal?"

"That depends how much you want for him."

"Consider Runt—I mean, Pal—a bonus for all the work you're doing. It's above and beyond anything I hoped for."

"Oh, no, you can't do that. I know this ranch is a business, and you can't give away a horse."

He gave her that smile, and she wished he wouldn't. "I can and I will if I want to. I told you before that my folks do things that they don't expect to be paid for. All they need is a thank-you."

"But I—"

"No, just take the horse when you're ready for him and send me a thank-you note. I'll share it with Mom and Dad." His dark eyes dared her to say anything else about money. "How's that?"

She swallowed her objections. "Thank you, Mr. Donovan. That's very kind of you." Then she curtsied.

He laughed out loud. "That's nice, very nice. I'll take that as full payment. Now let's get back to the house."

She turned to go to the door with him, but her pant leg snagged on the wire that bundled the hay. She stumbled, and Caleb caught her by her arm to keep her on her feet. He looked down at her, then his eyes roamed to her lips, and she thought he was going to kiss her. "It seems I'm always around when the Gabriel girls are going to fall," he said, then looked up to meet her gaze.

"It seems so. You also gave me a horse."

"I'm glad he'll be with you. You know what that means?"

"That he'll be on four acres instead of thousands?"

"It means I want visitation rights with Pal. You know, to check on him and make sure he's happy."

"You can do FaceTime with him on the phone, so you don't have to travel."

"If I show up in Cheyenne, would you let me take you out to dinner?"

"I'm so tied up with the company." Harmony felt the happiness of knowing she was going to take Pal, aka Runt, down to Cheyenne fading. "And I couldn't do that. You were...you *are* a client."

He stopped pushing. "I guess so. Keep everything neat and clean, no messes. You're right."

That was just what she'd wanted him to say, yet she hated that he'd said it. She shifted away from him. "I can send you pictures every once in a while to show you how Pal's doing."

"I'd rather see you and find out about Pal."

"He's going to be Joy's horse later on."

"I'm not asking to be involved with your daughter. I respect the way you feel about protecting her and—what was it?—balancing your life with her. I won't intrude on that part of your life."

She felt slightly sick. "You mean you

want your own part out of the whole, and you don't want any part of being around Joy."

"You make that sound terrible. I just wouldn't be around her to confuse her."

Harmony could barely take a breath and wanted out of the stables. "I'm not the one who made that sound terrible. It *is* terrible."

"The truth is, I was just trying to make things the way you would be comfortable with them. I told you truthfully that I admire you for what you've done. Truth. I don't know how you do it, but you manage to run your business and run after a toddler. Truth. I'm glad that you took her out of foster care and gave her a home. Truth. But you need a part of your life just for yourself. Truth."

"You don't understand, and I didn't expect you would. Joy isn't just one *part* of my life, she's my *whole* life."

He held up his hands. "I get it. I wish you well, and that your life is everything you want it to be. I really mean that."

She ducked past Caleb and out into the night. She sensed he was beside her when she headed across the empty parking lot over to the main ranch road. He didn't say anything, just fell in step with her. Then she turned onto the private road to the house.

Neither one spoke as they walked, but it wasn't a comfortable silence, with the night providing the sounds of nature. Harmony cast a sidelong glance at him. His hands were in his pockets, and his shoulders were slightly hunched forward as if he were walking into wind.

She tried to keep breathing, but beyond that, she didn't know what to do or say. She liked Caleb, and that went well beyond the crush she'd had on him when she was a lot younger, but she wasn't sure that had anything to do with reality.

They were at the house and Caleb stopped under the portico with Harmony. "Do you think you'll ever date again?"

She shook her head. "No. After Garth, I gave up on that."

He took one step that brought him within a foot of her. "I hope not," he whispered and before she understood what was happening, he framed her face with his hands, but he didn't kiss her. Instead, he leaned in and touched her ear with his lips and whispered, "I feel as if I've known you all my life, and I can't figure it out."

It took her a moment to realize what he'd said, and when she did, it chilled her.

You can't outride your past.

She opened her eyes and lowered her hands to press her palms against his chest. He frowned, then he drew back.

He wasn't touching her now, but she could almost feel his hands on her face, and she knew her time was up. Enough was enough. "There's something…" She stopped herself from saying the name Harriet Randall, just to get it over with. She couldn't bear the idea of Caleb looking at Les Randall's daughter with disgust. "I can't…"

"Caleb!" someone called out, and Ruby was at the door. "You two get in here out of the cold."

He looked at Harmony as he spoke to his mother. "I'm going to Cody first thing in the morning, Mom, about the break-in at C.D.'s."

"I heard about the mess up there. Are you staying here tonight, or what?"

"I'm staying, but I'll use your truck to take Harmony back to Pure Rodeo, if that's okay."

"Sure. But first she has to come in and see the picture Joy drew of your dad."

"We'll be right in," Caleb said, and Ruby moved back and shut the door.

When they were alone again, Caleb said, "We should have gone straight back to Pure Rodeo with the horses, then I could have picked up my truck."

"That makes sense now," she murmured and headed to the door. She'd barely stepped inside when Joy hurried into the entry space saying, "Mama, Mama!" Harmony scooped her up and hugged her.

She'd chosen Joy over Garth, and she knew she'd been able to do that because she'd never truly been in love with him. It had been wanting a life she thought he could give her, with belonging and building a family together. She'd never forget the way he'd just stared at her when she'd told him about wanting to adopt Joy, then him saying calmly, "That doesn't work for me." It had been over right then, and even though she'd cried about it, it hadn't been because he broke her heart.

With Caleb, it was a totally different situation knowing she could completely fall for him but still had to walk away to protect herself and Joy.

CALEB STAYED IN Cody until two days before Christmas Eve and drove back toward the ranch in the early evening. He'd stayed away from the ranch longer than he'd had to because he was still trying to absorb Harmony's rejection. He had no idea how it would all play out once he was back near her, but their ride to Pure Rodeo after the lighting of the tree had been silent and awkward.

Five miles from Flaming Sky, he saw the glow in the distance from the lights of the Christmas pine. Every previous year when he'd seen that ahead, he'd felt good about going home. This year, he felt uneasy. He'd done what he could, said what he could to Harmony, but none of it had worked on her. When they'd almost kissed, he'd wanted to see what might happen, but there had been no kiss and she'd backed away.

He went past the access road to the ranch gates and kept going to Pure Rodeo. The lights from the tree grew brighter the closer he got.

After he'd parked in the totally empty back lot, he went inside, and what he faced when he stepped out of the storage room almost made his jaw drop. The place had been transformed. The Christmas trees that Harmony had used to create boundaries were all fully decorated. He walked past them to the dance area where the stage had been enlarged and held an upright piano he'd never seen before. The instruments were all set up.

He moved around, taking it all in, from the tables with gold horseshoe vases holding a mix of poinsettias and daisies to the dark green table linens. He counted fifteen tables with five place settings each, plus the head table, which could seat twelve on one side.

The bar looked as if Christmas had exploded all over it. Garlands and lights were strung across the ceiling, a Christmas tree stood by the windows, and a Rodeo Santa statue decorated the bar top, making him laugh. In the entryway, a three-foot-by-five-foot poster of the picture Kyle had found of his dad's last championship graced the wall behind the welcome desk. Every guest would see it first thing when they arrived for the party. Kyle had truly outdone himself.

He wandered around some more, seeing things he'd missed the first time, then started over to the stairs. He was standing by one of the Christmas trees that edged the far side of the dance floor, looking at some photos set in handblown glass ornaments hanging on it when he heard a *click* followed by footsteps. He looked around the tree and saw Harmony coming out of his room, going across the walkway and stopping to sit down on the top step by the open safety gate.

He almost left by the front doors without saying anything, but just seeing her made him not want to leave yet. She was in a white oversize sweater, jeans and her red boots. The lighting behind her had dimmed, and the overhead lights were at half their power. She looked beautiful.

He braced himself and walked in Harmony's direction. He saw her shift to sit forward, resting her elbows on her knees and burying her head in her hands. She didn't move until he was almost to the staircase. Then she looked up, spotted him and sat straighter. But she stayed where she was. The gate at the bottom was open and he slowly took the stairs until he stopped two steps below her. "Can I sit for a spell?"

She nodded but stayed silent.

"Thank you," he murmured and sat down, careful not to brush against her.

He looked out across the bottom level. "It's impressive what you've done. It all looks like some sort of fantasy come to life. The pictures are great, and the trees... You really knocked it out of the park." When she didn't say anything, he glanced at her. Her eyes were shut, and her hands were resting on her thighs. "So, are you finished?"

She shrugged, a fluttery motion of her shoulders. "No."

"What else is there to do?"

"The caterers will be here early tomorrow morning to start their final prep and get ready to begin serving appetizers at five, followed by the meal at seven. Then there will be the toasts and presents to get through, and your parents' special dance. You mom picked an older song, but she said it speaks to the way she feels about your dad, about marrying him and making a life with him."

"What's the name of song?"

"It's called 'When I Said I Do.' I played it, and it's really about the two of them, from what I could tell."

He wasn't sure he knew the song, but if his mom wanted it, that was all that mattered. "So far there's no hint of snow in the forecast."

"I know. Dash has been checking on the weather constantly."

"I bet you're exhausted."

She finally opened her eyes but didn't look at him. She stared at her hands as she clasped and unclasped them in her lap. "I'm tired." She sighed, and then met his gaze.

"How about you? Did you get your mechanical bull fixed?"

"Yep, all done. I went through everything with Max, and I recognized the vandals. The thing is, they're good people who got stupid when they got drunk. Max worked out a deal where they pay all damages and he'll file it as a misdemeanor that will keep them out of jail but with a lot of public service demanded from them."

"They got lucky," she said in a low voice.

"Yes, they did. Max did a good job. Oh, I also fired my best bartender today before I left."

That got her attention, and she finally looked at him, instead of her hands. "You fired him at Christmas? Why?"

"He was caught on camera serving a minor. If someone had reported us, they would have shut us down. That kind of made it easy for me to show him the door."

"It could have been a mess," she said.

He knew all about messes. "I want to thank you for all of this, and let you know I'm real sorry for any hard feelings or misunderstanding between us." He hesitated.

"Some things just aren't meant to happen, I guess."

"I… I want you to know, it was me stopping everything. It has nothing to do with you. If things had been different, I don't know…" She stopped and bit her bottom lip, then waved that all away. "It's done."

Talking to her had shifted from being easy and fun to being almost painful, knowing that she would be leaving in a few days. He wished he could deal with being around her just as a friend, but he knew he couldn't even if she didn't want that anyway. "When do you leave for Cheyenne?"

"The day after Christmas." She stood abruptly. "I have to finish up."

"Do you need help?"

"No, I don't. I'm just adjusting the seating. I need to rearrange a couple of tables again."

"Okay, then I guess I'll get some things from upstairs and go over to see Mom and Dad. Are you sleeping here or at the house?"

"Where do you want to sleep?"

That was the last thing he cared about. "Here, I guess."

She nodded. "I'll stay at the house tonight, then stay here tomorrow night to go over everything before the party. Oh, Coop's going to get in the day of the party."

"Good. I haven't seen him for four, maybe five months."

She stood and said, "I'll see you later," and started down the stairs. Caleb stayed where he was, watching Harmony until she disappeared into the kitchen.

CHAPTER THIRTEEN

Harmony headed back to Pure Rodeo at dawn the next day, ready to open it up for the caterers and the band so they could run through their set. When she went around the back to park, the silver pickup was still there. Bracing herself, she went inside. She took the stairs up to the office and got the files she needed to sign off on delivery for the caterers at seven o'clock. The carpenter was coming to adjust the depth of the step on the side of the stage, and with any luck, the last important thing she had to do until the day of the party was to approve the drinks being stocked and do a bottle count.

She would actually have some free time during the day, and she wanted to spend that time with Joy. The next day, she probably wouldn't see Joy more than a few minutes here and there. She needed this time with her to feel the connection she valued so much. Going inside and up to the office, she glanced at Caleb's shut door. Maybe he was sleeping or maybe he had gone for a ride on Blue. It didn't matter. She sat at his desk keeping track of what was going on downstairs over the monitors while she went online to check on the limited-time liability insurance.

A while later, after everything was in motion—with the carpenter hammering the stair together and the catering teams taking over the kitchen—Caleb's door was still shut. She needed him to sign off on the addendum to the insurance policy by two o'clock. If it wasn't signed by the deadline, the party couldn't happen.

When she saw the logo of the insurance company pop on the computer monitor, she opened it and the papers were there. They needed signatures. She stood and headed across the walkway hoping Caleb was inside and not out somewhere riding. She knocked on the door. There was no response, and she didn't wait to knock again. She checked the latch, and the door swung open to reveal the mussed bed and no one in it. It was like a rerun of the last time she'd stood there and found Caleb gone.

She took out her phone and called his number. It went right to voice mail. "Caleb, it's me, Harmony. I need you to sign off on the final draft of the limited liability policy for the party. It has to be done before two o'clock today or they won't cover the party. Call me as soon as you get this."

She went downstairs to grab her jacket and hat off the newel post on the staircase, and then cut across to the storage room. She went through it and reached to open the back door, but it swung back before she even touched it. Caleb was there in his denim jacket, jeans and a hat she'd never seen him wear before, a black rolled brim with a leather strap around the crown. "Thank goodness, you got my message. Come on upstairs and we can take care of it."

"What message?" he asked as he came in and shut the door.

"The one I left on your phone when it went to voice mail."

"Oh, sorry," he said. "I didn't get it."

"It's not a problem now that you're here."

She went with him up to the office, thankful that seeing him again hadn't rendered her unable to breathe. It hurt, and she pushed that away. Everything was almost over, and this would end when she and Joy went home. Once in the office, Caleb took off his jacket and hat, laying them on a packing box by the folding chair. He sat behind the desk and looked at the computer monitor. "I didn't get any phone message because my phone died last night sometime." Then he read the page on the screen. "What's this addendum to the policy?"

She explained it, and fifteen minutes later, she and Caleb had signed the document online and he was sitting back in his chair. "Is there anything else I need to take care of?"

"There's something I'm curious about."

"What's that?"

"Your headboard. You said there was a story behind it, but you never told me the story."

"Oh, I forgot about that."

"It's pretty impressive," she said. "Where did it come from?"

"Uncle Abel has always been a treasure

hunter of sorts, and Coop and I were with him on the rez looking for metal when we found the headboard in a half-collapsed cabin that had been long forgotten. I don't know why I wanted it, but I did. I was maybe fourteen. Uncle Abel said I could have it. He'd clear it with the council, then he'd keep it safe for me until I settled down on this land. He figures I'm settling here now on Donovan land, and he got it out and worked on it. He made the frame from trees harvested on the ranch, and he gave it to me as soon as the suite was finished."

"What do the symbols carved in it mean?"

"My uncle didn't know and neither did my mother, but a friend of ours, Henry Lodge, a mechanic in Eclipse, said it's probably a storyboard, or was. It was a way to record family history and pass it down from generation to generation. Most likely, the family understood it, but no one else would."

She liked that idea. "It's so personal and permanent. It's not like chalk or ink or even paint."

"Dad thinks it was forgotten when the last of the lineage depicted on it died. There was no one left to pass it down to. That's as much of the story as I know."

"Thanks for telling me about it." She was glad she asked and stood, ready to go over to the house and be with Joy. She had an idea in the back of her mind about making their own storyboard, a special board that they could add to when they wanted. "I'll see you later. I'm going over to the house to get Joy and do something special with her."

"What are you going to do?"

"I don't know. I'll figure out something."

Caleb got up. "There might be something in Eclipse that she'd like. There's lots of Christmas going on in the town."

"That might be fun."

"I'll tell you what, Santa's there in person all day until tomorrow evening when he has to go to work."

She actually managed to smile at that, and she felt some of the tension she'd had thinking about Caleb coming back lessen. "Where's he hanging out?"

"Do you know where the general store is?"

"Sure."

"He's in the smaller store right beside it.

Word is that Farley, the owner of the general store, set it all up."

She remembered Farley from when she was twelve. He was a nice guy, a talker— the kind of shop owner who'd give a free lollipop to a child tagging along after their father who was complaining about the prices in his store. "I think I'll try that. I'll go over and pick up Joy, then head into town."

"I'm going in to pick up some things for the party. If you want to, you and Joy can drive in with me."

She didn't expect that. She'd thought that Caleb would want to keep a distance after what happened after the tree lighting. She'd kind of hoped he would, actually. "You don't have to do that."

"Hey, I want to see the old man in red, too. It looks ridiculous when a grown man stands in line by himself to talk to Santa about what he wants for Christmas."

Harmony couldn't help laughing at that. "I bet the free candy cane is a big draw, too."

"You bet it is. Now, why don't we get in the truck and go and pick up Joy?"

She wanted to do that, to have someone else there with them to take pictures for her and share the chore of waiting in line. "Yes, let's do that. Just let me inform the caterer how long I'll be and leave a message for Dub when he shows up to go over their playlist."

"Sure, go ahead, I'll warm up the truck," Caleb said.

"I'll see you out there in five," she said and hurried out of the office.

Caleb waited in the warm truck, wondering why he was doing what he was doing. He hadn't planned on it. He'd never thought about it, even, but talking to Harmony brought up the idea. She'd worked so hard, and she deserved a diversion.

He watched as she came out the delivery doors and went right past his truck to her SUV. At first, he was confused, but when she opened the back passenger door, he knew what she was doing. Sure enough, she took out a car seat and brought it around to place it in the truck bed, then quickly climbed into the passenger side.

"Heat, wonderful heat," she said.

He wanted her to talk, just so he could listen to her. "Feels nice, huh?"

"That's an understatement," she said on a chuckle. "I called Raven and she's going to have Joy ready to go when we get there."

"Good," he said as he swung around and drove off of the concrete toward the big pine in the distance. "Short cut," he said as they bounced over the dry earth, then he cut to the right before the trees and onto the hard dirt road they'd used to get to the tree lighting. He pulled onto the driveway of the house and up to the entry. The door swung open, and Ruby came out carrying the baby, who was bundled up in her one-piece snowsuit. Raven came after them and went around to the back passenger-side door of the king cab. Caleb grabbed the child seat out of the truck bed and went around to hand it to Raven. "I don't have any idea how to put this in there for her."

Raven laughed. "I could do it in my sleep."

She was fast and Joy was safely in the seat, looking around at the interior of the truck, then at Caleb. She frowned, and he looked away. "Are we ready?" he asked.

Harmony glanced back at Joy as Ruby and Raven hurried into the house. "Ready to go, baby?" she asked.

"Go, go!" the child said enthusiastically.

"We're ready," she said to Caleb.

"Okay." He drove to the private road and turned toward the main road that went to the gates and the highway.

"So, does she know about Santa?"

"I'm not sure. Dash has been wearing his Santa hat around her, and she likes that. He let her wear it once, but it was so big it went down over her eyes." She laughed. "Poor baby didn't like that as much."

His father was getting really involved with the little girl, and so was his mother. Maybe a trial run for the grandkids they talked about sometimes. "I'm glad they get along."

He looked at the baby in the rearview mirror and she was looking out the window. He hoped the thing with Santa went well. There was a picture somewhere of him and his brothers when he was about four years old, standing by Santa, who'd been sitting on a fancy throne. Max had smiled while the twins looked frozen with terror. He didn't remember that day, but maybe he'd blocked it out. Max was the one who remembered the incident and brought it up at the worst times over the years. No girl wants to hear that her date was terrified of Santa Claus.

"I appreciate you doing this," Harmony said.

"No problem. I was going into town anyway. Tell me, were you afraid of Santa when you were a kid?"

He thought she'd joke or say that she loved him, but she didn't do either. She said, "I never—" she paused then spelled out *believed* "—*b-e-l-i-e-v-e-d* in him."

"Never?"

"Never."

He slowed as he approached the gates and waited until they slowly swung open. He went through, down the entry road to the highway, then entered the southbound lane. "How can that be? In school they always had Santa things going on."

"I don't know. I wasn't in school regularly, and even if I'd wanted to...you know... I wouldn't have been allowed."

"Your parents?" he asked.

"My dad. He made very sure that I didn't get any stupid ideas."

Caleb knew he'd had a privileged upbringing, with parents who made sure their kids could be kids. He couldn't imagine a parent doing that to their child. "I'm sure sorry about that," he said.

"Me, too," Harmony agreed in a flat tone of voice.

"So you aren't doing that with Joy, of course."

"No, I want her to have a childhood where she can pretend and be allowed to read fairy tales and go searching for fairies."

"Did you do that?"

"Me? No, but I read a lot. I was lucky that my dad couldn't read very well, so he never paid attention to my books."

He felt pained at what Harmony had gone through. "Some people shouldn't be parents."

"That's for sure," she said just above a whisper.

He made himself not reach out and put his hand over hers. He noticed that she was clasping and unclasping them again. "Have you been in Eclipse before?" he asked.

"Yes, when I was small, but not for a very long time."

"It's still the same, except there are more touristy stores, like a gourmet chocolate shop, a whole store that only sells organic beef jerky, a few shops that sell astronomy-themed stuff and, of course, stores that sell all things Western for the dude ranch crowd."

"I barely remember it, but I have an impression of nice people there. There was this one lady who worked in a diner—she was so friendly. I can't remember her name." She exhaled. "I always thought it would be nice to live there, or maybe on one of the ranches nearby."

"You'd be right on that."

He slowed as they drove onto Clayton Drive, and there were the shops and businesses he'd just told Harmony about. "Up there," he said, and pointed out the general store that looked like an old, weathered barn. "That's where Santa's set up."

He approached it and pulled nose-first into the parking slot just to the right of the barnlike building. A big wooden sign on the walkway overhang read Santa's World.

Harmony took it all in. The windows had been decorated with faux snow as it if was piled up the wall from the boardwalk. Snowflakes glittered on the windows, and the door had Welcome To The North Pole painted on it. Pinecones hung along the fascia of the overhang, and as soon as Harmony opened the truck door to step down and get Joy out of the back, she heard Christmas music in the air.

Caleb came around to her as she undid Joy's seat belt, and then lifted her out. "This is great," Harmony said. "Joy, we're going to visit Santa."

Her daughter looked at her with caution in her eyes. She wasn't frowning, but she didn't look happy, either. Harmony moved to let Caleb shut the doors, and then she walked up the steps to the raised wooden walkway. The door to the Santa store opened and a short girl dressed like an elf with bells on the toes of her green slippers came out, smiling. "Welcome, welcome! Santa was just going to lunch, but he can see one more child."

The green-clad person came closer and spoke to Joy. "Hi there. Do you want to see

Santa?" The baby drew back and pressed against Harmony's shoulder. Joy stared at the elf who pulled a candy cane from her pocket and held it out to the baby. "Here, sweetie."

When Joy ignored it, the elf looked at Harmony. "Is she coming inside?"

"Yes, but she's a little cautious."

"Of course. Don't worry, Santa's good with kids," the elf promised.

Harmony looked behind her, but Caleb wasn't there. She wondered if he had gone to take care of his business as she followed the elf into the store. Green foil paper covered the walls, and shelves on both sides of the space had toys on display. A large Christmas tree was at the far end and Santa was sitting on a silver throne beside it.

He looked like the perfect Santa, with a velvet suit and boots trimmed with white fur. Harmony thought whoever was in the suit hadn't needed any padding for the stomach. Bright blue eyes behind round spectacles and a full white beard completed the package. The elf urged Harmony to move closer with Joy, and she slowly went forward. Maybe if the man playing Santa hadn't suddenly boomed out, "Ho, ho, ho! Merrrrryyyy Christmas," things would have gone better. But Joy was startled, and she twisted around, trying to scramble up onto Harmony's shoulder, or maybe jump off of it.

Harmony reached for her, trying to grab her arm or leg, but the baby moved so fast, she couldn't get a hold on her. Then she was gone, and Harmony spun around to find Caleb holding Joy, her face buried in his chest.

"I've got you, Joy," Caleb said. "You're okay. Santa's my friend. He's a nice man. If he was really smart, he'd tone down things and be really nice to you."

Harmony saw Caleb lock eyes with the man in the suit as he patted Joy. Santa nodded, then lowered his voice considerably to say calmly, "Hi, Joy. What a pretty name. I'm Santa. Maybe Mommy wants a picture of you with me."

Harmony doubted Joy would go anywhere near Santa. But Caleb moved around her with Joy and slowly went closer to the silver chair with the man in it. Santa smiled and was smart enough to keep quiet. That worked until Caleb and Joy were pretty close to Santa. That was when Joy leaned forward to look more closely at the man, and then she suddenly reached out and grabbed his beard, which happened to be very real. He yelled and Joy spun back around to bury her face in Caleb's shoulder again.

There wouldn't be a picture with Santa, but it had been an experience. Caleb stayed where he was. "Clay, you gotta be more gentle with kids."

"You're telling me," the man named Clay muttered.

"Do you have a stuffed horse toy in here?"

The elf pointed to a shelf to Caleb's left. "Perfect," he said and reached to take down a fluffy brown horse with a star between its eyes. He looked at Joy and held it close to her. "Joy, Gee-Gee?"

The baby slowly turned to look at Caleb, and then cautiously touched the toy. "Gee-Gee," she said in a whisper, then took the horse and hugged it to her. Harmony could hardly believe what had happened. Joy sighed, and Caleb smiled at her.

Harmony took out her phone and quickly took a picture. It was far better than any picture of Joy with Santa would have been.

"How much for the horse, Clay?" he asked.

"Just take it. It's on me," Santa said.

Two children came into the store, saw Santa and ran toward him. Caleb moved out of the way just in time to avoid a collision with them and turned to Harmony. "Time to go?"

She nodded. "Yes, it is."

WHEN MORNING CAME, Harmony woke alone in Caleb's suite and almost couldn't believe today was Christmas Eve, the day of the party, and she was ready for it. When she was dressed in her work clothes, a red sweater and jeans, she called to check on Joy. All was well at the Donovan home, so she headed downstairs to find things going smoothly. Dub was on the stage with his band, and Caleb was there talking to him. She hadn't expected to see him until the party.

She went past the men into the kitchen to check on the timetable for the meals.

When she stepped back out into the main area, she saw Caleb was now sitting on the top step by the walkway. He waved to her and motioned for her to come up.

She ran her fingers through her hair when she remembered she hadn't combed it yet. She took the steps to the top, and Caleb stood. "Come here," he said and led the way into the office. He shut the door behind them and turned to Harmony. "First, Joy was asleep when I left the house about half an hour ago."

She didn't mention her call to get the same information. "That's good."

"Is everything okay here?"

"Yes, everything's pretty much ready."

"Will you need any extra help? I can bring some servers down from C.D.'s if you need them."

"Thanks, but I don't need them. I had two of our backup staff come up yesterday and we worked it out last night. They'll be the ones to stay in the background but keep everything moving tonight. I'll oversee them from the office via the monitors. We'll open the front doors at four thirty in case some guests come early. Is that why you came over, to see if I needed any help?"

"No, not really," he said as he came closer to her. "I probably won't get a chance to see you alone again, and I wanted to make sure to tell you that I wish you and Joy all the happiness in the world, and that I hope your life is everything you ever wished for under your wishing tree."

She swallowed before she could speak. "I… I wish you all the very best in your life, too."

He came closer. "There's one last thing."

"What's that?"

He touched her chin with the tip of his forefinger and gently tilted her face up so his dark eyes met hers. "This," he said, and kissed her. The contact was tentative at first. Then his arms went around her and drew her closer to him as the kiss deepened. Harmony stood very still as her twelve-year-old-girlish crush went out the window and was replaced by feelings that canceled out sanity. She should be running as fast as she could to get away, but she didn't want to go anywhere except closer to Caleb. She lifted her hands to clasp them behind his neck and lost any will to be anywhere except right where she was at that moment.

Then he let go of her and it was over. He looked at her, the shock she was feeling mirrored in his dark eyes. His voice was edged with roughness as he said, "Goodbye, Harmony Gabriel. Have a safe ride home."

He hesitated, and then crossed to the door, his limp more pronounced than she'd seen it before. Without turning around, he went down the stairs, and just like that, he was gone.

Harmony sank down onto her folding chair and whispered, "Goodbye, Caleb Donovan." The first time she'd left the Flaming Sky, she'd been ashamed and frightened. This time, she'd go quietly, with no sheriff in sight, not frightened nor ashamed, just heartbroken.

By four thirty everything was in place. The greeters were by the door and the valet set up and waiting for the first guests to arrive. That big reveal was always exciting— that moment when she knew the client had what they'd asked for. But this time there was a flatness that hovered over everything, and she tried to ignore it so that the party would be perfect for Ruby and Dash.

She took one final look around, talked to Dub—a sturdy man with a great smile, graying hair and wearing silver boots—about the playlist for his band. Then she went upstairs to the office where she'd stay until just before the meal was scheduled to start. She'd use the security monitors to watch everything unfold below. Sitting in Caleb's chair, she saw people were already arriving, their clothes a mixture of fancy rodeo outfits and more traditional formal wear. The greetings went smoothly, with drinks and plates of appetizers that Dash had approved being offered to the guests. Many of the guests were seeing Pure Rodeo for the first time and moved around the space, taking it all in. When the band started up, a few couples headed out to the dance floor. Things looked like they were going splendidly.

She spotted a trio of older men in the entry area, looking at the big poster of Dash she'd had blown up. She actually recognized two of them, Judge Boyd and T-bone

Weston; they were in the newspaper files Kyle had sent her. Then they were grinning and pointing at the pictures that weren't covered by the poster. A glance at the outdoor cameras showed two women arriving just now, one pointing out the metal sculpture of Shadow on the roof.

Dash and Ruby arrived a few minutes later and were greeted by loud applause as soon as they stepped inside. Dash had transformed from a rough-looking gray haired cowboy into a stunning gentleman wearing a black Western-cut suit over a red shirt and red boots studded with silver. Ruby was at his side holding his hand. She looked as striking as ever in a tea-length Western styled dress with a flowing skirt, a sleek bodice and scooped neckline, fashioned in a gauzy red fabric. Her boots were identical to Dash's, and the two of them made a terrific pair.

Then she saw their sons coming in behind them: Max, Caleb and Coop. All three wore Western-tailored tuxedos with red rope ties, white shirts and red boots. Ruby had said Dash and the boys had picked out their clothes with her in mind. Red for

Ruby. Coop had rushed through an order for their boots at the last minute. Royce, Mandy's brother, a slender man, moved into the frame and started taking photos as he followed the Donovans into the main area.

They all looked great, but Caleb took her breath away, especially as he was smiling and hugging people. It hit her hard that she'd simply miss seeing him around. She looked away, swiveling her chair to look out the window at the big pine and its lights, shining in the falling dusk. She'd miss him when she left, but sooner or later that would ease, and he'd slip into the place of a memory.

She'd stay in the office and out of the way for now, unless she saw something going wrong down below. She kept the office door open so she could hear the band, and she tried not to watch Caleb doing what he did best, charming people, men and women both. Then she saw him take to the dance floor with a pretty woman, in an off-the-shoulder gold dress and white boots. They stayed out there for two dances, both slow. Harmony thought she might be

Heather; the woman Ruby had mentioned on the first day she'd arrived at the ranch.

She looked away and left the office to go to the bedroom. She was still in her work clothes, which she was going to trade in for a dress and shoes she'd asked Mandy to bring down for her. She had just finished zipping up her simple red sheath dress to go with her silver two-inch heels when a knock sounded on the bedroom door.

When she hurried over to open it, Raven was there. She walked into the room and Harmony couldn't believe her eyes. Caleb was coming toward her with Joy in his arms.

CHAPTER FOURTEEN

"Don't even ask," Caleb said as he handed Joy off to Harmony. "She saw me, and she almost dove out of Raven's arms to get to me. It was weird."

"But she didn't cry." She pointed out the obvious as Joy hugged her around the neck.

"I think she thought I was Coop. As soon as he got to the house today, he was playing with her. He actually sat on the floor with her and her blocks, building things just for her to knock them over. She loved it, and he kept doing it. She really took to him, and I'm surprised she didn't scream thinking he was me. She kept calling him Coo-Coo."

"Coo-Coo," Joy said as she held out her hands to him. "Coo-Coo," she said again, twisting in Harmony's arms to get to Caleb.

"I told you, she thinks I'm Coop." He

turned to Raven. "Do you want me to bring the bags up?"

"Yes, please," she said as she took off her jacket and boots. She waited until he left to say, "He is so nice, and so good-looking."

Harmony wouldn't argue with that, but she'd rather not discuss Caleb with the woman. "The Donovans are great, for sure."

Raven looked her over. "That dress is very nice, and it's great to see high heels instead of boots for a change."

"It's all I have," Harmony admitted.

"It's very pretty." Raven came over to take Joy out of Harmony's hold. "Let me get her ready for bed, so when she falls asleep, we don't need to undress her."

"You're wonderful, Raven. I wish you lived down around Cheyenne. Joy's so happy being with you."

"I love being with her."

Caleb came back quickly with a heavy-looking canvas bag, and the minute he stepped into the room, Joy ran right to him. "Coo-Coo," she squealed and threw her arms around his leg. Just as quickly, she let go of him and ran to the back window. She pressed both hands on the glass and started to bounce. "Yites, yites," she said over and over again.

Caleb watched the baby for a long moment. "She really thinks I'm Coop," he said wryly.

Harmony was just thankful Joy was happy and not screaming. "Seems so," she murmured and looked down at his feet. "Nice boots. Dash told me what you were all doing."

Joy turned quickly and went to Raven, who was sitting on the floor now, taking toys out of one of the bags. "Joy, look, it's Mr. Winky." That claimed the child's attention. She hurried over to Raven and took the stuffed unicorn out of her hands. A moment later, she tossed the unicorn and picked up the stuffed horse Caleb had given her. "Gee-Gee," she said as she held it up for everyone to see.

"Does she ever sit still?" Caleb asked.

"When she sleeps," Harmony said.

"Sorry. That was a genuine question. She never seems to stop."

"Don't look so scared," she said. "She won't bite. At least, she hasn't yet."

Caleb couldn't make a joke about that because Harmony didn't usually like his jokes. If he told her that the child was actually growing on him with her word repeats and her love of Christmas lights, it would sound too patronizing. So, he shrugged. "Let's hope she never does."

"Absolutely." Her features softened, and in that red dress and those heels, she looked more beautiful than any of the women downstairs in their fancy clothes. He was getting glimpses of what he would be losing when Harmony left. "Mom wants to know when you'll be down and to remind you that you're not just working tonight. She wants you to enjoy yourself."

"I will. I'll take a break when I can."

Joy got to her feet and ran at Caleb again. She wrapped her arms around his good leg, tipped her head back and said, "Coo-Coo."

With her blue eyes and blond hair, the baby was almost as pretty as her mother. The strange thing was, he kind of wanted her to know he wasn't Coop. "Caleb," he said. "I'm Caleb." She let go of his leg and looked up at him with a frown. Careful of his knee, he crouched in front of her. "I'm Caleb." He could see her confusion. "Coop's my brother."

"Coo-Coo," she said, smiling and nodding so vigorously that her wispy curls danced around her face. "Coo-Coo."

So much for that. He figured he'd be forever labeled Coo-Coo by the child. He shrugged as he stood, and Joy headed to the windows again, pressing her face to the glass and fogging it up. He glanced at Harmony. "I tried."

"She'd figure it out sooner or later if she was around you and Coop enough, but…" She shook her head. "It's not important."

It shouldn't be, but it kind of bothered him that the child was like most people when they were around him and Coop. Many of them never did see the differences between the two of them. "Yeah, it's nothing."

"I'm going down now. They'll be serving dinner in ten minutes, and I need to supervise the seating."

"If you need help, let me know," he said, then left to head downstairs before she did.

Caleb mingled with the guests, but he always had one eye open, hoping to see Harmony. When the announcement came asking people to find their assigned seats, he caught movement on the walkway. Harmony was walking across to the stairs. She came down to the main level, stopping to secure each gate behind her, then walked quickly across the dance floor and went directly to the kitchen.

Most of the guests had found their places, and the waiters started serving. Caleb sat to the right of his mother at the head table, Coop and Max were to the left of his father. His mom leaned over to him. "Where's Harmony? Didn't you tell her to come down and enjoy herself?"

"I did, Mom, but she's got so much to do. I don't know how she does it, honestly. Her daughter's a little whirlwind. She never stops."

"She reminds me of you boys when you were her age. Dawn until dark, you all never stopped."

Coop came up behind his chair and crouched to talk to Caleb. "You're going last for the toasts, since you're the youngest son, right?"

He nodded. "The youngest by minutes," he pointed out.

A voice cut him off, a voice he knew right away. Harmony stopped his conversation by getting the attention of the guests, and a hush fell over the group as she said, "Friends and family, it's time to begin the celebration dinner for Ruby and Dash. Each place has a bronze-sculpted placeholder with your name on it, and inside is a gift to each of you from the Donovans. Have a wonderful evening, and a very merry Christmas Eve."

The murmuring started as the guests reached for their placeholders, and then the sounds changed when they found the gift inside the keepsake. "Oh, dang! Really?" a man was heard to say, then another and another joined in.

Caleb watched the look on Harmony's face as she stepped back away from the party. It seemed to him that it was an expression of pure satisfaction. Then she moved out of sight and went into the kitchen. Caleb had forgotten Coop was still crouching behind him until his twin tapped his shoulder.

"Mom said that you and Harmony were getting along pretty well."

"We've been working together to plan this party, if that's what you mean."

"You know it's not. I spent time with her and her daughter today playing blocks and being hit by a stuffed horse toy Joy kept throwing at me. I have to say, Harmony's pretty nice. So, are you interested?"

He hated the way Coop could zero in on something and make a comment that sounded casual, not part of an interrogation, which it actually was. Coop wouldn't give up until he knew what he wanted to find out, so he gave him a quick answer. "I was but it didn't work out. Things just didn't fit right."

"It's the kid, isn't it?" Coop hit a bull's-eye again.

He couldn't say that. "We just don't fit."

"It isn't because of that pretty little girl?"

"No, I like Joy."

That stopped him dead. He did think she was pretty cute. The way she doubled her words amused him. When she'd cried after he saved her from doing a face plant on the floor, he'd actually been hurt that the little girl could be so upset with him. Then she'd smiled at him and clung to his leg when she'd thought he was Coop. How could he not like this little human who made Harmony so happy? But that wasn't enough for him to change his life plans, the ones he'd worked on for so long.

"Caleb, she's a cute kid, so what's not to like as long as they're someone else's kid?" he added.

"Same old, same old, huh?"

"I am what I am." He couldn't change the way things were, but then again, things changed on their own. That was one thing he'd learned after his accident. It wasn't what he'd planned, but it had turned out okay. He didn't regret leaving the rodeo. Maybe that was how Dad looked at his changes in life.

"We both are," Coop said wryly. "For better or worse." He straightened up and went back to his seat.

Caleb looked around at the guests while his plate of food went untouched. *I am what I am.* Someway that sounded horrible to him. His aunt Reese, Uncle Abel's wife, a heavyset woman who sat next to him, leaned in toward him.

"What a great idea giving those passes. We never would have been able to do that on our own. Now Abel and me are going to spend a full week together down there in July." She actually winked at him. "Like a second honeymoon. I know you're the one who thought of that. Thank you."

"You're welcome, but the event planner came up with that idea."

"Harmony? I've heard all about her. Thank her when you see her, okay?"

"Sure, I will."

His father's brother, Warren, who'd flown in from Utah, stood and tapped his fork against his wineglass. He wasn't as tall as his dad, or as lean, but he wore a tux well. "It's time to toast this wonderful couple." He turned to his brother and sister-in-law. "I always admired Dash for his fearlessness and his determination. But what I truly admired him for was him having the good sense to marry Ruby." People chuckled at that. Dash nodded and put his arm around his wife. "Here's to your smarts, Dash, Ruby's patience, and to another forty years."

Caleb joined in the toast, then Max stood, followed by Coop. Both said the perfect things, making their mother cry and their father beam. Then it was his turn. He stood with no idea of what to say, and then it came to him.

"Mom and Dad, I love you both, and I thank you for everything you've done for me over the years. You've set the goal post so high for marriage, it seems impossible to match it. I just hope that I can find a fraction of what you two found." He lifted his glass to his mom and dad. "Thank you for giving me life and for being there for me every step of the way."

The guests applauded, and as he looked out over them, he saw Harmony back by the kitchen entrance doors, clapping. They made eye contact for a brief second before she turned to her left, and Dub was there, taking off his flat-brimmed Stetson he wore with his denim jeans, a black T-shirt and silver boots. He got closer to her to say something. After a brief moment of conversation, Dub headed back to the stage and Harmony disappeared into the kitchen again.

Caleb spent the next hour going from table to table and speaking with the guests, all of whom raved about their rodeo passes and his parents. He smiled a lot and talked to old friends, and by the time he took his seat at the head table again, he really understood what Harmony had done for his family. She gave them a celebration that defined what he'd struggled to tell her back in the office: what he'd envisioned was exactly what she'd given them. It was a night to remember.

The servers were quietly clearing the dinner plates as the music ended and Dub spoke into his mic. "Family and friends, it's time for Ruby and Dash to dance to a song Ruby chose for the love of her life.

Let them start it off, then y'all are invited to join in." Dub grinned and made a motion toward the head table. "You two kids, get on over here."

Amid chuckles and murmuring from the guests, Ruby and Dash made their way to the dance floor. As the first chords of the song "When I Said I Do" started, they went into each other's arms and moved together perfectly. After they had made one trip around the dance floor, Dub said, "Come on, y'all!" and some of the guests headed over. "Join in."

Caleb stood, automatically scanning the room for Harmony, then she appeared coming down the stairs. He skirted the dance floor and stopped by one of the Christmas trees, the one decorated with glass ornaments that had family pictures inserted in them. All he could see was Harmony coming toward him. Her blue eyes widened when she saw him, and he had the crazy idea she was going to smile. That didn't happen, but she did stop in front of him.

"I've been looking for you," he said. Right then, he knew that whatever it took, he wanted to stay in touch with her. "I have something I want to give you, and I'd like it if we could talk tonight when this is over." He didn't actually have anything, but he'd figure something out before they talked. "Maybe meet on the top step?"

"Because the party's over doesn't mean I don't have work to do after the last guest leaves, you know."

"I'll help you with it, then we can talk."

"No, I don't think we need to," Harmony said, her voice oddly lacking emotion.

He'd played everything the wrong way since first meeting her, and he had a sinking feeling that there was no reason to try to pursue things any further. So, he knew what to give her: cold, impersonal money. A bonus for what she'd done for him and the family. "Okay, I'll have it delivered to your office after New Year's."

"No, please, you don't have to do that."

"It's a bonus for the fantastic job you've done." He'd send it to her and try to forget everything. "This is more than I ever hoped for."

"You gave me Pal as a bonus," she said.

"That was just part of it."

Her phone rang. She had her phone in her hand and lifted it to check the caller ID, then took the call. "Yes?" She listened, then turned and glanced up at the walkway. Raven was there, motioning frantically for her to come back up. She broke the connection, then turned without a word and half ran to the stairs, going up to the walkway and disappearing into the bedroom with Raven. He knew that something was wrong, and he went after Harmony, annoyed that it took him so long to get up the blasted stairs and to the bedroom door because of his leg. After knocking once, he opened it himself and stepped inside.

He was met with the baby crying, Harmony holding her, trying to comfort her, and Raven hovering over the two of them. The cries were half sobs, half gasps. Joy's face was flushed and her tiny hands flailing.

"Raven, she's burning up. We have to get her to a hospital or call an ambulance," Harmony said over the crying. "Please call someone."

That look of helplessness on Harmony's face cut into Caleb, and he couldn't bear to see her like that. "Raven, Boone's here. I'll get him."

He hurried out and stopped on the walkway to look down at the party. He found the man he wanted, took out his cell phone and called the doctor. He watched as Boone answered on the second ring. "Dr. Williams. What is—?"

Caleb cut him off. "Boone, it's me, Caleb. I'm upstairs, and I need you to get up here right now."

"I'm on my way." He was already on his feet when he spotted Caleb on the walkway. He held up one finger, then pointed to the back doors before disappearing out of sight.

Caleb went back inside. The crying kept up while Harmony tried to comfort her daughter. "A doctor's on his way," he said.

Harmony shook her head. "No, we can't wait—she's so sick. Just call an ambulance, please."

Thankfully, Boone came in and passed

Caleb and Raven to get to Harmony. "Your daughter?"

"Yes. Her name's Joy."

"Put her on the bed and undress her."

"Can't I hold her?"

Boone reached out his hands. "Not right now. Let me have her." He wasn't being mean at all, just focused on the child.

"Okay," she said.

The doctor took Joy and laid her on the bed as her screams increased. "Can you undress her for me please?" he said to Harmony as he opened his bag.

Harmony's hands were shaking as she tried to unsnap the fasteners on the baby's sleeper, and Caleb almost reached in to help her, but Raven was faster. She swiftly undid the baby's one piece and eased it off of her.

"Okay, give me room," Boone said.

When Raven moved back, Harmony didn't, and Caleb reached for her arm. "Come on, let the doctor take care of her. He's the best around. Give him space."

She didn't jerk away from him, but it took a moment for her to finally take a step back toward him. He felt her shaking and hated to let go, but he made himself.

"Tell me all about her," Boone said as he bent over the crying child.

"She's going to be two in April, and she's not a crier at all. She's so small. She got really hot all of a sudden."

"Does she have any allergies or chronic medical conditions?" he asked as he moved his hands over her stomach, then took a thermometer out his bag.

"Not that I know of," Harmony said while she clasped and unclasped her hands over and over again.

Caleb could tell how nervous she was as the doctor hovered the no-contact thermometer over Joy's forehead. He then exchanged that for a stethoscope and kept examining her as he spoke. Suddenly the baby stopped crying, went stiff and started to shake. "Get some towels or rags and something to hold cold water! Now!" Boone ordered.

Raven ran into the bathroom, and Caleb instinctively grabbed Harmony's arm to keep her from reaching for her daughter. "Let him help her," he said, and she didn't fight him. He kept her back as Boone managed to manipulate a wide tongue depressor into Joy's mouth to give her something to bite down on without hurting herself.

Raven was back with a plastic waste basket and set it down by Boone's feet. She had half filled it with water, and towels were soaking in it. She quickly reached in, took out a face cloth and wrung it out before handing it to Boone, who laid it on the baby's forehead. She took over quickly, putting more wet face cloths on Joy while Boone took out a vial of clear liquid and loaded a small syringe.

As he turned to the baby, Raven stepped back and the child went limp. Harmony gasped, and Caleb felt her shift and turned to press her head into his chest. He held her tightly as she sobbed, "No, no, please, no."

The doctor spoke quickly. "It's okay. The seizure's over and she'll sleep. It wears kids out, and that's normal. I'm going to give her an antibiotic in case there's an infection of some sort, but I'm pretty certain she's experienced fever convulsions. We'll keep her cool with towels for another round, then get her comfortable and let her sleep."

Caleb had felt the fear in Harmony, and he'd felt it, too. The baby looked so helpless and pale just lying there not moving, her chest barely rising and falling as she breathed. He would have done anything to help Joy, no matter what it took, and anything for her mother.

Boone gave the baby the shot without her even flinching, then Raven took care of the towels as he turned back to Harmony. Caleb was taken aback to see Boone was smiling. "She's going to be fine. Babies can have this happen for no reason we can find, and it's scary for parents, but I promise you, it's pretty common. We just need to get the fever down. I'll take care of that for you. She'll be okay when she wakes up."

"Can…can I hold her?" she asked.

"Not just yet. Let Raven finish with the towels and I need to check on her. But as soon as the fever breaks, you can hold her all you want to."

Caleb felt Harmony put her arm around his waist while he still held her against his side. "What do we need to do now, Boone?" he asked.

"Be thankful this *will* pass, and Joy will be fine."

Boone was checking on Joy while Harmony watched silently. "I'll be at Flaming Sky tomorrow in the afternoon for Ruby's Christmas Day Ride. One way or the other, I'll be there to check on Joy."

"Thank you," Harmony whispered.

Boone turned back to Joy, held the thermometer over her forehead, then turned, smiling again. "The fever's starting to come down. Raven can take off the towels."

"Can I hold her?"

"Let her sleep. But you can be with her, for sure."

Harmony leaned more heavily against Caleb, and he figured it was from relief.

Then she let go of him to move to the bed, sitting down to reach for the baby's hand. "Mama loves you," she whispered. "I love you so much. You'll be okay, I promise you." Joy's eyes fluttered, then looked up at her mother. "Oh, sweetheart," Harmony said in a shaky voice and her shoulders trembled. "I love you so, so much."

Boone leaned around Harmony to take the baby's temperature again. "Down two degrees," he said. Joy closed her eyes on a sigh and went back to sleep. "That's very, very good." He paused, then handed Caleb the thermometer. "If her fever isn't any lower in an hour, call me. I'll be downstairs."

"I certainly will. I don't know how to thank you for your help."

"The only thanks I need is seeing her get better and that's what she's going to do."

Boone left, and Caleb stood by Harmony. He couldn't make himself leave her. Finally, she spoke to him without looking away from her daughter. "You need to be downstairs with your family. Please, go."

He couldn't make himself leave Harmony and Joy up here while he ate cake, or whatever they'd be doing downstairs. "I will, but in a few minutes."

"Raven, why don't you go down and try to enjoy yourself for a while. I'll be right here."

Raven hesitated. "Okay, but you call if you need me."

"I sure will. We'll be fine."

After Raven took care of the wastebasket and the towels, she left and Caleb stayed where he was. Harmony looked up at him. "Could you turn that settee around to face the bed so I can sit there and watch Joy?"

"Sure," he said.

As soon as he repositioned the settee, Harmony went over to sit down. She pressed the side button that released a footrest and put her feet up on it. Caleb took the baby's temperature, then went over to Harmony. "It's down another degree."

"You're a good man, Caleb."

"I don't know about that, but I'm glad I found you to do the party, and I'm glad I got to know you some." He glanced back at her daughter on the bed. "I'm glad I met Joy, too."

"I'm glad you've started to call her by her name."

He sat down by her, released the other footrest and put his feet up. "I'm sorry for that. I didn't realize it before you mentioned it."

"Don't worry. She didn't get your name right. But what could she call you with that double-word habit she has?"

"I have no idea," he said, glancing at the baby on the bed. He had to admit that tiny human being had more power than he'd ever have. She'd managed to get to be with Harmony for the rest of her life, and all he could manage was to be with her for a handful of days on the ranch.

Questions were running through his mind, like what kind of father would he make working so much? What kind of life would a child have with him if he was gone a lot, and wasn't there for them? He'd never be able to match what his father had done for him and his brothers. Dash had been a constant presence in their lives, taking them with him when he was working. He trained them in every aspect of the ranch, supported their rodeo dreams and just plain loved on them. He almost laughed to himself when he thought about what kind of training he could provide for a child:

teaching them about pleasing all manner of people, about food, drinks and all things Western and rodeo related. But he'd never know the answers to those foolish questions because he'd never be a father.

When he glanced at Harmony, her eyes were closed and her breathing steady. She was worn out from all she'd done for him and his family, and what she was now going through with her daughter. He watched her, taking in everything about her, writing a memory to keep with him. She'd soon be back in her own world with Joy, and he'd be here alone. He reached to gently brush an errant strand of hair off her face and felt the silkiness of her skin under his fingertips.

She stirred and he drew back as her blue eyes opened to meet his. An uncertain smile touched her lips and he leaned toward her to kiss her. Another notch in the memory of this night, and he coveted it. It could have lasted forever or maybe the blink of an eye, before Harmony eased back. Her eyes were full of questions he had no answers to. He heard himself whisper, "I apologize," knowing he was lying and didn't mean that at all.

There was a rap on the door and Boone stepped inside. Harmony sat up and, snapping down the footrest, she stood and hurried over to where Boone was touching the baby's forehead. He held out his hand to Caleb, who got up and took the thermometer over to him. Boone took Joy's temperature and then said to Harmony, "It's almost normal. She's over it."

"I don't know how to thank you for what you did," Caleb said again and held out his hand. They shook, and then gave each other a partial man hug as Caleb realized how relieved and grateful he was to the doctor. Joy was Harmony's life.

"I like to win, and this was a win, so thanks for inviting me to the party so I could be here when I was needed. Are you coming downstairs anytime soon?" Boone asked.

He didn't want to go downstairs. He didn't want to leave Harmony. He didn't want to leave Joy. "I'm staying up here for a while."

"They're holding the cake cutting until you can join them."

"Tell them I'll be down later and to save me a slice. Kyle will take a great picture of the cake cutting, and you send me your bill for everything."

"No bill. It's Christmas Eve and I wish you all a merry Christmas. See you tomorrow," he said, and then headed out the door.

When they were alone, Caleb turned to Harmony. "I lied to you earlier."

"What are you taking about?"

"I apologized for kissing you, but I didn't mean it. I wanted to kiss you. I want to kiss you again."

Her blue eyes widened as he bent his head to touch her lips with his, and she didn't pull back. Her hands were on his shoulders, and then her arms were around his neck. She was leaning into him, and it felt as if she was holding on to him for dear life, the way he was holding on to her. He never wanted to let her go. But he had to when she slowly drew back and looked up at him.

"Don't, please don't," she said unsteadily.

"You should be down with your parents and brothers. This your parents' big night, and family is the most important thing in this world."

She'd said those words before, but this time Caleb had an epiphany that came out of nowhere, surprising him, yet making so much sense he wanted to share it with only one person. "You're right. Family is the most important thing in life. I can't imagine what I'd do without mine, and I can't imagine not wanting that myself, to build a family with someone I love. Friends are great, but a family is forever."

"That sounds like cowboy rules—family first, horses second."

He didn't laugh. He wasn't kidding. Now that he knew what he'd wanted all along, he wasn't going to joke about it. "I can't even believe that I'm saying this, but when I see myself having a family, I see it including you and Joy."

"No," she said abruptly. "Don't do that. It's not funny."

"It's not supposed to be. I'm serious. Harmony, I know I've taken every wrong direction and I stumbled into this moment by pure dumb luck. I almost went right past it, but I won't. I'm stopping right here with you. This is it for me." He exhaled roughly. "I'm trying to say that I love you. I think I've loved you since I first heard your voice on the phone."

"Caleb, no, you can't. You don't want a ready-made family in your life, especially not yet. Were you drinking too much tonight?"

"No, and don't say that. I've never felt this way before, and believe me, I've never said I love you to anyone and meant it as much as I do now with you."

Her shoulders dipped on a heavy sigh. "I love you, too. I honestly do, but it can't work." Joy stirred and her eyes opened for a moment, then she smiled over at them before she closed them again and settled back to sleep. "We're a package deal." Her voice was trembling. "You don't want the whole package. You don't love Joy, and that's a prerequisite. You can't make yourself love someone."

"It's been such a short time that I've

known you and an even shorter time since I met Joy, yet I love you. It's that simple. I knew I could love Joy tonight, when I saw her crying and scared. I would have done anything to help her and to help you. The fact is I think I love her almost as much as I love you."

She shook her head. "I have to say something, and you have to listen until I finish. Promise?" She clasped her hands tightly in front of her. "You know when you said you thought you'd met me before?"

"I remember."

"You did meet me before, about seventeen years ago."

He touched her lips with his forefinger to stop her from talking. "Don't."

"I… I have to. You need to know—"

"That you're Les Randall's daughter."

She gasped softly. "You knew? All this time, you knew?"

"No, I knew when you were telling me about the horse you used to ride, how much Pal is like him, that you told him your secrets. Then you called Pal, Duke, when we were together in the stable. And when you told me about your dad yesterday and how he treated you, I remembered a girl with freckles like yours, a quiet girl who looked as if she was trying to be invisible. Harriet Randall. That's when it all came into focus for me."

"If you know all that, why are you telling me that you love me, and you love Joy?"

"Because I do…totally, hopelessly, deeply, I do. Who you were doesn't matter one iota to me. In fact, knowing you were Les's daughter and how he treated you makes me want to love you even more, to blot out all of that. You deserve so much more, and so does Joy."

She studied him intently, then she touched his cheek with unsteady fingers as she brushed the tips of them across his beard shadow. "I believe you're a good man and you wouldn't lie to me. Or if you did, you'd confess to it, wouldn't you?"

He nodded. "You know me so well in a short time. I can only imagine how well you'll know me after years and years together, when our children give us a fortieth-anniversary party right here at Pure Rodeo.

Maybe a big barbeque where they invite the whole town."

A teasing smile touched her lips. "How many?"

"How many what?" he asked, dying to kiss her again, but waiting for her answer.

"If we're talking about getting married, which I assume we are, how many children would be planning that party?"

He chuckled at that. "Now, that's a trick question. I won't know the answer to that unless we can work on it together to find a solution we both agree on."

Harmony circled his waist with her arms as she said, "I'll agree to any number under six right here and now," she said, then reached up to kiss him before he could negotiate a much lower number.

He felt her warmth and softness against him, and he wrapped his arms around her. The kiss was magic, and by the time he moved back enough to look into her face, he knew that he'd made the right decision. "It's a solid no to six children, but I am open to bribery."

She laughed at the same time he heard

"Mama, Mama." They both turned to see that Joy had pushed herself up to a seated position on the bed. She smiled at them, and then held out her arms to Caleb.

"Coo-Coo."

He reached for her to hold her with one arm and circled Harmony's shoulders with the other. "I'm Caleb," he said.

She looked at him quizzically. "Coo-Coo."

Harmony offered a suggestion as she held Caleb's eyes with hers. "I think we may be able to make this whole marriage thing work, so how about Daddy? But only if you're okay with that."

"I'm very okay with that." Caleb knew he wanted this forever. "My name's Daddy," he said to the child.

Joy touched Caleb's nose, then regarded him intently. He almost held his breath until she said, "Da-Da."

He laughed and Joy clapped her hands. "I like that name," he said, then looked at Harmony. "What do you think?"

"I think that's perfect." She reached to kiss Caleb quickly then whispered, "Perfectly perfect."

EPILOGUE

For the last two months, life had just been getting better and better for Harmony. Joy flourished with her new family, and Caleb only became dearer and dearer to her. When he came up to his private quarters above Pure Rodeo, she was lying on the bed with Joy. It was almost midnight, and she knew it was time for her and Joy to go back to the main ranch house. That was where they had been staying while she made plans to expand her business. She would open and run an office in Cody while Mandy took over in Cheyenne.

"Hey, beautiful," Caleb said in a half whisper as he came to the bed. Harmony moved cautiously to the edge of the mattress hoping to not wake the baby. When she was close enough, Caleb swept her up into his arms. She loved him so much it almost hurt at times, but she'd worried about him making such a huge decision so quickly. Gradually, she'd come to see his commitment to her and Joy, and it only got stronger the more time that went by.

"Can we stay for a bit and just sit and…?"

He kissed her, then carried her over to the settee by the back windows. "Yes, we can. I need to talk to you about something really important."

That took her aback. She realized he wasn't smiling and his dark eyes were solemn. "I don't understand. What's wrong?"

"I wanted to tell you sooner, but I couldn't. Everything's been so great—perfect, actually—and I didn't want to hurt you."

She felt her heart sink, and she pushed away from him, scrambling back off his lap and onto the cushions. "No, you can't…" She bit her lip. "If you're over all of this, just say it. You want out."

She saw the shock in his expression, and he reached for her, taking her hands in his. "No, oh, no, Harmony. No. This thing we have together is forever. It's not a fly-by-night thing. I love you more than I did before…totally, completely. You and Joy are my life now."

"Oh, I'm so sorry, Caleb." She reached out and almost collapsed against him. He wrapped her in his arms. "Then what is it?" she asked in an unsteady voice.

"I'm sorry about this, but I talked to Max a week or so ago, and he told me something I know I need to tell you, but I've been afraid that it's going to upset you."

Harmony sat back but held tightly to his hands. She could see the concern in his eyes. "What did he tell you?"

"I asked him to check on Lester Randall." Her hold on him tightened even more. "He found out he was living in Oregon for years and worked on a ranch near the Washington border. Then he was arrested for swindling the owner out of a great deal of money in a horse scam. Apparently, he has quite a rap sheet of conning people, along with plenty of DUIs."

She could finally breathe right. "That's what you were worried about telling me?"

"I didn't want to upset you. I mean, he's your dad…"

She looked him right in his eyes. "Caleb, he's not my dad. Biologically, yes, but in no other way. Dash has been more like a dad to me than Les ever was. I was an annoyance to Les, or a prop so people would think he was a good guy. He wasn't. The day the sheriff took me away from the ranch, I was terrified... I didn't know what was going to happen to me. Then they found Letty, and everything changed for the better. The best day in my life back then was knowing Letty wanted me.

"Then I found Joy and had another best day in my life. Then you called me at the office, another best day. Every day with you and Joy is the best day. Les never once made a day the best day for me. Not once. I am so sorry that I thought... I'm just sorry. I love you so much."

She was back in Caleb's arms again, right where she belonged, and she just took in his presence in her world. He kissed the top of her head and whispered, "You and Joy are my family, my life, and that's never going to change."

She looked up at him, and the smile on his face made her heart swell. She forgot all about Les. "Oh, guess what? Uncle Abel talked to someone near Wind River who knew about the storyboard. The last person in the family's lineage did die, and the story was sealed. But Uncle Abel carved his own symbol into it. He said it was a wish for you from him. It looks like overlapping hearts, with swirling lines around them. It's right in the middle at the top of the headboard."

"What does it mean?"

"It means that love makes two hearts beat as one. But Uncle Abel said that he's going to alter it for us if we ever get married. He wants to put a small heart where the two of them meet to represent Joy and future children as the years go on. He just wondered how many you think he'll have to add."

He grinned at her. "We never did settle that, did we?"

"No, you said we'd do it when we got married or something like that."

"I think I did. I do have something to make you happy, I hope."

"What's that?"

He moved and reached in his jeans pocket, then showed her his closed hand. "I made a wish today under the tree and I hope it comes true."

"What was it?"

"I'm not happy with this arrangement. You and Joy at the main house, me up here all alone. I want to fix it."

"How?" she whispered.

He opened his hand and a gold ring lay in his palm. It had a beautiful heart shaped diamond. His smile made her heart skip. "Please, will you please marry me? I know I want you to be my wife, but are you ready to set a date and make this forever?"

She looked at him. "Yes, yes!" she said.

He slid the ring onto her finger, then kissed her quickly. "Now, we can talk numbers. But I can tell you again that anything six or over is still out."

"Okay," she said and moved closer to him. "That's a good starting point."

"Yes, it is," he murmured before he kissed her again. When he drew back, he said, "Let's not worry about that now. We have a while to figure it out. Just tell me when we can get married."

"When it's warmer, maybe around June or July." She looked out the window at the snowy night. Since New Year's Day, snow had broken the drought and then some.

"When the snow melts because I want to have our wedding under the wishing tree."

"Perfect," he said. "Perfect."

"Mama, Da-Da?" they both heard at the same time and turned to look back at the bed. Joy was awake and sitting there rubbing sleep from her eyes. Then she was up on her feet and thankfully Caleb intercepted her before she got close to the edge of the bed.

He put out his hands to swoop her up, and she flew into them. "Dang, you're getting to be a pro at keeping her safe," Harmony said.

When he lifted her with his hands under her arms, the baby laughed as if it was the funniest thing ever. Then Harmony was there, laughing too. "No crying anymore," Caleb said.

"I told you she just had to get to know you, and to know you is to love you. That's the way it was with me—first when I was twelve, then I fell in love again the moment I came here and saw you standing in the doorway of the office."

"Really?"

"Yes, really and forever," she said as she

wrapped her arms around her whole world;
Caleb and Joy, everything she'd ever wished
for under the wishing tree.

* * * * *

*Don't miss the next book
in Mary Anne Wilson's
Flaming Sky Ranch miniseries,
coming July 2023 from
Harlequin Heartwarming.*

Get 4 FREE REWARDS!

We'll send you 2 FREE Books plus 2 FREE Mystery Gifts.

FREE
Value Over
$20

Both the **Love Inspired®** and **Love Inspired® Suspense** series feature compelling novels filled with inspirational romance, faith, forgiveness and hope.

YES! Please send me 2 FREE novels from the Love Inspired or Love Inspired Suspense series and my 2 FREE gifts (gifts are worth about $10 retail). After receiving them, if I don't wish to receive any more books, I can return the shipping statement marked "cancel." If I don't cancel, I will receive 6 brand-new Love Inspired Larger-Print books or Love Inspired Suspense Larger-Print books every month and be billed just $6.49 each in the U.S. or $6.74 each in Canada. That is a savings of at least 16% off the cover price. It's quite a bargain! Shipping and handling is just 50¢ per book in the U.S. and $1.25 per book in Canada.* I understand that accepting the 2 free books and gifts places me under no obligation to buy anything. I can always return a shipment and cancel at any time by calling the number below. The free books and gifts are mine to keep no matter what I decide.

Choose one: ☐ **Love Inspired**
Larger-Print
(122/322 IDN GRHK)

☐ **Love Inspired Suspense**
Larger-Print
(107/307 IDN GRHK)

Name (please print)

Address   Apt. #

City   State/Province   Zip/Postal Code

Email: Please check this box ☐ if you would like to receive newsletters and promotional emails from Harlequin Enterprises ULC and its affiliates. You can unsubscribe anytime.

Mail to the **Harlequin Reader Service:**
IN U.S.A.: P.O. Box 1341, Buffalo, NY 14240-8531
IN CANADA: P.O. Box 603, Fort Erie, Ontario L2A 5X3

Want to try 2 free books from another series! Call 1-800-873-8635 or visit www.ReaderService.com.

*Terms and prices subject to change without notice. Prices do not include sales taxes, which will be charged (if applicable) based on your state or country of residence. Canadian residents will be charged applicable taxes. Offer not valid in Quebec. This offer is limited to one order per household. Books received may not be as shown. Not valid for current subscribers to the Love Inspired or Love Inspired Suspense series. All orders subject to approval. Credit or debit balances in a customer's account(s) may be offset by any other outstanding balance owed by or to the customer. Please allow 4 to 6 weeks for delivery. Offer available while quantities last.

Your Privacy—Your information is being collected by Harlequin Enterprises ULC, operating as Harlequin Reader Service. For a complete summary of the information we collect, how we use this information and to whom it is disclosed, please visit our privacy notice located at corporate.harlequin.com/privacy-notice. From time to time we may also exchange your personal information with reputable third parties. If you wish to opt out of this sharing of your personal information, please visit readerservice.com/consumerschoice or call 1-800-873-8635. **Notice to California Residents**—Under California law, you have specific rights to control and access your data. For more information on these rights and how to exercise them, visit corporate.harlequin.com/california-privacy.

LIRLIS22R3

Get 4 FREE REWARDS!

We'll send you 2 FREE Books plus 2 FREE Mystery Gifts.

FREE Value Over **$20**

Both the **Harlequin® Special Edition** and **Harlequin® Heartwarming™** series feature compelling novels filled with stories of love and strength where the bonds of friendship, family and community unite.

YES! Please send me 2 FREE novels from the Harlequin Special Edition or Harlequin Heartwarming series and my 2 FREE gifts (gifts are worth about $10 retail). After receiving them, if I don't wish to receive any more books, I can return the shipping statement marked "cancel." If I don't cancel, I will receive 6 brand-new Harlequin Special Edition books every month and be billed just $5.49 each in the U.S. or $6.24 each in Canada, a savings of at least 12% off the cover price, or 4 brand-new Harlequin Heartwarming Larger-Print books every month and be billed just $6.24 each in the U.S. or $6.74 each in Canada, a savings of at least 19% off the cover price. It's quite a bargain! Shipping and handling is just 50¢ per book in the U.S. and $1.25 per book in Canada.* I understand that accepting the 2 free books and gifts places me under no obligation to buy anything. I can always return a shipment and cancel at any time by calling the number below. The free books and gifts are mine to keep no matter what I decide.

Choose one: ☐ **Harlequin Special Edition**   ☐ **Harlequin Heartwarming**
(235/335 HDN GRJV)   **Larger-Print**
(161/361 HDN GRJV)

Name (please print)

Address   Apt. #

City   State/Province   Zip/Postal Code

Email: Please check this box ☐ if you would like to receive newsletters and promotional emails from Harlequin Enterprises ULC and its affiliates. You can unsubscribe anytime.

Mail to the **Harlequin Reader Service:**
IN U.S.A.: P.O. Box 1341, Buffalo, NY 14240-8531
IN CANADA: P.O. Box 603, Fort Erie, Ontario L2A 5X3

Want to try 2 free books from another series? Call **1-800-873-8635** or visit www.ReaderService.com.

*Terms and prices subject to change without notice. Prices do not include sales taxes, which will be charged (if applicable) based on your state or country of residence. Canadian residents will be charged applicable taxes. Offer not valid in Quebec. This offer is limited to one order per household. Books received may not be as shown. Not valid for current subscribers to the Harlequin Special Edition or Harlequin Heartwarming series. All orders subject to approval. Credit or debit balances in a customer's account(s) may be offset by any other outstanding balance owed by or to the customer. Please allow 4 to 6 weeks for delivery. Offer available while quantities last.

Your Privacy—Your information is being collected by Harlequin Enterprises ULC, operating as Harlequin Reader Service. For a complete summary of the information we collect, how we use this information and to whom it is disclosed, please visit our privacy notice located at corporate.harlequin.com/privacy-notice. From time to time we may also exchange your personal information with reputable third parties. If you wish to opt out of this sharing of your personal information, please visit readerservice.com/consumerschoice or call 1-800-873-8635. **Notice to California Residents**—Under California law, you have specific rights to control and access your data. For more information on these rights and how to exercise them, visit corporate.harlequin.com/california-privacy.

HSEHW22R3

THE 2022 LOVE INSPIRED CHRISTMAS COLLECTION

Buy 3 and get 1 FREE!

May all that is beautiful, meaningful and brings you joy be yours this holiday season...including this fun-filled collection featuring 24 Christmas stories. From tender holiday romances to Christmas Eve suspense, this collection has it all.

YES! Please send me the **2022 LOVE INSPIRED CHRISTMAS COLLECTION** in Larger Print! This collection begins with ONE FREE book and 2 FREE gifts in the first shipment. Along with my FREE book, I'll get another 3 Larger Print books! If I do not cancel, I will continue to receive four books a month for five more months. Each shipment will contain another FREE gift. I'll pay just $23.97 U.S./$26.97 CAN., plus $1.99 U.S./$4.99 CAN. for shipping and handling per shipment.* I understand that accepting the free books and gifts places me under no obligation to buy anything. I can always return a shipment and cancel at any time. My free books and gifts are mine to keep no matter what I decide.

☐ 298 HCK 0958   ☐ 498 HCK 0958

Name (please print)

Address   Apt. #

City   State/Province   Zip/Postal Code

Mail to the Harlequin Reader Service:
IN U.S.A.: P.O. Box 1341, Buffalo, NY 14240-8531
IN CANADA: P.O. Box 603, Fort Erie, ON L2A 5X3

---

*Terms and prices subject to change without notice. Prices do not include sales taxes, which will be charged (if applicable) based on your state or country of residence. Canadian residents will be charged applicable taxes. Offer not valid in Quebec. All orders subject to approval. Credit or debit balances in a customer's account(s) may be offset by any other outstanding balance owed by or to the customer. Please allow 3 to 4 weeks for delivery. Offer available while quantities last. © 2022 Harlequin Enterprises ULC. ® and ™ are trademarks owned by Harlequin Enterprises ULC.

Your Privacy—Your information is being collected by Harlequin Enterprises ULC, operating as Harlequin Reader Service. To see how we collect and use this information visit https://corporate.harlequin.com/privacy-notice. From time to time we may also exchange your personal information with reputable third parties. If you wish to opt out of this sharing of your personal information, please visit www.readerservice.com/consumerchoice or call 1-800-873-8635. Notice to California Residents—Under California law, you have specific rights to control and access your data. For more information visit https://corporate.harlequin.com/california-privacy.

XMASL2022

Get 4 FREE REWARDS!

We'll send you 2 FREE Books plus 2 FREE Mystery Gifts.

FREE
Value Over
$20

Both the **Romance** and **Suspense** collections feature compelling novels written by many of today's bestselling authors.

YES! Please send me 2 FREE novels from the Essential Romance or Essential Suspense Collection and my 2 FREE gifts (gifts are worth about $10 retail). After receiving them, if I don't wish to receive any more books, I can return the shipping statement marked "cancel." If I don't cancel, I will receive 4 brand-new novels every month and be billed just $7.49 each in the U.S. or $7.74 each in Canada. That's a savings of at least 17% off the cover price. It's quite a bargain! Shipping and handling is just 50¢ per book in the U.S. and $1.25 per book in Canada.* I understand that accepting the 2 free books and gifts places me under no obligation to buy anything. I can always return a shipment and cancel at any time by calling the number below. The free books and gifts are mine to keep no matter what I decide.

Choose one: ☐ **Essential Romance**
(194/394 MDN GRHV)

☐ **Essential Suspense**
(191/391 MDN GRHV)

Name (please print)

Address   Apt. #

City   State/Province   Zip/Postal Code

Email: Please check this box ☐ if you would like to receive newsletters and promotional emails from Harlequin Enterprises ULC and its affiliates. You can unsubscribe anytime.

Mail to the Harlequin Reader Service:
IN U.S.A.: P.O. Box 1341, Buffalo, NY 14240-8531
IN CANADA: P.O. Box 603, Fort Erie, Ontario L2A 5X3

Want to try 2 free books from another series! Call **1-800-873-8635** or visit www.ReaderService.com.

---

*Terms and prices subject to change without notice. Prices do not include sales taxes, which will be charged (if applicable) based on your state or country of residence. Canadian residents will be charged applicable taxes. Offer not valid in Quebec. This offer is limited to one order per household. Books received may not be as shown. Not valid for current subscribers to the Essential Romance or Essential Suspense Collection. All orders subject to approval. Credit or debit balances in a customer's account(s) may be offset by any other outstanding balance owed by or to the customer. Please allow 4 to 6 weeks for delivery. Offer available while quantities last.

Your Privacy—Your information is being collected by Harlequin Enterprises ULC, operating as Harlequin Reader Service. For a complete summary of the information we collect, how we use this information and to whom it is disclosed, please visit our privacy notice located at corporate.harlequin.com/privacy-notice. From time to time we may also exchange your personal information with reputable third parties. If you wish to opt out of this sharing of your personal information, please visit readerservice.com/consumerschoice or call 1-800-873-8635. **Notice to California Residents**—Under California law, you have specific rights to control and access your data. For more information on these rights and how to exercise them, visit corporate.harlequin.com/california-privacy.

STRS22R3

#451 THE COWBOY'S RANCH RESCUE
Bachelor Cowboys • by Lisa Childs

Firefighter paramedic Baker Haven will do right by his orphaned nephews—even keep his distance. He couldn't save his brother, and he can't give his heart to the ranch's beautiful cook, Taye Cooper, either...despite the hope she brings to their home.

#452 HIS PARTNERSHIP PROPOSAL
Polk Island • by Jacquelin Thomas

Aubrie DuGrandpre and Terian LaCroix were rivals in cooking school—and now they're vying for the same restaurant property! When Terian approaches her about a partnership, she agrees. Can a past grudge lead to a lifetime commitment?

#453 A RANCHER WORTH REMEMBERING
Love, Oregon • by Anna Grace

Matchmaker Clara Wallace avoids skeptics—and Jet Broughman, her new client's best friend, is the ultimate nonbeliever. He's also her teenage crush! Now Clara must help Jet's friend find love *without* falling for the gorgeous, stubborn rancher she's never forgotten.

#454 THE OFFICER'S DILEMMA
by Janice Carter

Zanna Winters and Navy Lt. Dominic Kennedy wanted to escape the small town of Lighthouse Cove. But Zanna's surprise announcement might tie them there...and to each other. Can two people who dream of adventure find one with family?

YOU CAN FIND MORE INFORMATION ON UPCOMING HARLEQUIN TITLES, FREE EXCERPTS AND MORE AT HARLEQUIN.COM.

HWCNM1122

HARLEQUIN
PLUS

Announcing a **BRAND-NEW** multimedia subscription service for romance fans like you!

Read, Watch and Play.

Experience the easiest way to get the romance content you crave.

Start your **FREE 7 DAY TRIAL** at
www.harlequinplus.com/freetrial.

HARPLUS0822